Captain of I

CAPTAIN OF HORSE

Book 2 in the English Mercenary Series

By

Griff Hosker

Captain of Horse

Published by Griff Hosker 2024
Copyright ©Griff Hosker

The author has asserted their moral right under the Copyright, Designs and Patents Act, 1988, to be identified as the author of this work.
All Rights reserved. No part of this publication may be reproduced, copied, stored in a retrieval system, or transmitted, in any form or by any means, without the prior written consent of the copyright holder, nor be otherwise circulated in any form of binding or cover other than that in which it is published and without a similar condition being imposed on the subsequent purchaser.

A CIP catalogue record for this title is available from the British Library.

Dedication

To Roger Jennings, a dear friend and a true collaborator who helped me many times in my research. I shall miss you in the pub on Fridays. Rest assured that the first pint will always be a toast to you.

Captain of Horse

Contents

Prologue 5
Chapter 1 8
Chapter 2 18
Chapter 3 27
Chapter 4 38
Chapter 5 48
Chapter 6 60
Chapter 7 69
Chapter 8 84
Chapter 9 99
Chapter 10 108
Chapter 11 119
Chapter 12 132
Chapter 13 144
Chapter 14 155
Chapter 15 167
Chapter 16 178
Chapter 17 188
Chapter 18 199
Chapter 19 212
Chapter 20 222
Epilogue 238
Glossary 240
Historical Background 241
Other books by Griff Hosker 243

Captain of Horse

Real People in the Book

Protestant Leaders
King Frederick V of Bohemia
King James 1st of England and Scotland
King Christian IVth of Denmark - King James' brother-in-law
King Gustavus Adolphus of Sweden
Axel Gustafsson Oxenstierna - Chancellor of Sweden
John George of Saxony - Elector of Saxony
Samuel von Winterfield - German Quartermaster
General Hohenlohe - Bohemian general
Georg Friedrich - Margrave of Baden-Durlach
Christian the Younger of Brunswick
William - Duke of Saxe-Weimar
Sir Horace Vere - King James' commander in the Palatinate
Ernst von Mansfield - Mercenary leader
Prince Maurice of Nassau
Prince Frederick of Nassau
Prince Philip William of Nassau
George Villiers - Duke of Buckingham
Prince Francis Albert of Saxe-Lauenburg
Lennart Torstensson - Commander of the Swedish artillery
Gustav Horn - Swedish general
Johan Banér - Swedish general and diplomat
Karl Gustav Wrangel - Swedish general
Bogislaw XIV, Duke of Pomerania
Wolf Heinrich von Baudissin - German cavalry commander under King Gustavus
George William - Elector of Brandenburg
Charles William - Leader of Magdeburg
John Leslie - Scottish general
John Hepburn - Scottish general
Robert Munro - Scottish general
Sir James Ramsay - 'Black Ramsay' Scottish general
Marquess James Hamilton, 1st Duke of Hamilton
Torsten Stålhandske - Commander of the Hakkapeliitta (Finnish light horsemen)

Catholic leaders
Johannes Tserklaes, Count of Tilly - Commander of the Catholic League armies
Emperor Ferdinand II, King of Spain and Holy Roman Emperor

Captain of Horse

Albrecht von Wallenstein of Friedland and Mecklenburg - Imperial general
Charles Bonaventure de Longueval, 2nd Count of Bucquoy - Imperial general.
Colonel Dodo zu Innhausen und Knyphausen - German mercenary
Tommaso Caracciolo, Count of Roccarainola - Spanish mercenary
Graf zu Pappenheim - Imperial general
Heinrich Holk - Danish mercenary leader

Others
Cardinal Richelieu of France
Sir Richard Young - aide to King James
Sir Théodore de Mayerne - King James' Physician
Edward Zouch - Knight Marshal
John Felton - soldier
Prince Charles of England
Princess Henrietta of France
John Sigismund - Elector of Brandenburg and Duke of Prussia

Captain of Horse

Germany 1630

Prologue

When I returned from the wars in Germany, that first year living back in England was a whirlwind. I had returned having served the Protestant cause. The Danes and the Dutch had lost, and the empire now ruled vast swathes of Germany. The emperor had used the vast resources of his huge empire to buy victories. I had been a mercenary and without a paymaster I needed an income. That was now even more important for I was married. The cottage was more than adequate but I knew that I wanted more for my wife. As soon as I saw the plot of land that Roger had offered, I began to plan, and Charlotte was with me for every moment of that planning. We did not argue, and both saw solutions from any problems that arose. Two months after I had begun the plan, the builders were digging the foundations. I used some of the money I had accumulated when I had been a mercenary. It coincided with the time that Sir Giles asked me to begin to train his soldiers. It was not a full-time job. I only had them every Saturday. However, after the first week I realised that I would have to work a great deal harder than I had expected to. They were not what one might term real soldiers and had little discipline. It took two or three days each week to plan what to do with them and to ensure that they progressed.

It meant that Charlotte spent every day supervising the builders and when, a month after I began training the militia she collapsed, I felt guilty. I learned it was nothing to do with me overworking her, she was with child. She had a strong will and once she realised the cause of the collapse then she dealt with it herself.

So, the first year passed in what seemed like moments. As that first year of our marriage came to a close, I was relieved that the house was ready but still unfurnished and Charlotte, according to the doctors and, more importantly, the midwives of the village, thought that the baby would be due in a month. Despite Charlotte's objections I decided not to move into the house until it was furnished and the plaster completely dry. Our baby would be born in the cosy cottage that was our old home.

Charlotte put the relatively easy birth down to the hard work in the early days of her pregnancy. I was not the one who said it was easy. It was the doctors, midwives and Charlotte herself. My son, William, took just two hours to be born. To me that seemed like a long time but apparently it was not so. The baby was healthy as was Charlotte. Roger and his son Peter joined me to, as they said in the village, wet the baby's head once the baby was born.

Christmas was a delight. Roger would not hear of Charlotte cooking, and we were invited to his grand house where we enjoyed a perfect Christmas. We had no work and were waited on hand and foot by Roger's servants. My father's best friend was a rich man. Our lives were perfect. William was not a demanding baby and Charlotte soon recovered from the birth. We moved into our new home in March and that coincided with the renewal of the training of the militia.

The pay I received was not enough to live on, but I still had coins I had earned as a soldier. Roger told me not to worry about money, but I would not be a charity case. Charlotte suggested asking her father for money. She assured me that he thought well of me, and it would be forthcoming. I was adamant we would live on what I earned. He was not a rich man and as a clergyman had little money to spare. When we hired a cook and a servant we began to eat into my savings. I earned a little extra by teaching men how to fence. I was a good swordsman, and I found that I was a good teacher. It deferred the problem, but I knew that once William was old enough then he would be an expense. He would need a school and that cost money.

One night, after Charlotte had put our son to bed and we were speaking about the future, I told her that I worried we would not be able to live as well as I hoped. She laughed, "James, you think that because I speak well and know how to dress that I was brought up as a lady. You are wrong. I was brought up as the daughter of a clergyman. We rarely had more than a housekeeper and oft times the housekeeper would be me. If money becomes a problem, then I shall take in commissions for needlework. I am a seamstress. I can take in washing."

I was shocked, "I cannot allow my wife to take on such menial tasks."

She put her hand on mine and looked me in the eyes, "James, I did not know your father, but I have spoken to Roger. He was a man who had an idealised view of the world. He wanted to be a gentleman and tried to live that lifestyle. He gambled and he lost. I fear that you may be heading down that same road. I married a soldier. I never expected to be rich in terms of money, but I think I am rich beyond words as the life I lead is the one I want in a place that I love with people whom I like. That is enough for me."

I did not know what or who had thrown Charlotte into my life, but it was the best thing that ever happened to me. She was right. I was stepping down the road that had destroyed my father. Her words were timely, and I changed the way I thought about life in general and mine in particular.

.

Chapter 1

William was almost one year old when Sir Giles died. He drank too much. The food he ate was too rich and he lived a life that was doomed to end early. I had not liked him at first and even at the end I would hardly say that I thought we were friends. I learned to live with his foibles. I suppose that is how men get by. His death brought me a thousand guineas in his will. That was unexpected but it also brought to an end my employment. He was no longer the Lord Lieutenant and his replacement, Sir Walter Blousefield, had his own man he wished to appoint to train the militia. My salary ended immediately and until I was paid from the estate we were without an income. We learned all of this after the funeral and the reading of the will. I was unemployed and I began to worry about our future.

That fateful morning, I had been woken by William demanding food and left the house early to walk through the village having been disturbed. There had been a frost, and the ground was hard. With a cloak wrapped around my shoulders and a hat upon my head I enjoyed the walk to the river and the bridge there. I descended to the river to watch the river heading east. I threw the odd stone into the water. I needed time to think about my future. The inheritance would soon disappear. I needed an income and a regular one at that. I had to have some occupation that paid better and was more reliable than the training of militia.

I heard the hooves on the bridge above me and I made my way back up the bank. Riders at this time of year were rare and those on horses even rarer. The rider who came into the village looked like a soldier. I had been a soldier and recognised the well-worn comfortable boots, the serviceable oiled cloak and, most tellingly, the pair of horse pistols in the saddle. I saw him before he saw me. When I reached the bridge, I saw that the man was speaking to John Cunningham who lived in the house close to the bridge. I could not make out the words but recognised that he had a foreign accent. I had made enough enemies in the Palatinate and the Netherlands for me to regret walking about unarmed.

John spied me and pointed. He called out, "There is Captain Bretherton, Sir."

The rider turned and watched me as I approached him. I saw that he made no move to reach for a weapon, but I was cautious in my approach. Old habits died hard and a stranger in my home was something that made me wary.

"Captain, this foreign gentleman was asking after you." I heard the suspicion in John's voice. We had few foreign visitors, and any visitor was viewed with wariness, foreigners doubly so.

I smiled, "Thank you, John. A cold morning, eh?"

He nodded, "Aye, Captain. Just going down to the river to collect more driftwood." He chuckled, "Easier than walking to the common wood and chopping, eh?"

"Aye, John."

He slung his axe over his shoulder and headed down to the river. At that time of the year, we sometimes had large trees brought down the Tees. The Pennines endured some vicious storms in winter.

The rider had dismounted and walked his horse over to me. He took off his glove and held out his hand, "I am Sigismund Friedrich, and I have come, Captain Bretherton, to offer you a commission." I studied his face. He was about my age and there was a scar on his face that could have come from a wound. I said nothing and he smiled. "You are right to be suspicious. I come to you having spoken to Colonel Berghof."

I had known the colonel when he was still a captain. He was a Dutchman. I said, "If you met him then what did you notice about him?"

"You mean apart from the fact that he has a wound and can no longer take an active command on the battlefield?"

He knew the Dutchman. "Come inside. It is too cold to stand outside." I had no servants to help me, and I led him to the stables. There were just my two horses within, and I watched him as he unsaddled his horse. He was a soldier for he did so with great care. He looked at the bag of oats and then glanced at me. He wanted permission to feed his horse. "Of course." As he fitted the nosebag, I took a pail and handed it to him. "There is a well." When I had supervised the building of my house, I had ordered a well to be dug.

That done I led him inside. The kitchen was warm. I knew that Charlotte would be in the parlour with William and so I pointed to the table, "We shall eat here."

The cook, Elizabeth, looked curiously at the visitor. "Will you dine here too, Captain, or with the mistress?"

Just then Margaret, the other servant, entered and I said, "Margaret, tell the mistress that we have a visitor. We will dine here and then I will need the parlour."

She bobbed a curtsy, "Yes, Captain."

"Take off your cloak, Sir, or you will not feel the benefit when you leave." As he did so I went to pour two mugs of ale. Elizabeth was stirring the porridge. The bread was baking in the bread oven outside. I put a poker in the fire that heated the kitchen and the oven. My visitor had said nothing. If nothing else that confirmed he was a soldier. Everything about him, his clothes, his sword, his manner marked him as a professional. Working with the militia had shown me amateurs. The young gentlemen who had fine swords and dressed as though they were soldiers soon had their pomposity pricked. This soldier was the very opposite of that. I heated the ale and Elizabeth dropped in two knobs of home-made butter. I handed one to the soldier and sat. He drank it appreciatively.

When he spoke, Elizabeth turned at his foreign accent. "I have had a long journey to find you, Captain. I spoke with your man Edgar in London."

I laughed, "Edgar is anything but my man."

"Nonetheless, he spoke of you in glowing terms and confirmed what we were told by Colonel Berghof." I nodded and said nothing. "This last part, from York to this river, was a lonely one. I left the inn in Richmond well before dawn for I was anxious to complete my commission. I have been away from my homeland for too long."

Elizabeth ladled two portions of porridge into our bowls. I took the honey pot and pushed it towards him, "First, we eat and then we can speak in the parlour."

The porridge was good. It is not easy to make well, and Elizabeth knew my taste. While we ate, she went to the bread oven and returned with a basket covered with a cloth. She took a steaming loaf and placed it on the bread board that sat in the middle of the table. It steamed and the smell was enticing.

Margaret returned with an empty bowl and Elizabeth said, "Take a loaf for the mistress."

Margaret said, "Captain, the mistress says she will vacate the parlour for you now."

Shaking my head I said, "There is no need yet. We will eat first."

By the time we had cut and sliced the bread, slavered it in butter, topped it with carved ham and eaten it, I deemed that Charlotte would have finished her own breakfast.

"Come."

As he stood the soldier bowed, "Thank you, cook. That was as fine a breakfast as I have eaten in England."

It was only then that I realised how good his English was. It was accented, of course, but his grammar and vocabulary were perfect.

Elizabeth beamed, "Thank you, Sir."

Margaret had taken William to our room and Charlotte awaited us. She was seated in a chair and I knew that she wished to stay; Margaret would deal with William. I sighed, "Sigismund Friedrich, this is my wife, Charlotte."

She held out a hand for him to kiss and said, "I pray that you sit, Sir. I hope you have an interesting tale to tell for we are well away from the main thoroughfare of life. We crave news."

Our visitor looked at me with an unspoken question in his eyes. I nodded to him and said, "I have no secrets from my wife. Sit and tell me what has brought you the length of this land to seek an audience with an old soldier."

"Further than that, Captain. I have come from Brandenburg."

Thanks to my service in the war against the Catholics I had a good sense of the geography of that part of Germany. "That is a prodigious distance. I am flattered that I merit such a journey."

He spread his hands, "Captain, I am anxious to return to my homeland. I am a blunt soldier and not a diplomat. I will come directly to the point. I serve the Elector of Brandenburg. As you may, or may not know, his son-in-law is King Gustavus Adolphus of Sweden."

I smiled, "We may be a backwater here, as my wife says, but I have heard of the Snow King."

The nickname of the Swedish King brought a nod from the German, "Then you should know that the king has recently defeated the Poles and that allows him to come to the aid of the German Protestants." He paused and looked directly at me, "King Gustavus Adolphus has heard of you. Christian of Brunswick spoke well of you." The German leader had fought against the Catholics, and I knew him. He had died before I left for England. "The king would have you join his army as a captain of horse. My master, the elector, will pay you a stipend of a thousand reichsthalers a year."

The amount staggered me. However, I was cautious. "A generous offer but, it seems to me there are worthier candidates for the position already in Germany."

He shook his head, "You showed, so I am told, great skill. You outwitted the enemies of the Protestant cause and that is what the king requires. He needs men who are adaptable. He has new ideas about war and does not need old fashioned men who want to fight in tercios."

I looked at Charlotte. She smiled, "Sir, it is a worthy offer, but the war is being fought far across the sea. My husband has a family here."

"The king is aware of that. The payment for the captain's services will be paid directly to you. There is an agent at Hartlepool who will ensure that it is delivered here, in advance. The captain would be allowed to come home for one month each year. The king knows the value of such a gift."

The offer of money was a generous one, the leave less so. It might take me a month to get home from Germany. As desperate as I was for the income, I did not wish to leave my wife for so long.

The German saw my hesitation, "Captain, you may resign the commission at any time after the first year. Initially the king seeks a year of your services. He wants you to take charge of the English and Scottish mercenaries who are in Germany already. He believes that you could make them a better force in a year." There was something of a warning in his words. What was wrong with the men I would command? He smiled, "He hopes that at the end of the year you would, after a brief return home, be committed to the cause."

I stiffened, "Sir, I fought the Catholics at every turn. I lost many good friends in the conflict. My commitment is not to be questioned."

"I apologise if I have offended you. As I said, I am a soldier and not a diplomat." Silence filled the parlour. The crackling of the logs in the fire and the distant singing of Margaret as she lullabied William back to sleep, were the only sounds to be heard. "However, time is pressing. I am a soldier and if you cannot or will not come then I must return to Brandenburg. The organising of the English and Scottish companies is needed and if you cannot do it then…"

Charlotte knew my dilemma and she reached over to touch my hand, "James, take the commission. The coins will ensure that we live well, and, at the end of a year, you could return home. William and I will miss you but when I met you, I knew that you were a soldier. That I have enjoyed your company such a long time is more than I hoped."

I looked at the Brandenburger, "And when would we leave?"

He gave a sad smile, "In a perfect world, by noon, but I am a practical man and can wait until the morrow." He shrugged, "My horse needs the rest."

"Let me speak with my wife. Can you find your way back to the kitchen? Elizabeth can tend to your needs."

He stood, "As I said, I am a soldier. A good soldier can find his way to a kitchen, blindfold." He bowed, "Mistress." He left and closed the door behind him.

Charlotte held my hand in both of hers, "Since the reading of the will and the loss of your post you have not slept well. You rise early and you drink far more than you once did."

"William…"

She laughed, "Do not blame our son. You toss and turn in the bed, and you are worried. This is the answer to our prayers. You are a soldier. It is what brought us together. We have begun to eat into your savings already. Take this offer. At the very least we have a year without having to worry about an income."

"Are you sure?"

"I am certain."

Once that was decided, Charlotte went to pack my clothes for me. I would see to my weapons myself. I went to the kitchen, "We will leave tomorrow."

He looked relieved, "How far is it from here to Hartlepool?"

"Thirty miles."

"Then we will be in time to speak to the agent in Hartlepool and to take a ship."

"That may not be as easy as you think, Sigismund."

He smiled, "It will. I arrived in England across the Channel for I only had the name of the inn in London as a guide. The Swedes, Danes and Germans use Hartlepool frequently. It is why the King of Sweden keeps an agent there. That, and the fact that more than half of our mercenaries come from Scotland or the north of England."

Margaret appeared and curtsied, "Captain, the mistress says that I am to show your guest to the guest bedroom."

He stood, "I will fetch my bag."

He left.

Elizabeth said, "You are going to war again, Captain?"

"For a while but I trust that you two will keep both my wife and son safe."

Elizabeth looked indignant, "As if you should have to ask, Captain." She softened, "But you take care of yourself too, eh?"

She was right. The last time I had engaged in anything warlike was when I had rescued my wife on the road to York. That had been more than two years ago. Was I ready?

The first thing I did was to see to my horses. I now had two. Jack was a good war horse. He was fearless and strong. Bluebell was an old fashioned sumpter. She had a quiet nature and a broad back. She would easily carry my bags. I led both of them to Alf, the smith. I could not remember the last time I had shoed them both. Alf was a good smith, and I would not be rooked.

"Leave them with me and they shall both be ready by supper time." He smiled, "A visitor, eh?"

We were a small place and word spread. "Yes, from Germany."

He shook his head. Alf had never left the village. "And if you need these two to be shoed then you shall be leaving too."

I nodded, "For a while."

"Well, you take care but while you are gone, we shall watch your home and family for you."

It was gratifying to know. I then headed to my father's old friend, Roger and Peter, his son. When I told them of the commission Peter looked excited, but Roger frowned, "James, you are no longer a boy who went off to war. You have a wife and a son. Is this wise?"

"It is for a year and then I will be home. It is good pay."

"Not if you are dead." I had no answer to that. He sighed and then smiled, "Fear not, Peter and I will ensure that your family prospers while you go to war."

As I headed back to my home, I reflected that everyone seemed as concerned about my family as I was. That seemed, to me, to be a good thing.

My wife was in my bed chamber sorting out my clothes. William was asleep in the cot at the side of the bed. It meant we both worked in silence as I opened my chest to take out my weapons. I laid my cloak upon the bed. I always handled my weapons carefully but knowing that I might wake my son made me even more diligent. I took out the hat I would wear and shaped it before placing it on the cloak. I took my sword and sword belt. I placed them with the pistols. The sword was sharp. I had sharpened it before the last militia training, and I had not used it since. I took out the four wheellocks. They would need to be cleaned. I carefully carried them downstairs and laid them on the kitchen table. Elizabeth frowned but said nothing.

"Where is our guest?"

"Margaret said that he was on the bed asleep. She told him to take off his boots."

I smiled. The two women were like that.

I went back upstairs and took out the powder horn and bag of balls. It felt heavy enough. I assumed that powder and ball would be provided. I had enough for the journey. I laid my two holsters on the bed. I took the knives I would use. One would be in my belt, a second in my boot and the third one in my saddlebags. I checked the leather on the breastplate. I had taken it when I had first gone to war. I had not always worn it, but I thought that this campaign might need it. I took my tool kit and headed back downstairs. It took until noon to clean and service all four weapons. When Elizabeth told me, in no uncertain terms, that they were no longer welcome on the table, I nodded and took two out to place in the saddle holsters. The other two I carried back upstairs, Elizabeth's voice ringing in my ears, "Tell the mistress, Captain, that lunch is ready, and we will serve it in the dining room. I will send Margaret to tell the German."

William had woken when I reached the bedroom and Charlotte handed him to me. "I will wash my hands. Take him down to the dining room and put him in his chair."

I could strip a handgun easily and reassemble it. I could sharpen a sword but carrying an infant downstairs and placing him in a chair would tax me to the limit. I was lucky that, when I reached the dining room, Margaret was there to help me. I marvelled at how easily she found it to handle my son. I was afraid I might break him.

While we ate, I questioned the German about the coming campaign. "We will sail directly to meet the king on the island of Usedom in the Baltic. He was gathering an army there at a place called Peenemünde."

"Then that means I will be training the men while we go to war."

He nodded, "Do not worry, Captain, I will be there to help and advise you. The king is the greatest general that I know. He is remarkably far-sighted, and you are an example of that great vision. It was not just Colonel Berghof and Christian of Brunswick who spoke well of you, Prince Maurice of Nassau also did. King Gustavus knew these men well and learned of you and your skill while you still fought in Germany."

"Then why send for me now?"

He sighed, "The regiment that you are to command…well, let us say that they are unique, and the king needs an Englishman to lead them. He has too few soldiers under his command to waste this regiment because they are…difficult."

He was being careful in his choice of words, and I wondered what the problems were. As I ate, I reflected that two of those men who had recommended me were now dead and the third could not go to war. It seemed to me that I was putting my life in peril by returning to this bloody conflict.

Charlotte was astute and she smiled. Perhaps she read my mind. "I have read, husband, that there are lucky leaders and unlucky ones. From what you have told me, you have skill and luck."

She had witnessed that luck when I had been wounded on the road to York. What she could not know was just how confused a battle could be. I smiled, "Thank you for those kind words. I pray that you are right."

Chapter 2

Hartlepool 1629

As much as I wanted to spend as long with my family as I could, I knew that travelling at this time of year to Hartlepool could be a longer and slower journey than it would be in summer. We left at dawn. I am not even sure that William was aware of my departure. He was asleep. He would be happy with the three women in the house caring for him. I hugged Charlotte and whispered in her ear, "It is unlikely that I will be able to write to you. The next time I see you might well be when I walk through that door."

"Then I will look at William and see you. I shall talk to you each night and know that the prayers I say will be for you. God will watch over you for you are a good man and do God's work."

I led Bluebell. As we rode, I learned about the German who would be my guide and my adviser. He had fought the Imperial armies and lost more times than he had won. He told me, with a wry look on his face, that since he had been appointed to the king's staff, the ratio of losses to victories had changed dramatically. He had followed King Gustavus in Poland and helped the Swedish king recover the lost lands of Sweden. He told me of the innovations that the Swedish king had introduced into battle plans.

"The king wants leaders who can be a musketeer as well as a horseman. He wants every leader of men to know how to fire a cannon. He likes those skills in the men who lead his regiments. He wants men to be flexible and to be able to think. The king likes flexibility in his battle lines. We have more musketeers than pikemen and we do not fight in the huge tercios. The king likes smaller, more flexible formations. Tilly is a good general, but King Gustavus is better. He is a real leader. He leads from the front and does not sit at the rear watching a battle; men will follow him anywhere. But for the Poles he would have joined the coalition much earlier. You remember I said that his wife is the daughter of the elector?"

"Is that how you came into his service?"

"The elector saw something in me and my skill with languages meant that I was the perfect man to liaise with his son-in-law. I have not regretted my move for one moment."

I was silent for a few miles, and I think the German must have thought that I was having doubts. I was not. I was just thinking back to my time with Maurice of Nassau. He had been an innovative leader, and it looked like I would have one that was not only full of ideas but charismatic too.

"You now that the stipend you have been given is just the start? There will be opportunities for you to make more money."

I frowned, "How? I will not rob the men that I lead." I had known some leaders who did that. Even a good leader might hold back some of his men's money as a sort of insurance.

"Nothing like that, Captain Bretherton. We both know that leaders who steal from their men risk a knife in the back. No, the king will be successful, and it is what you take from the battlefield that will make you rich. The men who fought alongside the king against the Poles discovered that. Some of the mercenary leaders made enough coins to retire and live a life of peace."

I thought back to when I had fought alongside Edgar for the first time. He had made it clear that taking from the dead that you killed was part of war and expected. At first, I had baulked at it. It was theft or seemed to me like theft. Later I realised that if the men were dead, it did not matter if their goods were taken.

As we neared Hartlepool, passing the village of Greatham, he told me of his immediate employer. The elector did not bother with day-to-day matters. Samuel von Winterfeld was the First Minister in Brandenburg who had sent Sigismund to find me. He now worked closely with King Gustavus to help the elector recover his lands. I realised that the expenses incurred would have been very high. They really wanted me.

We passed through the gates of the port. We were only asked our names and nothing more. Having spoken to the Brandenburger I realised that many mercenaries passed through the port on their way to the war. We were not unusual. Sigismund had never been in the port and neither had I. We had to ask directions for the agent who lived close to the Middlegate and St Hilda's church. It was almost dark when we knocked on the door of the address that the captain had been given. The house was set slightly apart from the others, but it was small.

When George Smith opened it, I was taken aback for I had not expected what I saw. He was a huge man, and he towered over us both. He had a white opaque left eye, and he had a stump instead of a left hand. I had been told his name was Smith but when he spoke, his words were heavily accented.

When the Brandenburger said his name, the agent bowed. Sigismund was clearly held in high regard. "Come, gentlemen, I am honoured." He gestured for us to enter but I hesitated. We had three horses. He smiled, "There is a stable. It is empty at the moment, but I will take them there."

"They are good horses. They need feed." I wanted my horses looked after, for when we went to war, I would need good animals.

"And when I have attended to you two gentlemen, I will see that they dine too."

As we entered, I saw a woman in the shadows. She curtsied, "I am Gilda. Follow me please." Unlike George she had no accent. She was English.

The house, which had a narrow frontage, was deceptive. She led us down a corridor and there were small rooms on either side of the passage. There were no sconces but there was light emanating from a room at the end. She opened a door, and I saw a cosy room with a fire, table and five chairs. Four were around the table and the fifth was close to the fire. This was the living room and the dining room.

"We wondered when you would arrive. There is food but I must prepare it." As we sat, she scurried out and returned with a jug and two beakers. She poured the ale and without a further word disappeared into the kitchen. A few moments later George appeared with our bags. Mine was larger than Sigismund's as it contained my breastplate.

"I will take these to your room. I fear you must share. There are two beds albeit small ones." He smiled apologetically, "Our visitors are rarely as grand as you are."

Sigismund nodded, "Hopefully, it will not be for long."

I heard the front door close and I guessed that George was going to buy feed for our horses. The port was close by, and I deduced that horses were used to transport goods from ships to warehouses. I could smell food cooking. It had been a long day. We had stopped in Stockton and had ale and a pie at noon but that seemed a long time ago. I had forgotten how hungry a day in the saddle made a man.

I said, quietly, "What is this man's story?"

Sigismund shook his head, "Like you I have never met the man, but I am intrigued. He looks like a soldier, and he is not English. Perhaps the conversation while we eat might be entertaining."

I was not bothered about being entertained but I had seen the danger in strangers. Don Alphonso had sent men to attack me on the road. I was wary of foreigners whilst in England. I expected a variety in London but in the north such strangers were few and far between. I wanted to know George's story but mainly to ensure I had a good night of sleep and did not need to keep a dagger close to hand.

George arrived back before the food was ready. I heard him in the kitchen as he poured water to wash his hands and then he entered, smiling, "Your horses have oats and water. They are content and the food will arrive soon."

"And a ship, George, when will that be ready?"

He nodded, "The **'*Maid of Oslo*'** arrived in port today. She leaves on the last tide tomorrow. She is loading local coal and is heading for Denmark."

Sigismund frowned. "We need to get to get to Usedom."

"And you shall for the ship lands at Kopenhagen and there are many ships that leave from there to sail to Usedom. Captain Pedersson is a good man, and he will arrange the passage. I have spoken to him already."

The answer seemed to mollify the Brandenburger. As the food was ready then the conversation naturally ended. Gilda brought in a bowl of what looked like stew. George laid plates and spoons on the table and Gilda hurried back into the kitchen for bread and a bowl of butter. The bread was rustic but I knew that the fine bread I had enjoyed at home would be rare in the future.

Gilda surveyed the table and seemingly satisfied, left us. I said, "Will your wife not be joining us?"

George was impassive as he said, enigmatically, "She is not my wife. She will eat alone."

The stew was wholesome. I could not identify all the meat that was in the stew, but I recognised some rabbit and some ham. It was mainly made up of vegetables although there were some pieces of fish as well. It was tasty and the butter for the bread was freshly made. Soldiers always eat as quickly as they can, and Sigismund and I were soldiers. George ate as quickly and I deduced, especially from his maimed hand, that he had been a soldier.

While we ate, we chatted, and George asked enough questions to learn a little about our backgrounds. I also learned that Sigismund had served as a musketeer and a horseman. We had similar backgrounds.

When we finished George took out his pipe and, after pouring more ale, filled and lit it. I said, "George, what is your story?"

"My story?"

I took a swallow of the beer. It was good. "What is someone who is clearly not English doing living here in Hartlepool?" I used the beaker to gesture at his hand, "And that looks like an old wound to me."

He nodded, "I was a soldier. I am German by birth, and I wielded a two-handed sword." He smiled, "I think the days of such weapons are long gone, Captain, but in any case, the Pole who took my hand, and my eye ended that career." He gave a grim smile, "The Pole did not survive long. I was well thought of for I had lost the hand defending the standard and I was kept on. When King Gustavus' father attained the throne, he remembered me." He had a wistful smile on his face, "He was a good soldier. He asked me if I would be his agent in England, here in Hartlepool. He was wise as well as bold and he saw that trade with England could only help Sweden. I came here fifteen years ago. At first, I was viewed with suspicion but now…"

Sigismund finished off the sentence, "But now you are accepted…"

George laughed, "Accepted? No. I am tolerated and no longer viewed with suspicion. They call me George the German. Even changing my name to Smith did not help. Still, I get on with the people. They speak plainly and are honest. I am happy here." He looked at me, "You are a soldier, Captain, you know what it is like to lose comrades and I am the last of the two-handed swordsmen who left Swabia to serve as mercenaries. Sweden and Poland held too many ghosts for me. Here there are no ghosts and I sleep easier at night."

I understood him a little more and I enjoyed a better night's sleep than I had anticipated. Warfare had changed since the time George had served. Now handguns made even half trained men more dangerous than a swordsman who took a lifetime to learn the skill. Even archers were becoming rarer. A good archer trained his whole life to learn the skills of the bow but a musketeer could learn his skills in months. Musketeers were cheaper. Soon the vaunted archers for which England was renowned would be a memory.

We did not see Gilda again but when we went to our beds, I realised that she had put warming stones in the bed to take away the dampness. George had not enlightened us about her, and we had not pried. It was not our business. Before I slept, I knelt and prayed. I knew that Charlotte would be doing the same and that thought seemed to make me feel closer to her. I slept well.

The smell of kippers frying in the kitchen woke me. Smoked fish was a tradition on the east coast and the smell made me hungry. There was also porridge and we dined well. George said, "We might as well head to the port now for it will take time to load three horses."

I put my hand to my purse to pay George for his hospitality. He frowned, "I am well paid, Captain Bretherton. I am paid by Sweden and I am no innkeeper."

"Sorry, George, I meant no insult."

The frown disappeared and the smile filled his face, "I should apologise. That was rude of me. You should know that I will be the one who takes the gold to your home."

"On your own?"

"No, Captain, I will hire men. I believe that the gold will be on its way soon." He looked at Sigismund.

"Yes. As soon as we reach Usedom it will be sent. King Gustavus is an honourable man. He would have been happy to send the money with me but my master, Samuel von Winterfield, is a prudent man. He hoped I would succeed but…"

Captain of Horse

Samuel von Winterfield was not a soldier. He was a counter of coins. Gilda put a cloak around her shoulders and came with us as we headed the short distance to the port. She was going, George told us, to buy fresh fish from the fishing boats that had been returning since dawn.

The ship was a carvel. With a high bow castle and stern castle, she could be defended but I saw no sign of soldiers. Having said that the sailors looked more than capable of handling trouble. Captain Pedersson was smoking a pipe and supervising the loading of sacks of coal. George did not disturb him. The coal was the primary cargo and would need to be loaded first.

When he was satisfied the captain tapped out his clay pipe and walked over to us. He was a small stocky man. I guessed that he was perfectly built to stand at the steering board during a gale and still be well balanced. He was a little older than me but not by much. His golden hair told me that he was probably Danish.

"Master George, these are the passengers?" His eyes took in the two of us and our horses.

"They are. They will need passage to Usedom when you have reached Kopenhagen."

"It can be arranged." He looked at the two of us, "You know that your horses will have to be tethered on the deck. The hold will be filled with coal."

I was not sure that my horses would enjoy that, and I frowned. Sigismund said, "Captain, would it be easier if we did not take our horses?"

I saw the relief on his face, "Much and it would also be easier to have you taken to Usedom as foot passengers rather than men with three horses."

I was not sure I liked this, "But what would happen to my horses?" I was not bothered about Sigismund's.

He smiled, "George will need to transport the gold to your home. This way he can ride my horse and return yours to your wife. King Gustavus will provide horses for us. In my experience transporting horses does them little good."

I had not planned for this, and I was a man who liked to be in control. However, it made sense. I turned to George, "And the horses would be well cared for?"

"Captain, it is in my interest to do so. This saves me expenditure as I would have had to hire two horses. I save money from my commission. I am happy and I promise that the animals will be well looked after."

"Then all is well." The other three looked more relieved than me but I was not happy. I knew Jack and Bluebell. The horses that would be provided would be new to me. I took my saddle holsters but left the saddle on Jack and George led them away. We walked up the gangplank and boarded the ship. Already the plans I had made were changed. I did not like change.

When the storm hit us in the middle of the German Sea, I was glad that the plans had been changed. This was not the Atlantic but nasty storms could erupt and the one that tore at our sails and tossed us around as though we were a piece of flotsam was terrifying. Not only would the storm have terrified the horses, but the sailor who was washed overboard demonstrated that I might have lost one or both of my horses. They were safer where they were. We limped into Kopenhagen. Captain Pedersson would not be sailing any time soon.

Here I was in the hands of Sigismund. I had a few words of Danish but not enough. Had I been alone then I would have been lost. Despite his problems, the captain took the time to find us a ship. It was a small knarr. These ships had plied the Baltic since the time of the Vikings. She was taking ball for pistols to the army and we could be accommodated. However, the knarr had no cabins and we had to endure the open deck for the one-hundred-and-twenty-mile voyage across the sea that was the hunting ground of the Swedish navy. It took more than twenty hours to make the voyage. I slept fitfully beneath my cloak, but I was not rested. To take my mind off the storm I had Sigismund give me lessons in Swedish and German. I had a skill in languages, which was thanks to my mother but Swedish was a new one to me. When we reached the island even, I was not prepared for the army that was assembling for the invasion of the Holy Roman Empire. Tents and horse lines stretched in every direction. It was as though the whole island was an armed camp.

Captain of Horse

I slung my heavy bag over my shoulder, donned my hat and followed Sigismund towards the standard that marked the house that was used by King Gustavus Adolphus. I was at war once more.

Chapter 3

Sigismund told the sentry at the door our names and that we had recently arrived. We could, I suppose, have entered. I had been summoned by the king but Sigismund cautioned me as we waited in the shelter of the wall that ran around the house. The wind was coming from Russia and was a lazy wind that did not go around a man but tore through him. "Not all those who surround the king are loyal. Some resent him. I met a few of my countrymen before I left to summon you and they wonder why we should be led by a Swede."

I frowned, "But, Sigismund, the Lutheran cause is losing. The great leaders like Christian of Brunswick and Maurice of Nassau have died and the ones that remain… Even Horace de Vere is back in England. He was not a great leader, but he knew his job. If half of what you say is true then the perfect man to lead the Protestant cause is King Gustavus Adolphus."

He smiled, "You are right, and I can see that the king has summoned the right man, but keep an impassive face. I know you are a soldier; can you be a diplomat too?"

"You mean lie and adopt a false face."

He seemed to miss the tone I used and grinned, "That is it, James, just so!"

We were admitted. The sergeant who escorted us asked us to drop our bags outside the front door, "I will make sure that they are safe. I can see that you are both soldiers." He spoke in German. On the journey east and across the sea I had encouraged Sigismund to speak to me in his native tongue. I was more confident now.

It was not a court but the king was the focus of the attention of the men in the hall. The house had obviously been chosen for the king as it had belonged to a rich man and could accommodate the leader of this burgeoning army. The hall in which he sat had a long table and must have been the place the owner held feasts.

I worked out which man was the king. King Gustavus Adolphus sat in the centre, rather than the head of the table. It enabled him to speak to more men directly. However, I would have picked out the king even had he not been sat where he was. He had a steely eye and a commanding presence. I learned more about him as the campaign wore on but in that first meeting, I saw a leader who could lead.

He stood, "You must be Captain Bretherton." He nodded to Sigismund, "Thank you, Captain Friedrich for undertaking such an arduous task." He looked at me and waited for an answer.

I had practised my words on the boat and answered, "I am Captain James Bretherton, and it is an honour to serve the Protestant cause once more."

He smiled. As he gestured with his right hand, I saw that two fingers looked stiff. Sigismund had told me that the king had been wounded in the Battle of Dirschau. A ball was lodged in his muscle and could not be removed. The paralysed fingers were the result. He spoke in rapid German, most of which I understood. He addressed the leaders who were seated around the able, "This man comes to us with a great reputation. He has fought and defeated the Imperialists. He fought at the Battle of the White Mountain." I saw the nods from those who remembered the battle. "He is English but a loyal Protestant. I would have all of you make him welcome." He smiled at me, "And now…you have had a long journey. Captain Friedrich, there are quarters for you in the town. I will speak with you both this evening but for now," he smiled apologetically, "we have a campaign to plan. We have just four thousand soldiers at the moment and face tens of thousands of Imperial soldiers…we will need my mind and your swords, eh?"

When we reached the door Sigismund turned to me and his face was aglow, "Have you ever met a leader like him? Why I would follow him to hell and back if he asked."

"Aye, he seems to be a good leader, but four thousand men, Sigismund? It is not enough."

The smile disappeared and he nodded, "I know. More will come but…"

A flurry of snow had joined the biting wind and Sigismund put the cowl of his cloak over his cap. "Let us find our chamber." He turned to the sergeant, "The king said that there was accommodation for us?"

"Yes, Captain." He pointed to a building over which fluttered a Swedish flag. "The senior captains and colonels are over there." He added, "You two are amongst the last to arrive." His words told me that we would have the worst of the rooms. I was a soldier, and we would endure.

I slung my bag over my back, and we headed for the house. The flurry of snow was becoming heavier and by the time we reached the house it had begun to lie. We opened the door of the house. Like the larger one occupied by the king, it had to have belonged to an important merchant. The war meant that many merchants had taken homes in safer locations. This one had a small chamber next to the front door. A soldier stood as we entered. We quickly closed the door for snow had blown in already.

"Yes, gentlemen?" He was a grey-haired soldier. The grey was thinning, and he had a scarred face.

Sigismund said, "Captain Friedrich and Captain Bretherton. We have been sent by the king."

He frowned, "I fear, captains, that most of the rooms and certainly all the best ones have been taken." He suddenly smiled, "A strange thing, is it not, that a soldier like me should end his career as makeshift innkeeper?"

I could not help but think of Edgar who had willingly chosen that particular career.

Sigismund said, "Like you, my friend, we are soldiers and even a room with paillasses would be acceptable."

He nodded, "Then I have such a room. I was commanded to reserve it for the servants of Prince Francis Albert of Saxe-Lauenburg, but you are soldiers and besides," he lowered his voice, "I like neither man."

He led us up what had to have been the stairs used by servants and we heard voices from the room. The soldier knocked on the door and then opened it, "Gentlemen, I fear that this room is now needed by two officers."

Any reasonable man would have accepted the words for the house was intended for officers and these were servants but the two of them struck arrogant poses. One of them said, haughtily, "We serve Prince Francis Albert of Saxe-Lauenburg and are more important than these two."

Until that moment Sigismund had been a quiet and calm man. Nothing on the journey seemed to upset him but the words of the two servants did. He grabbed the shirt of the man who had spoken and pulled him close. Spittle flew from his lips into the face of the servant as he spoke, "Listen, little man, I care not who you serve, you are a servant, and we are soldiers. This house is for soldiers and not poxy little rodents like you. Get out now before I kick you out."

The terrified men grabbed their clothes and ran out so fast that one of them tripped at the door and fell sprawling.

Sigismund shook his head, "I am sorry about that, but we are an army. Bringing servants to war is unnecessary." He looked at the soldier, "I am betting that the king has but one servant."

The soldier smiled, "Aye, but he is more of a bodyguard. You did the right thing, Captain, but be prepared for the prince. He has a high opinion of himself. His servants are a mirror to the man."

Sigismund nodded, "I know."

"If you need anything then ask. Food will be served at five."

"Thank you, my friend."

When the door was closed, I began to unpack. The room was a cosy one and there were just the two paillasses on the floor. There were a pair of rails on either side of the chimney breast, and I used them to hang the clothes that had lain in my bag since Charlotte had packed them. They were damp from the journey across the sea but the heat from the chimney would dry them.

"Who is this Prince Francis Albert of Saxe-Lauenburg? He has a grand title."

"And he has grand ideas. His lands were taken by the Imperialists, and he joined the king last year. The rest of his family fight for the emperor and the prince seeks victory so that he can take over the Dukedom. He does not fight for religion as most of the army but for personal gain. He is one of those young men who aspire to be a soldier but do not know what that means. He has a fine horse, a good cuirass and an expensive sword. You and I know that you need more to be a soldier. I think the king felt sorry for him. In the Polish campaign he kept him close and gave him no commands. He is not even good enough to be a battlefield aide." He smiled, "Let us forget him and descend. If I am any judge there will be ale and it will be good to meet the other captains."

"Should we change?" Both of us wore the same sea-stained clothes that still retained the stink of horse sweat despite the crossing of two seas.

"These are soldiers. If we are judged for stinking, then I will be surprised."

He was right. We went down the servants' stairs and the soldier came from his cubby hole to point us in the direction of the dining hall. We could have found it without his guidance as there was a buzz of noise punctuated by laughter.

The corridor leading to the hall was cool but once we opened the door we were hit by a wall of heat and noise. There were just twelve men inside the hall, but they sounded like many more. The sudden silence as we entered was caused by our arrival.

A portly warrior with a belly that showed he liked his beer strode over. He had a mug of ale in his hand, and he had the florid cheeks and nose of a trencherman. "Two more soldiers." He turned and said to the others, "And that means those two unpleasant little men have been evicted." There was laughter and I guessed that the two servants had been less than popular with the other senior officers. He turned back and beamed, "If that is the case then you are doubly welcome. This is a warriors' home for we go to do God's and the king's work!" We both bowed and he continued, "I am Count Wolfgang Otto von Hohenlohe."

"Captain Sigismund Friedrich of Brandenburg."

"Captain James Bretherton."

"An Englishman, good. We need someone who can talk to these wild men from the north of your land. They are good soldiers, if a little ill disciplined, but they speak not a word of German!"

I began to see why I was needed.

One of the other officers, clearly well on the way to becoming drunk said, "Count, show him your hat." He tapped his nose, "His most prized possession!"

The count nodded and picked up the hat which looked like mine except that the brim at the front was raised. "This was given to me by the king himself. How many other men wear the hat of a king, eh?"

It was a merry welcome and company. Sigismund and I were accepted from the first. Perhaps Sigismund's handling of the servants helped, I do not know but whatever the reason I was happy for the week or so we spent in the house as we waited for Christmas to pass and the New Year to begin. We learned that more soldiers were on their way, but King Gustavus would not wait to begin to reclaim the lands lost to the Imperialists. The weather meant that it would be June before we could begin to move into Saxony and Brandenburg.

It was not until the 1st of January that the king sent for me. This time there was just myself, Sigismund and the man I learned was the quartermaster of the army and the one who had sent Sigismund for me, Samuel von Winterfield.

We were alone in the small office commandeered by the king, "I know you have been cooling your heels, Captain Bretherton, but I know my Scottish soldiers. They like to celebrate what is it they call it, Hogmanay? I thought it judicious to let them do that before you began to work with them. They are a wild bunch of men and need to be led. We have tried German and Swedish leaders but to no avail. We hope that one who speaks their language might be what is needed. The men are vital to our plans. The captain who led them in Poland, well, he has left us and I believe he serves the emperor now although that is just a rumour. They have been without a leader since the autumn and they need you." He nodded to the quartermaster who spread a map out. The king jabbed a finger at Brandenburg. "That will be our first target." He smiled at the quartermaster. "Lord von Winterfield and Captain Friedrich will be anxious for us to try to reclaim their homeland." Sigismund had told me that von Winterfield was the First Minister of Brandenburg and had taken on the role of quartermaster to help the king begin to reclaim the lost lands. "Once that is done, we will head to Saxony. Tilly has enjoyed a free hand for too long."

He leaned back and put the fingers of his two hands together. I saw the two paralysed ones quite clearly. He would be severely hampered in battle for they were on his right hand. How would he fire a pistol or wield a sword?

"Now, your role. Initially you will bring some order to the men who, at the moment, make up the British Horse." I nodded.

"They are from what is called, I believe, the Borders and are not the heavy cavalry that we favour here. They are light horsemen and there are five hundred and ten of them. I believe that they may prove invaluable as scouts even though they do not know the land. We need you for your language skills and your leadership. Once they are trained you will operate largely unsupervised. The king wishes you and your regiment to be the scouts for the army and to not only hide our presence but give us information about the enemy. Your past performance suggests that you will be eminently well suited to the role. Now we have a disparate group of soldiers. I am afraid that the regiment you have been given is a rabble, almost a warband. They need discipline. I want them to be part of my army. They need to look like soldiers and not a band of brigands who prey on the weak."

His body told me that it was time for me to speak.

"I am honoured that I have been chosen. May I ask about Captain Friedrich's position?"

"He is your second in command. As we will begin by operating in Brandenburg then his knowledge will help."

I nodded, "Good. And to whom do we answer?"

"Me, of course. I will be with the vanguard. I will issue commands."

His words pleased me. "As we will be operating ahead of the army could I ask about supplies?"

The king deferred to Samuel von Winterfield who said, "There will be powder, ball and food for the start of the expedition but then you will have to find your own."

I frowned, "But as we will be in Brandenburg does that not mean we will be taking from the very people we are supposed to be helping?"

I saw the king smile. The Brandenburger nodded his head, "Regrettable but necessary."

The king said, "Of course if you could take from our enemies then so much the better."

I was not happy, but I was being paid and I would, if at all possible, take from the Imperial Army not least because I did not want to incur the wrath of the locals.

"The captain and I have no horses."

The quartermaster said, "We have some fine animals. You can choose your own."

Sigismund said, "Two each?"

"Of course."

The quartermaster asked, "And would you like servants?"

I shook my head, "Two more mouths to feed and two more horses to find. The captain and I can cope. There will be men in the regiment who can serve as servants if we need them."

The king said, wryly, "I have heard how you treat servants, Captain Friedrich." He waggled a playful finger at the Brandenburger, "The prince is less than happy with your treatment of his servants. He asked for you to be dismissed."

Sigismund was not put out by the criticism, "King Gustavus, like you I am a soldier. Perhaps I am bluffer than most but if you wanted a diplomat then you would have chosen another."

"You are right and as you will be ahead of the army then it is unlikely that you will come into contact with the prince. Your duties begin once you reach your camp. Until then I suggest you find your horses and study maps. You will, of course, be leaving the house to join your men in their camp. It is two miles from here."

The quartermaster added, "As far from other regiments as it is possible. It is less trouble that way."

"You will need to be ready to leave in the middle of April. I am hoping to move the army in May or, perhaps, June, we shall see."

He looked down and we were dismissed.

The quartermaster came out with us. There were clerks and servants working on orders, "Stephan, take these two officers to the horse lines. They are to choose their own horses."

"Yes, my lord."

The servant grabbed his cloak as he led us from the warmth of the room out into the biting cold. As we walked, I asked, "Why is such an important man as Samuel von Winterfield acting as quartermaster? I would have thought that he was far too important for such a position."

I had asked the question of Sigismund, but it was the clerk, Stephan Hard who answered, "Until the army recovers all of Brandenburg then he has no power. I am a Brandenburger, and I look forward to the time I can return to a civilised place and not this pustule at the back of beyond. This wind comes all the way from Russia."

Sigismund chuckled, "My countryman is right. This is a bleak place that the king has chosen to begin his campaign, but it means more men can easily be sent from Sweden or Denmark."

We reached the stables and the frown on the face of the horse master when Stephan informed him of our needs told me that he was not particularly happy about having to simply hand over four horses. There was no profit in that for him. The frown quickly changed to a smile as he led us to the far end of the lines.

I stopped Sigismund, "Let us save ourselves a walk and choose from here, closer to the stables." Stephan had told us that the stables contained the horses which belonged to the senior officers.

The horse master blustered, "I know my horses, Captain. The best horses are down here."

I adopted an innocent look and said, mildly, "You keep the best horses far away from the stables? I think not, my friend, and as we were asked, by the king," I emphasised the word, "to choose our own then we shall do so. If we choose badly then we will have to live with the consequences, eh?"

Sigismund caught on and nodded, "Aye, let us look at this end."

The first four horses, the ones who had the shelter of both the wall and the roof of the stables were good horses. Their coats showed that they had enjoyed attention lavished upon them. They were not as lean as the ones I could see ten horses down. Two of them were also big horses. If they were to carry me, a saddle, horse pistols and my cuirass then they would need to be big. As I took the halter of the chestnut the animal neighed and bobbed his head. I knew that was the horse for me. Charlotte had spoken of luck there was also something called fate and this horse spoke to me.

"This one."

The face of the horse master fell, "Marcus? He is an awkward horse, Captain. He threw his last rider."

I nodded, "Then I shall be more careful."

I handed the reins to Stephan, "Hold on to this wild animal for me, eh, Stephan?" He grinned as he knew what the horse master was up to. I could see that Sigismund was choosing between the next two and so I went up to the fourth horse. It backed away a little. I smiled, "Then if you do not like me I shall leave you. The fifth horse stood its ground and our eyes met. This was not as big as an animal as Marcus. It was a hand smaller, but it had a broad back. It was strong. Marcus would be a good horse for battle, but this one would be a good riding horse. "This one."

That I had not chosen the fourth horse pleased him and he gave a half smile, "Ran, is a solid enough horse, Captain, and she came from Sweden. Her last owner died of dysentery."

If he thought that would change my mind, he was wrong. "And her name?"

Stephan answered, "Ran was a goddess of the sea according to Norse legends."

Sigismund chose his. The Brandenburger then said, "Saddles, bits and horse furniture."

Before the horse master could speak Stephan pointed inside the stables to the tack room. There were saddles hanging from hooks. The horse master scurried in. "The ones on the lower hooks are taken already." Sigismund put his hands on his hips to stare at him. The man shook his head, "I swear, Captain. See, the names are burnt into the wood." I saw the names.

Nodding I took a ladder and climbed up to one without a name. It had seen service and that was good. The leather would be softer. I was not as precious about the saddle as the horses. I was confident that we would encounter Spanish troops, and they had the best saddles. Whatever saddle I chose would be a temporary one until I could pillage better. As I carried it down the ladder I was already thinking ahead. We would be living off the land. I was loath to take from ordinary people. It was not in my nature, and, in any case, I thought that was always a mistake. It was better to take from your enemies. I intended to do the task we had been assigned aggressively. I would seek out the enemy. I knew that, as scouts, we had to find the enemy. What better way of keeping our own position hidden than taking from our enemies?

With our horses, saddles, reins, halters, bits and blankets, we headed back to the house. Stephan was keen to get back into the warmth of the office he shared with the other clerks. As he turned to enter, I said, "Maps and directions to the camp, Stephan, and then you are done."

His shoulders sagged, "Come within, where it is warm."

Sigismund smiled, "I will wait with these horses. I would not have them pilfered before we begin."

Once inside the clerk took me to some maps. He sought one and said, "This is the land through which you will travel initially." I went to pick it up, but he shook his head, "This stays here. You will need to memorise it."

That was not good enough and I reached into my purse and took out a pair of English shillings. They both bore the image of King James. "Would this allow you to make me a rough copy and bring it to our rooms?"

He shook his head and grinned, "No, but three would." I took out a third and handed them over. They disappeared in a flash. I doubt that any other saw the transaction. "I will have them delivered to you this evening, Captain."

Chapter 4

January 1630 Peenemünde

We left the comfort of the officers' house the next morning. The best that could be said of the weather was that the snow had stopped. It was still bitingly cold, and the wind was still from the east. I rode Marcus. Ran seemed happy to be carrying my war gear. Until I could find panniers the bags were hung across her back. We had, according to Stephan, just under three miles to travel to reach the camp. We passed tents that were spread at the side of the road. I could see where houses had been commandeered and the best camp sites were those that were close to the houses. When the camps began to thin out, I wondered if we had been misinformed. The stink of horse dung half a mile from the last camp told me that we were getting close. The noise confirmed it. I heard the baleful wail of bagpipes and a cacophony of shouts and screams. That told me there were men from the north ahead.

Sigismund reined in three hundred paces from the camp. For the first time since I had met him he seemed uncomfortable. We could see that the camp was not a tidy one. Worse, there was a ring of men who were clearly fighting. Sigismund said, "These men we are to lead, are they cavalry or have we stumbled upon a band of brigands?"

I shook my head and pointed to the horse herd. The camp might be a mess, but these men knew how to hang on to their horses. There was a fence with a gate around them and four men stood guard. The horses were what we called in England, nags. "Look at the horses, Sigismund. They could not face up to real cavalry. These men hit and run. They will be doughty fighters and be brave, but the king will not be using them to charge. They are not men who ride in serried ranks, fire their weapons and perform the caracole. We will find the enemy and we will chase them. If you hoped for glory, then this regiment will not afford you the chance." I dug my heels into Marcus, "Come, let us exercise our authority. I think we are in for an interesting time."

The attention of the whole camp was on the fight. Two men were fighting and there was a huge disparity in their sizes. One was a giant and the other was almost a dwarf. Both were well muscled and, despite the cold, they were bare chested. The blood on their hands and their faces told me that they had both been exchanging blows for some time. I did not dismount but drew a pistol. I patiently loaded and primed it. Even as I watched, the dwarf managed to fell the giant who roared and spat out a tooth. He put his head down and barrelled towards the smaller man. Raising the pistol, I fired it into the air. The effect was astounding. The two men stopped fighting and silence fell as every eye turned to watch us. I was pleased that our four horses had not baulked at the pistol's crack. They were war horses. The smoke drifted before us.

I said, "I am Captain James Bretherton and I am here to take command of this regiment." I paused, "Although, at the moment it seems like a rabble. Where are the corporals?"

The two bare chested men stood and raised their right arms. The giant said, "I am Corporal Alexander Stirling."

The shorter man said, "And I am Corporal Richard Dickson."

I dismounted and handed my reins to the nearest man. "Hold these." I began to reload my pistol. "I realise that you have just celebrated Hogmanay but that is now over. Whatever has gone on until this moment is in the past and we start the New Year afresh." I smiled, "Let us all resolve to make this rabble into a regiment of which Captain Friedrich and I can be proud. Before we inspect the camp, I will give you this morning to make it look neater. I will see the two corporals in the command tent." I turned to the horse holder, "Which one is that?"

He looked confused and said, "There isn't one."

I sighed, "Then which are the corporals' tents?"

He pointed to the two extremes of the camp, "There and there, Captain." His accent told me he came from the English side of the Tweed.

"Captain Friedrich, find us a large tent. Evict whoever is in it."

"Yes, Captain." He was grinning.

I turned to the regiment, the corporals apart they were standing there. The two fighters were heading for their tents and that boded better than I had hoped. They had obeyed my orders without question. "What are you all waiting for? I gave an order."

A man, clearly Scottish by his Tam O'Shanter, laughed, "And why should we obey the orders of a poxy little Englishman like you?" He laughed and others joined in.

He was just ten paces from me and raising the pistol I fired it at his hat. I aimed just above his head hoping to scorch the hat, but the ball took the hat from his head. I smiled as he stared at me, "Because this poxy little Englishman will shoot anyone who does not obey his orders. How is that?"

Every man took to his heels and ran.

I turned to the horse holder who had his mouth open. "What is your name?"

"Alan Summerville, Captain, from Bellingham."

"Then follow me, Alan."

I led him and my two horses towards the tent of the giant corporal. He had dressed quickly and was wating for me. "Stirling, follow me."

"Sir." He marched as well as a man who has just been fighting could march. He was behind me, but I heard him spitting out gobs of blood or teeth. I could not tell which. We reached the large tent and I saw that Sigismund had evicted the three men who occupied it.

"Where do we go, Captain?" One of them asked.

Sigismund said, "I am sure there will be room in other tents."

"But not for three of us."

I laughed, "Make new friends eh?"

"Summerville, Stirling, wait here." I strode over to the tent of Richard Dickson. Like the other corporal he was dressed. He held a cloth to his nose to staunch the bleeding. "Corporal, with me."

I led him back to the command tent. I saw that between them the three had tethered the horses. They were all unsaddled and my gear was in the tent. I pointed to the inside, "The two of you, inside. Captain."

"Sir." Sigismund shepherded them inside making sure that he was between them.

"Summerville, you seem a likely lad. Tell me, are there any other corporals in the regiment?"

Captain of Horse

He shook his head, "No, Sir. Captain Deschamps took the two sergeants and the other corporal when they left at the end of the Polish campaign." He looked up as though reading the dates in the snow flecked sky, "That would have been about the end of September, Sir. Since then we have had just two."

The officer and his senior men had left at about the same time that Sigismund had been sent to find me. Summerville seemed an honest man and he was no longer young. I took him to be about my age. "You are promoted to Lance Corporal."

"Is that a rank, Sir?"

"It is now." Stand guard outside the tent and close your ears, do you understand?"

His eyes flickered to my pistol, and he nodded, "Oh aye, Sir, I understand."

When I entered I saw that the two corporals stood ramrod straight with their eyes facing ahead.

I shook my head, "The only two officers left in the regiment, and I find you fighting. By rights I should have you stripped of rank and punished." They said nothing. "Well, out with it, what caused the fight?"

They looked at each other and the Scottish soldier smiled, showing where he had lost teeth, "Go on Dick, you tell him."

The shorter man nodded and began, "It is like this, Sir, this regiment is made up of men who, if they were back in the borders, would be fighting each other. When we are at war, well, there is fighting enough for any man. We reached here in December. The journey cost us twenty men who deserted. Once in camp then the trouble started. It blew up on New Year's Eve. Men were drunk and there were fights. If we hadn't intervened, then there would have been bloodshed. Men would have used knives and not fists. So, we agreed to have a fight and that would decide it."

"Decide what?" I think I began to understand it, but I wanted to be clear.

"Who would run the regiment and who were the best fighters, us or them."

Sigismund's jaw dropped open, "You were fighting to decide who ran the regiment?"

Alexander Stirling nodded, "More or less."

"But you were half killing each other. You are both a mess."

They nodded and said, together, 'Yes, Sir.'

Sigismund shook his head. I said, "As of now I am in command, and we will have discipline. The fight is over."

"Of course, Sir."

"I want the word to be spread that any fights will result in a flogging."

The Scotsmen shook his head, "The men willna like the idea of a flogging."

I sighed, "If they do not fight then they will not be flogged." Despite the circumstances they seemed good soldiers. They had done what they had to save the regiment. I took them into my confidence. "King Gustavus wants to use us as the eyes and ears of his army. When we head south, in a month or so, we will be foraging ahead of the army. It is our intention, Captain Friedrich and I, to do so aggressively. I can promise the men as much fighting as they can handle but the enemy will be Imperial soldiers and men of the Catholic League, not each other." At that they both smiled. "Now go and get yourselves cleaned up. Spread the word. I will hold a parade at noon. You two apart are there any other soldiers with responsibilities?"

Dickson frowned, "Responsibilities, Sir?"

"Horses, food, cooking, you know the things that help the regiment run smoothly."

The Northumbrian said, "Davy Campbell is the one we ask about horses."

Stirling nodded, "And Alistair Wilson is the best of the cooks, but we generally just cook for ourselves, Sir, with our tent mates." He leaned forward, "You upset three of the lads when you took over this tent."

He said it in a reasonable manner, and I smiled, "I suppose we could just sleep in the open eh, Corporal?" I asked, "What happened to the officer's tent?" There had to be regimental papers and the like.

Dickson shrugged, "They took everything. They did a moonlight flit, Sir. One minute they were here and the next they were gone."

"Flit? I have not heard this word."

I turned to Sigismund, "It means they left and took everything without saying a word." I took in the significance of Dickson's words. "The colours too?"

Both their faces hardened, and Stirling almost spat out, "No one ever liked the French bastard and his officers but when we found out that the colours had been taken…"

"Even the company standards?"

Dickson nodded, "Between you and me, Sir, I think he joined the other side, the Imperial Army. He didn't mind slaughtering Poles, but I reckon the captain and the others were Catholics." He nodded, conspiratorially, "They all had crucifixes. They kept them hidden but…"

I had much to do, "Very well, parade at noon. Send Campbell and Wilson to me."

"Sir." They snapped to attention, and I followed them to the entrance.

I followed them and said to Summerville, "Take our horses to the others and then return here."

"Sir." He paused and then nodded at the backs of the two corporals, "They are good lads, Sir. They would have stopped the fight when one of them was knocked out. They wouldn't have killed each other."

I smiled, "That is gratifying to hear, Summerville."

I went back inside, and Sigismund shook his head, "You have been given a poisoned chalice my friend. I am sorry that I got you into this. Had I known the extent of the problem…"

"You could have done nothing about it. I understand the fight and I do not think it will impair the ability of this regiment. If anything, it tells me that they can fight but we have more work to do than I expected. When we have spoken to the men at noon, I want you to go to the quartermaster. We need colours. We need more tents, and we need food. We can build up the regiment, but we need tools to do so. When time allows, I wish to speak to the king. If this Captain Deschamps took the colours he needs to know."

"Yes, I can see that. What colour and design do you have in mind, James?"

"The colour? We passed no green standards on the way here so green. As for the design…I will give that some thought."

From outside I heard a cough and then Summerville's voice, "Captain Bretherton, Campbell and Wilson."

"Come in, all three of you." They stood at attention, and I smiled, "At ease. I have given Summerville the rank of Lance Corporal and I would offer you the same promotion. With the rank comes more pay and responsibility. I hope, in the fullness of time, to make all three of you corporals and there will be sergeants. That is for the future." They did not know what to say but their faces showed a mixture of pleasure, they were being paid more, and trepidation, what would they have to do to earn the pay? "Campbell?"

The shorter of the three and the youngest nodded, "That is me, Sir."

"You are good with horses, I understand?"

He looked relieved, "Aye, Sir, I always liked animals."

His name sounded Scottish, but his accent was Northumbrian, "Campbell?"

"Aye, Sir, my dad was a Scot, and he settled in Rothbury."

I nodded, "I would like you to be in charge of the horses. Summerville brought you the four we were given."

"Oh aye, Sir, fine animals."

"And your animals, what of them?"

"Not so good, Sir. They are all underfed. We chose this campsite because I told the corporals that the grazing was better, but they need oats, Sir."

Sigismund had a wax tablet, and I said, "Captain."

"I have made a note, Captain."

"Do we have remounts?"

"No, Sir."

"We will try to get some."

I turned to Wilson, "Now I understand you can cook."

"Most of the lads can cook, Sir, but I suppose I enjoy it more than most."

"Then you will be in charge of food. How do you get supplies?" He and the others exchanged guilty looks. I sighed, "You steal. Whilst that might be handy in enemy land here it is not. When Captain Friedrich goes to the headquarters, Wilson, go with him."

"Sir."

Captain of Horse

"Captain, try to get a cart. Let us use whatever favour we have now, eh?"

"Sir."

"Summerville, you will act as servant and orderly to the captain and I."

He looked pleased, "Sir."

"Now, before you go back to your tents tell me about the regiment. I want to know about weapons and equipment, as well as the actions in which you have fought."

After an hour I learned that they had not fought in any battles but had skirmished and chased. I did not think that they had been either well led or well used. When I was told of their weapons and equipment I was appalled. The only consistent items were the swords. They varied from hangars to proper swords. Some had firearms. There were twenty matchlocks. They were lighter and shorter than those used by musketeers. A few men had handguns and ten had spears. There appeared to be no uniform at all.

After I dismissed them, I said to Sigismund, "We cannot face Imperial horsemen with twenty matchlocks and a few handguns. We need weapons." He nodded, "And food and uniforms." I lowered my voice, "At the moment these are a rabble and brave as they are would not be able to face Imperial cavalry. We do not have a long time to mould them. Colours, uniforms, weapons and food will do that. As for the rest…" I smiled, "That is down to the two of us and the five officers we have."

He nodded, "I have heard of this English optimism. When King Philip of Spain sent his mighty armada to crush England was it not a handful of small ships that took them on?"

I nodded, "It seemed hopeless, but God was on the side of the English and good seamanship and the aid of the weather defeated the Spanish but, Sigismund, the battle was almost lost because the English were not given enough cannonballs by the queen. King Gustavus will have to be more generous than was Queen Elizabeth."

The five men who were my officers had to have been busy for when the regiment paraded before me they were all dressed, with caps upon their heads and their weapons in their hands. They stood in their companies. I saw that they were equally divided between Scots and English. I did not like that but I knew that was something I could not change.

I had made my point with my pistol already and I kept my weapons in their holsters, unprimed. Sigismund stood behind me and to the side the five men who were the officers. Sigismund and I had made decisions in the short time we had been alone.

I held them in my gaze as they stood at a loose attention. The wind whistled from the east. It was no longer flecked with either icy rain or snow but it was still cold and the men were not close to their fires. I saw that few could meet my stare. When I spoke, I saw a few men start.

"I am Captain Bretherton and the new officer who will lead you into battle. Hitherto, you have had no name but from now on you shall be Bretherton's Horse. As you will bear my name, I expect no more of the nonsense that greeted me on my arrival. As I said to your officers, that is in the past. The past is, like your homelands, a country you have left. This regiment begins now." I let that settle in and then spoke again. "King Gustavus has high hopes for this regiment. He intends us to be his eyes and ears. At the moment a blind, deaf and toothless hound would be of more use. Captain Friedrich and I will spend the next months changing that state. When we leave, in the spring, this regiment will be unrecognisable. It will be disciplined. Any who do not wish for discipline or cannot accept it should leave this day. There will be no recriminations. If you stay, then every order will be obeyed instantly. Is that clear?" Some nodded. I said, "You are not asses and donkeys, you are men and have voices. I asked if that was clear?"

There was a mumbled, "Yes Sir."

I shouted, "I cannot hear you. Is that clear?"

They all roared back at me, "Yes Sir!"

"Good. The orders for the rest of the day are this. I want every man except for my officers to clean and prepare his weapons. They will be examined by me and my officers. Every horse will be groomed and paraded. I want to examine every piece of horse furniture. Captain Friedrich and Corporal Wilson will go to find more equipment for us. We will have organisation. You will each have duties assigned and all of us will stand a watch. This will become a military camp. You will be roused by a drum and parade each morning." I smiled, "You are, like it or not, soldiers now. I want you to behave like soldiers. Dismiss."

When they left there were more smiles than scowls. Sigismund and I had wanted a horn but knew that the chances of having a man who could play one were remote. Summerville would be able to use a drum once we had acquired one.

I turned to my officers. "Our success will depend as much upon you five as on the captain and me. I am relying on you. When we are successful then your purses will be full." I knew that these men were, like me the first time I had gone to war, mercenaries. They might believe in the Protestant cause but they were fighting for money. I was honest enough to know that I was too. The coins I earned were for Charlotte and my son.

Dickson nodded, "We won't let you down, Sir. With respect, Sir, Captain Deschamps never thought much of us. He led by sending us into action first. We had fifty more men than you see now a year ago. Any coins we found went into his purse."

I nodded, "Well know that I shall lead from the front and all," I emphasised the word, "that we take will be shared." They all smiled. "It will be hard work, but hard work makes men into soldiers." When the five had gone I said, "What we need, Sigismund, is action."

"I know. When I take Wilson to Headquarters, I will see what I can discover."

"Good."

I was alone after he had left and I surveyed my command. I was a Captain of Horse and I had my own regiment but it was like a blunted and rusted sword. Whilst in its scabbard it looked dangerous but when it was drawn it might shatter. We had to clean and hone the blade that would be Bretherton's Horse. If not, my wife might be a widow and my son fatherless.

Chapter 5

March 1630 Kotelow

Sigismund managed to get both food and weapons as well as cloth for colours but there were no horses to be had and only half of the men were issued with weapons. They were the shorter dragoon matchlocks. He also found powder and ball. It was a start but that was all. As I toured the camp, I made a point of speaking to every man I met. I had learned to judge men quickly. Occasionally I made a misjudgement, but it was rare enough for me to trust my instincts. I was also sharp eyed and as we examined the tents at the furthest extremity of the camp, I noticed that the two tents were tidier than the rest. The eight men who were there also seemed somewhat nervous. Until I had married, I might have been oblivious to the signs of a woman, but Charlotte had taught me how women liked to be organised. I spied the clothesline with drying clothes, and I nodded, "A fine and neat camp."

They relaxed and the one who seemed to be the leader of one of the tents, I learned his name was Paul White, nodded and smiled, "Thank you, Sir. We try." He had a northern accent.

I smiled back and said, "And if you would like to bring out the women who made it so I should like to meet them."

Their faces fell. "Women, Sir?"

"White, I am not a fool. I have not seen the women yet, but I know they are here and do you think you can hide them from me?"

The two women had been lurking behind the tent and they came out. One shook her head and said, "I told you, Paul White, this one is different from the Froggy." She curtsied, "I am Jane Brown, Captain, and Paul White's wife."

"Married?"

"We jumped the broomstick, Sir."

I nodded, "Then when we find a chaplain we shall make it a marriage in the eyes of God, too."

That made the couple smile. Jane looked to be in her early twenties and while her skin was red and chafed from the wind her hair was clean and neatly tied back and she had a pretty face.

She was what Paul and the others would have called bonny. I looked at the other one. She was thinner with blond hair and her features looked Slavic. She could not have been more than seventeen. "And this is?"

The leader of the other tent said, "Gertha Zalinski, Captain. We found some Poles trying to…" he shook his head, "They are dead now. She cooks and cleans for us, Sir. She is a good girl." He leaned forward, "No one touches her, Sir."

"Can she speak English?"

"After a fashion, Sir."

I smiled and said, in German, "Welcome Gertha. Are you happy here?"

She beamed and I saw that she was pretty, despite the thinness of her frame, "Yes Captain. They are good men."

I nodded, "Now I do not mind these two women being here but when we leave the camp, what then? Will they travel with the tross?" The tross was the name given to camp followers. They endured a hard life and, often, a short one.

They all looked at each other and Jane Brown frowned, "We follow the men, Sir."

"We will be in much danger." I sighed. While I had wondered about such a problem I had not come up with a solution. "In the short term there is not a problem but when we leave…" I suddenly had an idea, "Jane, can you sew?"

"Why yes, Sir. I mend the men's clothes."

"Good, then I shall pay you to sew the regimental colours."

She beamed, "It would be an honour, Sir."

Later that night, as I sat in my tent after the meal drinking with Sigismund, I realised that the visit to the two women had enhanced my reputation. My threat with the pistol when I had scattered the mob had cowed them but my reasonable behaviour to the women seemed to make me one of them.

I chose a red cross to be sewn onto the standard and the company flags. It reflected England and contrasted well with the green. I knew that the green, which was pale, would fade in the summer sun but the red cloth of the cross was vibrant and would last longer. Gertha helped Jane and I could see that the two women took pride in their work. Their needlework was impressive. I sent White and his tentmates to find the wood for the standards and the company banners. It proved a wise decision for they found ash and the branches they brought were straight and true. It was a start.

While they hunted, I worked with the rest of the men. I made up new companies giving each one a name rather than a number. A number or letters suggested a hierarchy and I wanted them all to be equal. I used animals from the north for the eight companies: Stag, Wildcat, Badger, Fox, Hunting Dog, Otter, Wolf and Hawk. They seemed happy enough with the titles and when each tent leader asked Jane to sew the animal design on their company flags then I knew I had made the right decision. As they paid Jane and Gertha the two women were happy. I also mixed the companies. I knew that I would need three more leaders and Paul White had already shown himself to be capable. There was no need for haste and I used the times we trained to identify potential officers.

I kept the training simple at first. I had them ride and wheel in formation. We had neither enough weapons nor ball and powder to waste and so we mimed firing the weapons. I had them practise so that while one half of a company fired their weapons the others reloaded. The ones without firearms protected those with firearms. We also practised fighting on foot. Our horses were not much use in a cavalry battle, but I believed that the men I led would be better as men who used stealth to attack. If we were the eyes and ears, then it would be better if we were invisible. I made a game of it. One company would hide and the other seven would seek them. The men who were the last to be found were noted by me. They would be the scouts.

By the end of the first month when the blizzards had ceased and the ground was becoming a muddy morass, I was happy with the progress. Sigismund and I were summoned to headquarters to update the king on our progress. That he had men who had spied upon us was clear from his comments, but he was happy with my organisation.

"King Gustavus, we still need remounts and more weapons."

He nodded, "As you can see von Winterfield is not here. He has gone to Sweden to bring more men. He will try to find you some but…" He spread his hands apologetically.

"King Gustavus, do I have your permission to lead a raid into the Imperial held lands?"

"You are ready for such a raid?"

"My men are better trained but I want to give them some action, and if we can take what we need from the Catholics while they think we are still hunkered down for winter then so much the better. It will also pave the way for the time we do scout for you."

"Then I give you permission for a limited raid." He stroked his beard as he studied the map. "When we do take on the enemy it will be to the south. Perhaps a foray to the south and west might serve its purpose. It would also be useful to know what forces we face." He raised his head, and his eyes met mine, "Captain, we have too few men to be wasteful of them. I can understand why you need to do this but when we move forward to relieve the suffering of the people I will need every man. Understand?"

"I do, King Gustavus, and that is my intention too."

As we rode back, I said, "Sigismund, I will take one hundred men only. I want the ones who have shown that they can scout and have weapons."

"A good idea."

"I will need you to maintain order in the camp."

"I should be with you."

"Yes, you should, but we cannot take both senior officers on this raid."

"And will you take one of the junior ones?"

I was silent for a moment. If I chose one to come, then they might take that as a sign that I favoured them. I did not want that. "No, this will be a chance for me to see who shines. We have three companies without officers."

Back at the camp I did take the other five into my confidence. Like Sigismund they all wished to come. I explained to them my reasons for not taking them. "This will be the chance for a small group of men to work together. I need the rest of you to help Captain Friedrich to continue to train the men in my absence. I hope to return intact and with supplies. More importantly, I will have learned how best to use this unique regiment."

Alan Summerville frowned, "Unique, Sir, how so?"

"We are not cavalry, and we are not mounted dragoons. I am not sure how the king wishes to use us if we find our enemy. I do not think he knows himself. Your Captain Deschamps clearly did not. I have ideas how we can be used but I need to test those theories. This will be my chance. Now, the men…"

The one hundred men were easy to choose. We all knew who they were. I let the others tell the men and I gave them just three days to get ready. They all had a firearm, but I hoped we would not need them. The knives and swords they carried would be better weapons. We did not take the colours. When they were revealed then our identity would be known. Until the campaign began, I wanted anonymity. I wanted us to be ghosts. To that end we all wore dun-coloured cloaks and the beaver skin hats favoured by the men of the north. I also wore one.

We slipped away from the camp after dark and skirted the rest of the army. I was in command and the king had given me licence. I intended to use that licence. The first part was, in many ways, the most dangerous. I intended to have the men swim their animals across the channel to the mainland. When the campaign began the king would use a pontoon bridge. I wanted to cross where no one expected us. When we reached the water, it was both dark and foreboding. I had chosen Ran rather than Marcus. She was nearer in size to the others, but I had also been told that she was a good swimmer. I turned in my saddle, "When you enter the water slip your feet from the stirrups. Your horses will swim. Hang on to your saddles. Keep your horse's nose as close as possible to the tail of the animal in front."

"Sir?"

I had learned the names of the men I led, "Yes, Longstaff?"

"What about our firearms? They will be rendered useless by the water."

"Before we raid, we will clean them. Remember, if we use our firearms then we will attract attention. We need secrecy."

I turned Ran and headed into the water. As I had expected it was icily cold but bearable. I slipped my feet out of the stirrups and focussed my eyes on the opposite bank. It stood out as a white line of sand. Ran was a good swimmer and as I glanced behind, I saw that she had pulled away from the horse behind. It could not be helped for she was the best swimmer. As soon as I felt her hooves find purchase on the sand, I put my boots back in the stirrups and turned. The nearest rider, Peter Jennings, was just fifteen feet behind me. Once on the beach I dismounted and held Ran's reins. While I waited, I emptied my boots of sea water.

I glanced up, "Well done, Jennings."

As each man joined me, I praised them. They did as I had done, and we all waited for the last men to arrive. The very last man, Archie Dalgleish, was a good forty feet behind the man who had reached the beach before him. I sensed the concern in all of the others, and it was with some relief that we saw his horse appear.

As he dismounted, he shook his head, "Sorry, Captain. I lost my way a little."

"Never mind, you are here. Now tighten your girths and be prepared to ride. Jennings, take the lead and find us a road that heads south and west."

"Sir."

We found a road, but it went due south. It was unfortunate as it compromised my orders. However, I consoled myself with the fact that I could gather valuable intelligence for the king. Jennings reined in an hour or so before dawn. We had passed a crossroads, and a sign had told us that the village of Kotelow lay ahead.

He said, quietly, "Sir, I can smell woodsmoke." I nodded, "And I think I heard horses."

Horses meant enemy soldiers. I turned, "Longstaff, keep the men here. Jennings and I will return soon. Have them prepare their weapons."

"Sir."

"Lead on."

We walked along the road in the dark. Jennings knew his business and when he turned to head into the forest I followed. I could now smell the woodsmoke and hear the horses. As the sky lightened in the east I saw the village in the distance. The animals were between the village and us. Jennings looked at me and I mimed for him to dismount. I tied Ran's reins to a tree and drew my sword. I led this time, and I picked my way along what looked like a hunter's trail. I saw pinpricks of light appear. There were campfires. The neighing of horses from my right told me where their horse lines lay. This was a military camp and I needed to know how many men were here before I made any decision. I moved from tree to tree, trusting in Jennings' skills behind me.

The German who appeared was just ten feet from me and I froze. When I heard the sound of water splashing and caught the smell of urine, I knew that he was making water. His companion said something that was, to me, unintelligible and the man laughed and said, "Good one, Johann." I saw his face as he raised his head. It stood out against the dark. "I do not know why we stand a duty."

The other man had come closer and I heard his words. "As for me, Karl, I do not know why we are in this little shit hole at all. Why are we not at Neubrandenburg with the rest of the regiment?"

The one called Karl laughed, "That is simple. Our corporal upset the captain, and we are punished. He said it was to keep watch for the Swedes but that is nonsense. They are all still in their little camp at Usedom. Come let us get food before we wake the others. It is the only benefit of a night duty."

As they walked away, I followed and saw that the camp was not a large one. It was a small company. There were ten tents and they each looked to be big enough to hold just four or five men. The two men I had heard were standing with a third at the fire and one was stirring a pot. I saw no stacked matchlocks but noticed that one of the men had a wheellock harquebus. They were harquebusiers. I turned and gestured for Jennings to follow me. We reached the horses, and I whispered, "Bring the men. Have them dismount here. No firearms. I want swords only."

He nodded and grinned. He left. I watched the sky grow a little lighter. Dawn would be less than thirty minutes away. The camp would soon awake. I heard the rustling behind me as the men appeared. I was pleased that they were all leading their horses.

I pointed, "Jennings, take ten men and secure the enemy horses. Dalgleish, take five men and guard our horses." They both nodded. "The rest of you draw your weapons. There are fifty or so Germans ahead and they are about to wake. Use your swords and knives. Spread out in a line and keep behind me. I want their camp, their weapons and their horses."

They nodded and I saw that they were eager. These were warriors and fighting was in their blood. I walked with my sword in my right hand and my dagger in my left. We were at the edge of the trees when one of the men who had been on watch put a trumpet to his mouth and began to blow. The camp would be awake in moments. I ran and my men followed. The three men turned at our approach and the trumpet wailed to a halt. Even as one of them tried to shout a warning I slashed my sword across the trumpeter's head.

"Alarm!"

The other two night guards fell as quickly as the trumpeter. As men emerged from their tents so my men fell upon them. When I saw the flash of a wheellock and then heard the report I knew that it was not one of my men but a German. I heard a cry from behind me.

A German voice shouted for them to rally and I ran at the man who had given the command. He had a sword, and I realised he was the officer, the corporal. He saw me and came at me with his sword. I saw that it was a heavy cavalry sword with S-shaped quillons. He would stab at me with it. He roared a challenge and came directly at me. As I had expected the lunge came at my neck. In the half light of dawn, he would not know if I wore a breastplate or not. My neck and face were my most vulnerable targets. I flicked the sword away with my dagger as I slashed at his side. My sword was shorter but had a good edge and I sliced into his side, scraping off ribs. Falling back, he tried to use the edge of his sword, but my left hand darted in and my dagger found his neck. He died quickly.

I was suddenly aware that the sun had peered over the eastern skyline and the village. Around me my men stood over the dead Germans. Eight had their hands in the air. They had surrendered. The rest were dead or dying. Sleepy men were easy prey. It was not pretty but it was war.

I shouted, "Dalgleish, fetch the horses. Longstaff, take ten men and secure the village."

"Sir!"

"Come on, you men, follow me." One of them looked at the dead man he had just killed. Longstaff said, "You heard the captain. We will all get our share. Don't you worry."

I sheathed my weapons and said, "Anyone hurt?"

A voice said, "Munroe was hit by a ball, Sir."

I turned and saw that David Munroe was having his wound cleaned. He grinned, "Just nicked me, Captain. No harm done."

The horses were brought, and I nodded to Jennings, "Come with me." We walked to the disconsolate prisoners. I spoke to them all, but I looked at one man who stared at me as I approached, "You are all my prisoners, and your fate lies in my hands. I know that you are a detached company of harquebusiers, where is your regiment?"

I knew the answer already, but I wanted them to think that they could fool me. The man who stared at me pointed to the south-east, "Schönberg."

I nodded, "Good." I turned to Jennings. "Take their boots from them and their weapons but let them keep their cloaks."

"Yes, Captain Bretherton."

"When my men have disarmed you then you may leave."

Jennings was no fool and he had six men with confiscated and loaded harquebuses aimed at the men as they were searched and their boots removed."

That done I pointed south and east, "You may leave."

They headed off and I said, quietly, "Dalgleish, follow them and then return when they have turned to the west."

He gave me a curious look but nodded. "Sir."

I cupped my hands, "First, we eat and then we will take this camp apart. I want us to leave by dark. Have Longstaff and the men in the village relieved when the first men have eaten."

Jennings showed that he was officer material when he nodded and said, "Do we take from the villagers, Sir?"

I nodded, "Yes, but not everything."

I headed for the largest tent. It was the one from which the corporal had emerged. I went inside and saw some maps and parchment. I took them. There was also a purse hanging from the cot and when I picked it up, it was heavy.

One of my men came in and said, "Sorry, Sir, I didn't know you were here."

"It is no matter," I tossed him the purse. "Take this and put it with the other coins we collect. We will divide it up before we leave."

He grinned, "Yes, Captain."

I knew that my action would ensure that no one kept coins for themselves. I was trying to build up warriors who would fight for their fellows and that meant sharing all. The corporal had four good wheellocks. They were more valuable than gold. Even if the rest of this company only had two such weapons each, we would be able to give another hundred or so men a firearm. Added to the swords we had found the raid was a success and I knew that we could return to the main camp directly and we would have done our job.

Dalgleish soon arrived back. He shook his head, "How did you know they would head west, Captain?"

"I knew that their regiment was based at Neubrandenburg. This way the men we released will tell their officers that we are headed for Schönberg. They will have a wild goose chase following us while we head home." I knew that I had impressed the men. Soldiers always like to have clever officers. I had seen enough stupid ones to know that.

It was noon by the time we had cleared the camp. The tents and weapons would be carried on the captured horses. There were fifty-five of them and they were all cavalry mounts. I would divide them amongst the companies when we reached our camp. I had the men build a pyre for the bodies. When we left, we would burn them. I did not want the stink of flesh to spoil our sleep. I divided the men into five groups and set a watch. Four would all sleep while the other watched. I took the last watch. I slept remarkably well considering that the ground was hard and it began to rain not long before I finally woke.

When I was woken, I set my men to cooking food. We had taken some perishable food from the village, and we made a hunter's stew. The rain meant that we would have to use some powder to begin the funeral fire. It could not be helped.

It was almost dark when we mounted. I had half of the men leading a captured horse and booty. I lit the funeral pyre and waited until the flames licked up the sides before we left.

Jennings said, "North, Sir?"

I shook my head, "No, Jennings, west. I want to see Neubrandenburg."

They were surprised but our success meant that they were willing to give me the benefit of the doubt. It was a main road but, at night, empty. The villages through which we passed kept their doors closed. They were unmolested by us. We skirted the town of Friedland. It was midnight when we saw the walled town of Neubrandenburg. We knew that from the bells of the churches. This was Catholic Germany. We watched from the eaves of the forest. The bulk of my men were a hundred paces in the forest, and I just had Jennings and Longstaff with me. We were hidden by the trees.

"What are you watching for, Sir?"

"I want to see what kind of commander they have here. The town has a wall and small towers. It can be defended. Is it an aggressive commander or a passive one?" I saw Longstaff frown. "Those prisoners would have reached here not long ago. We rode and they were walking. It is twenty odd miles but marching with no boots is hard. We will wait for an hour or so. The horses can use the rest. If no one emerges then we know that it is a commander who is cautious. If men emerge that is a different story."

In the end we had to wait, by my estimate, no more than thirty minutes. We heard noises from the town and then the gates opened, and horsemen appeared. There were cuirassiers as well as dragoons and harquebusiers. I counted more than two hundred as they thundered along the road we had taken not long earlier. When the gates slammed shut, I wheeled Ran and said, "Now we find a road north and head home."

We had a long and weary thirty odd mile ride through rain which had begun as drizzle and ended as a rainstorm that insinuated its way through oiled cloaks. This time we headed for the pontoon bridge begun by King Gustavus' engineers. A last boat was fitted to allow us to clatter across. As the last man passed, the final pontoon was removed. There would be spies watching and my ruse at Neubrandenburg would be discovered.

"Jennings, and Longstaff, lead the horses back to our camp. I will report to the king."

"Sir." As they rode off, I saw that every trooper rode proudly. They were soldiers now and not the rabble I had found just a short time earlier. There was still work to do but the rougher edges had already been polished off and we had the beginnings of a regiment.

Chapter 6

I had to wait for half an hour to speak to the king. He was meeting with his generals. When he emerged, he saw the blood spatter on my jacket. He frowned, "You are back quickly, Captain, and there is blood on your jacket. What happened? Failure?"

"Quite the contrary, Your Majesty." I gave him the details of the raid and subsequent scouting expedition. As I spoke the frown was replaced by a broad smile.

"I was told that you were a clever officer. If there are at least three regiments at Neubrandenburg, then that is where we will begin our campaign."

"King Gustavus, we skirted Friedland because that was also defended. If we approach Friedland openly then word will reach Neubrandenburg, and they will be prepared."

"And their defences will be ready." I nodded, "Could your regiment cut the road?"

"They can now, Sir. They have shown me that there are all capable men who obey orders. What I was told before I took command was misguided."

He gave me a sad smile, "And that is my fault. I believed what I was told by Captain Deschamps. I should have realised he was dishonest before he fled. You have a month before we leave. I trust that is enough time."

I nodded, "We have fifty-five good horses and a hundred or more wheellocks and swords. We even took four pot helmets. We will be ready," I hesitated.

"Go on."

"I wish to pay my officers. I have five and I need eight, at least."

"Quite right, too. I will have a chest sent over to you."

"Thank you."

"By the way, do you have colours?"

"Yes, King Gustavus. A red cross on a green background."

"Good. It was the cross used by the crusaders and we are on a crusade here, Captain. A crusade against the Papists."

When I reached the camp, it was sunset. As soon as I was seen there was a huge cheer from the regiment. I was taken aback. It was a far cry from the greeting when I had first arrived. Sigismund and my other officers stood like an honour guard before my tent, their swords raised in an arch. As I dismounted, Jack Wallace, who acted as an assistant to Lance Corporal Campbell, took Ran. There was another cheer as I walked beneath the swords.

I took off my hat and made a sweeping bow, "There was no need."

Dick Dickson said, forcefully, "There was every need, Captain. In a couple of days, you have brought us more glory, treasure and prestige than the years we served that Froggy. We can do anything with you as our leader."

"Well, I thank you. Is there food? I could eat a horse…with the skin on."

Lance Corporal Wilson said, "Aye, the lads found a couple of seals asleep. Added to the rabbits we have trapped we have a tasty stew."

"Good. On the morrow we shall have an officer's call after breakfast. I now have a better idea of the quality of our men and how they can be led."

Sigismund had found a large flagon of wine and the two of us enjoyed a feast. Archie Dalgleish and a couple of troopers came along with a trio of sacks. They deposited them on the ground.

"What is this, Archie?"

"All the treasure from the raid. No one has touched it, Sir."

"Thank you. I shall divide it up in the morning."

"No rush, Captain. There isn't a great deal to spend it on in this wind ravaged hole."

As they left Sigismund shook his head, "Who would have thought such a change could have been made so quickly?"

I said, "Let us not be hasty. I am pleased with the change but who knows how deep it runs. Perhaps our first failure might undo all the work we have done. We are taking baby steps, Sigismund."

I then went through my plans and ideas. He was happy with all of them. I began to understand why I had been chosen to lead the regiment. Sigismund was a good soldier and I did not doubt a fine leader but he lacked my background. The wars for the Dutch and in the Palatinate had made me a better officer.

The next day the five officers came to my tent. We met inside for the wild wind from the Baltic was unrelenting. I spoke plainly. "I have decided that you two, Dickson and Stirling, will be made up to sergeant with the accompanying pay." They beamed. "You shall also have first choice of the horses and weapons we took. As you two are senior I will let you choose your own companies."

It was clear that they had discussed this for Dick said, immediately, "I will have the Wildcats and Alex the Wolves."

"Good." I turned to the other three. "You three are all promoted to Corporal. You each get to choose your own horse and weapons. Like the sergeants you can pick your companies."

These three had not expected that and they looked at each other. Eventually Corporal Wilson said, "Most of my tentmates are in the Otters. If it is alright with you two, I would like those."

Alan nodded and said, "Then in that case I would like the Stags, for the same reason."

Corporal Campbell said, "Then it is the Foxes for me."

I smiled, "That was easy. Now we need another three officers. They will all be corporals. I have my own ideas, but I am happy for you to make suggestions. I want harmony."

They nodded.

"Peter Jennings impressed me on the raid."

Dick said, "Aye, he is a good lad."

I looked at the other faces, "Any objections?" They shook their heads. "Paul White and David Seymour seem like good soldiers too."

Sergeant Stirling said, "The problem is, Captain, that they are good mates. They both come from Dunbar."

I frowned, "So just one of them?"

"Aye, Sir. That way you have a natural second in command. They won't mind."

"You are sure?"

He nodded to Sergeant Dickson, "Dick knows the English lads, but I know the Scots. Trust me, Sir. David Seymour is the natural leader."

"Then Seymour it is."

Captain of Horse

The sergeant said, "His mates are in the Badgers, Sir."

"Then that will be his company and as I intend the Hunting Dogs to be our scouts then that will be Corporal Jennings' company. Longstaff impressed me."

"Aye, Ralphie is a good lad. He comes from Durham. His dad fought for the queen."

"Then Longstaff has the Hawks. Corporal Summerville, go and bring them to me."

"Sir."

When they had gone Dick said, "Sir, we were talking while you were on the raid. The lads would like the animal sewing on their company guidon. Would that be alright?"

"I thought they had already done so."

He shook his head, "No, Sir, they just made each guidon look different."

"It is more work for the ladies."

"They are loving it, Sir. The lads pay them, and they can buy nice things."

"And now we divide up the booty."

Sergeant Stirling said, "Is it just going to the ones who went on the raid, Sir?"

"I thought so, but would that not create bad feeling?"

"No, Sir, the opposite. You and the lads took the risks. We all benefitted from the food you brought and the weapons and the horses will be for the regiment. No, Sir, this is right." He chuckled. "Besides, half of them will gamble it away and it will be shared that way, through foolishness."

I still had to decide what to do when we began the campaign. I had a month left to make my decision. The three men were delighted with the promotion, the horses and the weapons. After they had chosen them, I paraded the regiment and announced the promotions to everyone. When Paul White beamed, I knew that Sergeant Stirling had been right.

"The other recently acquired animals and weapons will be awarded as rewards to those who impress your officers and myself."

Their smiles told me all.

I gave my officers a week to work with their new companies while Sigismund and I made copies of the maps I had taken. I would hand over the originals to the clerks, but I wanted the benefit of this treasure for myself. Corporal Campbell found men in his company who were like himself, men who liked horses. They took on the duties of watching over the extra horses. The officers had been lucky in that we had taken the holsters when we had routed the Germans. However, we had not taken holsters for all the pistols. Sigismund explained that the Germans liked to use their boots as saddle holsters when they rode into battle. We would either have to emulate them or find holsters from somewhere else. The Germans used a different boot from us. When we had raided, we had some of them and they had been distributed already.

The training took on a greater intensity. Everyone now saw a purpose to the training. There was more discipline in the camp and the duties of sentry were taken seriously. The raiders had told the others how we had caught the Germans because of a lack of vigilance. On our weekly visit to the headquarters Sigismund and I saw that more men and materiel had arrived. However, the men were still few in number. What had arrived, however, were the cannons that the king liked. As Count Wolfgang Otto explained to me at one of these meetings, they were an innovation of the king himself.

"He likes to have six smaller cannons attached to each regiment of infantry. They are just three or four pounders. They are relatively light but pack a punch. These do not trade balls with the larger cannons the Imperial Army uses but they are there to deter the enemy horses. They can thin out a charging force of men. It is a clever tactic."

Sigismund and I discussed the matter back at the camp. My fear was that once the enemy saw the efficacy of such a defence, they might use it against us. "I know that we are not intended to charge enemy infantry but who knows when we may be ordered to do so. We need the men to practise charging, not knee to knee as the cavalry do but use their natural skills as light horsemen. I cannot see a gunner wasting a ball on one or two men. We both know that a cannonball works best against a solid block of men. It can carve its way through."

He smiled, "James, you have fought in larger battles than I have. I will take your word for it."

Captain of Horse

We used the slightly warmer weather and drying ground to practise with our horses. As well as the caracole, sections of men charging a line, discharging their weapons and rolling to the back of their company, we also made a game of trying to capture mock guns we made up. It would be a deadly game when we used it in battle, but they enjoyed the fun of outwitting other companies.

I was also aware that, like Sigismund, the officers in my command lacked battle experience. Captain Deschamps had clearly not been a good leader. He had not used his men well and certainly never involved them in the planning of an attack. Once a week I met with my officers at my tent. We shared ale and food while I explained my philosophy of war and our tactics.

"We cannot match either pikemen or musketeers. We can however pin them. They will not waste ball and powder on a couple of men. When we are close to musketeers, I want loose and open lines."

Sigismund frowned, "But if their cavalry attacked us, they would simply crush the smaller numbers."

I smiled and shook my head, "Captain, do you think we can face Imperial cavalry? When we attacked the camp at Kotelow we found cavalrymen on foot without armour and weapons. The horses we captured are four or five hands taller than ours. If cavalry come at us, then we run."

Sergeant Stirling shook his head, "Sir, it goes against the grain of our men to run."

"Better that than a certain death. We need to teach our men to fire a pistol, turn and run. Our horses are nimble and have endurance. Those that could harm us, the heavier units will tire. If we can draw enemy horsemen to pursue us, then there will be holes in their lines. King Gustavus can exploit that."

Alan Summerville was a thoughtful soldier, "So what are our tactics, Sir? What is our purpose?"

"We find the enemy without being seen. We pick off their sentries and night guards. We take their supplies. We mask the movements of our army."

Dick Dickson nodded, "Hit and run, eh, Sir?"

"It is our best chance of survival."

Alan persisted, "But, Sir, there are almost five hundred of us. How do we hide?"

"No, Corporal, there are eight groups of sixty odd men. I doubt that all of us will move together."

It was then that David Seymour saw a problem, "And what about the women, Sir?"

The two camp followers had not been an issue before and most of the regiment had been able to ignore them. The sewing of the standards had made them part of the regiment. Every eye switched to me. I sipped my ale and said, "I have not come up with a complete solution yet, but I thought to have them travel with the baggage train of the army."

Corporal Campbell said, "There is another problem, Sir, the remounts. We can't scout and guard them."

He was right and I had overlooked the problem. It was David Seymour who gave me an answer, "Sir, we could detach men from every company, say two or three. They could lead the remounts with the baggage train." I nodded. He added, "And they could keep their eyes on the women and our tents."

I had forgotten our tents and the supplies we would need.

Corporal Wilson said, "We need a wagon." He turned to David Seymour, "The two women would be more comfortable in a wagon."

Sigismund poured water on the idea, "Wagons will be in great demand. I cannot see that we would be able to find one that was not a wreck already."

He was right and we all knew it. We were on the periphery of the camp and the least important of King Gustavus' regiments. Men like Prince Albert would ensure that their regiments had first choice of wagons.

"Then we make one, Sir."

We all looked at Corporal Longstaff. "Make one?"

"I know at least one wheelwright in the regiment, and I am guessing there will be men who know carpentry. We could," he smiled, "find wood and just make one. We have spare harnesses. All we would need would be to find some halters."

I smiled too. I knew that find was a euphemism for steal. The faces of my officers told me that they would have no issue with that. I nodded, "I leave it to you, then. We have to be quick for

Spring approaches." They nodded, "Captain, see the company commanders and find the men who will be the wagon and horse guards when we move."

"Sir."

I knew that they would be the ones with the worst equipment and the ones who were older. Some of the men in the regiment had grey hairs and balding pates. It would be work for which they were well suited. Surprisingly the extra work was not seen as a bad thing but a pleasurable activity. As well as the skilled tradesmen Longstaff had alluded to, we also had men who knew how to steal and over the next week halters, traces, leaders and wood arrived in the camp. All of it was well hidden.

When Sigismund and I arrived at headquarters for our weekly meeting we were greeted, before we entered the king's hall, by Stephan Hard. The quartermaster, Samuel von Winterfield, was no longer in the camp and had been sent, so we heard, to negotiate with the French for men and money. Stephan Hard had been appointed as temporary quartermaster. He enjoyed his position.

"Captain Bretherton, may I have a word?"

"Of course."

He coughed and said, "There have been a number of thefts from camp. Has your camp suffered any such thefts?"

"Theft?" I adopted an innocent look.

"Wood, harness, halters, you know…"

I shook my head, "We have little to steal but, to be honest, Quartermaster, my men would not take kindly to any who tried to steal."

He nodded and a thin smile appeared on his face, "Then I shall inform the other captains and colonels to be more alert and do as you have done. They should protect what they have."

"A good plan and whilst we are on the subject, we will need more supplies for the king wishes us to be the advance guard. It would be a shame if we were unable to do as the king asked because we lacked supplies."

"I will see to it."

"Shall I send men to collect them?"

He said, hurriedly, "No, no! I will send them to you. Safer for all that way."

That was also the day when the king gave us his strategy and his plan. I felt as I had when I had first served Prince Maurice of Nassau. I was a small fish in a very large pond. The king's generals had arrived: Gustav Horn, Johan Banér, Lennart Torstensson and Karl Gustav Wrangel had all arrived with another five hundred Swedish horsemen. Along with the colonels and other senior leaders we were the most junior men in the room and, as such, largely ignored. That suited me.

The king had an easy manner when he spoke. He used German as the majority of the men below the rank of general could all understand it.

"We are about ready to embark on this crusade and free the Protestant people of Germany from the oppressive yoke of the Papists." Men banged the tables in approval. "Count Tilly is in Saxony which is many leagues away and our plan is to make northern Germany safe. When more men and supplies arrive, we will be more adventurous. Our first target is Neubrandenburg. Thanks to our English scouts we know roughly the dispositions there." A few officers glanced in our direction and nodded. "Those scouts will keep us concealed from the enemy." He smiled, "Indeed, they are crucial to ensuring that we lose as few men as possible."

He went on, using a map, to illustrate how we would work south during the summer until the lands around Brandenburg were back in Protestant hands. He often deferred to General Horn who explained how we would move. He had planned to guard the baggage train with a regiment of dragoons and that pleased me. When we fought, the dragoons would be needed and other men would guard the baggage. Our horses and the two women would be safe, so long as we did not lose.

Chapter 7

May 1630 Neubrandenburg

It was the middle of May when we left. It was later than had been planned but a week of torrential rain had meant we had to let the roads dry. The king and General Horn had personally briefed us. "We have spies in the enemy camp, and they tell us, Captain Bretherton, that your raid had an effect. The enemy know your name and the make up of your regiment. You angered them and they wish to take revenge. I will use that to our advantage. As you suggested we need to take Friedland. You will leave first and prevent men leaving the town when we advance. When that is done, I want you to scout Neubrandenburg." He smiled, "It would be useful if you did it badly."

I smiled, "You wish them to see me."

"I told you, Gustav, this is a man to watch. Yes Captain. I want you to lead the enemy horsemen whom I hope will pursue you, into a trap. We know that there is a garrison in Neubrandenburg, but their best troops are their horsemen. If we destroy them then we can easily take the town and that will be the base we shall use to move south. You see the importance?"

"I do and it is clear that I should just use one company of men."

"Exactly. You raided with a company, and they will, we hope, think that you are going to do the same again. The rest of your men can be commanded by Captain Friedrich, and they can be part of the trap. I have no doubt that they will benefit well from the encounter." He smiled, "From what I have heard your men are more than resourceful."

He was right. We now had a wagon with four wheels and a spare. The captured tents and equipment, along with our original tents, could be transported and the two women would be spared the rigours of a march. As Jane was now with child that was even more important.

Once back at the camp I summoned my officers. "The first task is to take Friedland. The Hunting Dogs will lead the regiment. Corporal Jennings has made them into a set of skilful scouts. When we have closed off the road then we will slip away and announce ourselves to our enemies."

Sigismund might have wished to object but he had heard the orders himself. Captain Bretherton had to be seen.

The day we left was the first time the banners and standards were unfurled. The men who carried them would be the next men I promoted. It would be a dangerous duty as carrying the standard meant they could not use an offensive weapon. We left before dawn as we would be the first to cross the pontoon bridge. The Hunting Dogs would ensure that any enemy spies fled before the main army crossed. We were a distinctive regiment and looked more like a warband than an army. The standards were the only mark of regular troops. I followed the Hunting Dogs. John Gilmour from Newbiggin carried the standard and rode behind Sigismund and me. The green banner with the red cross fluttered gaily in the fresh breeze, lit by the sunrise. The sun broke the eastern sky and promised a fine day. It enlivened my spirits and from the looks on the faces of the Wolf Company who followed, it did my men too.

While the Hunting Dogs galloped off in the distance my other companies spread out in a fan. We covered a large area, and any spies would be seen and dealt with. We had barely travelled a mile towards Friedland when we heard the sounds of pistols. Jennings and his men had found spies.

When the messenger from the king arrived, I halted, "You can now complete your mission, Captain Bretherton. The king has landed."

We had taken a trumpet at Kotelow and Dermot Murphy, our sole Irishman, would sound the signals. "Dermot, sound recall."

The notes rang out. We had devised our own calls. We knew the ones that the king would use but we were a unique unit, and I wanted special calls for us. The training showed it had been well learned and within half a mile we had a column of horsemen in company order, four abreast. Bretherton's regiment was going to war.

The Hunting Dogs knew to ignore the call. They had to get into position on the road from Friedland to Neubrandenburg first. It meant that I led, with Sigismund, Sergeant Dickson and Sergeant Stirling, the rest of the regiment. We passed houses and farms. Jenning's men had alerted them to the presence of an army. What they did not know was which one. They would look at the green flag and the red cross and wonder. When the Swedish standards carried by King Adolphus' guards came, they would know but as we passed, they peered fearfully at us. We were horsemen and could not be outrun. I turned in my saddle, "Sergeant, tell the men to smile. We are here as liberators and not oppressors."

I am not sure if it worked but we had tried.

When we passed the hamlet of Boldekow I knew it was time to leave the road. "Off you go, Captain."

He led his three companies to the right, and I waved my arm to take the other four to the left. We would use natural cover to encircle the town of Friedland. It would be almost impossible to hide four hundred or so men but as Jennings would be on the road beyond Friedland, it was not a major problem.

"Gilmour, furl the standard."

"Sir."

The standard would not be needed for a while, and he rolled it and placed it in its case. It hung from his saddle and meant he could now use his right hand for a weapon.

There were Protestants in this land, but we would have difficulty identifying houses that belonged to them. The Catholics all wore crosses and used that same emblem in their homes. The war had ensured that they kept them hidden. King Gustavus had said to err on the side of caution. The people hid as we rode across the land. We were clearly invaders, and they would begin to hide their food and their treasure. It was a sad state of affairs but understandable. We spied Friedland to the west. Sigismund would be closing the net from the other side of the town, and I was sure that Corporal Jennings would have secured the road that led to Neubrandenburg.

As we passed a small road that led east, I waved to Corporal Seymour and the Badger Company. "Hold this road."

"Sir! Dismount. Horses to the shade and you six go up the road a ways." I smiled at the efficiency. Thanks to the weeks of training every man knew their task. I knew from passing through the other camps that the rest of the regiments had just enjoyed free time. Perhaps they could afford to do so but we could not.

I spied the town just half a mile away. I said, "Stag Company, guard this section."

"Sir."

I led the Otter and Wolf companies to the road that ran south. I saw that Jennings was in position. He and his company had done well for it was clear that they had hidden their horses and secreted themselves in the hedgerow and trees. Had I not been actively looking for them then I might have missed them. We, on the other hand, had been seen and I heard a bell sound from the town. It was just the half a dozen riders with me that were seen. I heard the alarm as it spread through the large village. I shouted, "Otters, dismount and prepare to use your firearms. Wolves, hold fast."

I stayed mounted but drew and primed two of my wheellocks. A dozen horsemen burst from the town and, brandishing weapons, galloped down the road towards us. Corporal Wilson shouted, "Prepare your weapons. Do not aim at the horses." I could not help but smile. The corporal could see that the men could not possibly get past us and if we could capture their horses then we would have more remounts.

I levelled my pistol at the leading rider. I was a good shot and my weapon was accurate. I aimed at the rider's chest. A heartbeat before Wilson shouted, "Fire!" I pulled my trigger. There was a flash, a puff of acrid smoke and then the bang. As usual my sight of the man was obscured by the smoke from my weapon but when his riderless horse's progress was stopped by Corporal Jennings, I knew he had been hit. When the wall of smoke evaporated there were two more riderless horses and a wounded man holding his arm. The rest had fled back to Friedland.

"Secure the horses and the prisoners. Tend to their hurts. Sergeant Stirling, take your company a mile down the road and make camp there."

"Sir." The plan was for the king and the army to occupy Friedland. We would camp beyond the village and ensure that our army was not spied upon.

Sigismund rode in with the Hawk Company. "Any trouble, Sigismund?"

He shook his head, "We heard the firing and came as quickly as we could. The plan worked then?"

"It did and now we see if the next part will work. I will wait until the king has taken the town and then consult with him." I pointed down the road, "Send the spare companies to Stirling. He is making a camp."

I could not help but feel satisfied. We were in control and the plan appeared to be working. When a messenger came from the town wearing the uniform of the Smaland Cavalry regiment, I knew that the town was ours. "Captain Bretherton, the king wishes to speak with you."

He and his generals had taken over the largest hall in the town. He smiled when I entered, "No one escaped?"

"Some tried and paid the price. My men are camped a mile from the town."

"Good, then you may return and rest for tomorrow you need to annoy the horsemen in Neubrandenburg." I nodded, "And the signal that you are approaching?"

"Three blasts on my horn."

"Then let us hope that this ruse is successful. If it is, we can gain a walled town and eliminate a powerful threat to our lines of supply."

As I rode back, I reflected that the supply lines were an issue. Here we were less than half a day from the sea and our supplies. The further south we went the more likely it would be that our lines could be cut. The king relied heavily on powder and ball. An old-fashioned army using largely pikes and swords could forage from the land and still fight. We could not. He needed Neubrandenburg for if we could take it then with a garrison it could be held.

The Wolves had occupied a farm. Already fires were lit to prepare the food and I dismounted. I handed my reins to a nearby trooper, "Take Ran and see that she is watered and fed."

He nodded, "Sir. The sergeant is inside the house, Sir. They were Papists."

I entered the house, which appeared, at first sight, to be well furnished. I saw the crucifix in the alcove as soon as I entered.

Hearing me Sergeant Stirling called, "Here, Sir, the room to your left." I went into a room and my original view was confirmed. This house had belonged to a wealthy farmer. "It was empty when we arrived but had only been recently vacated.

There were still pots of food being cooked. The stables were empty but there was evidence of about four or five horses."

Already our plans were falling apart. They had to have heard the firing from the crossroads and deduced that an attack had taken place. We would have to leave for Neubrandenburg before dawn. "Have riders bring the rest of the companies here."

"Sir."

I took off my gloves and hat. There was a jug of wine on the table and I poured myself a goblet of it. This was my command, and I had to deal with the problems that had been created. I drank half a goblet. It was good wine. The Catholics liked such fine wines. I saw, in the corner, an ornately decorated desk and I went to it. I found a quill and ink. Scrabbling through the letters that lay on the top I found a piece of parchment. I began to write.

Sergeant Stirling and Corporal Wilson entered. I did not look up but said, "Help yourselves to wine."

I heard them talking, "I reckon there will be some treasure hidden here. This is a rich house, and they had to have fled with just what they wore."

"We can search it now, Sergeant."

I signed the paper and said, "You can do that but first I want a meeting with my officers. Have the other companies arrived?"

"Just waiting for the Badgers, Wildcats and Foxes. Captain Sigismund has arrived with the Hawks."

I stood and held out the letter, "Corporal Wilson, send a reliable man to the king with this letter."

"Sir."

He left. Alexander Stirling emptied his wine and wrinkled his nose. He preferred brandy or ale but, like all the men, alcohol was alcohol. "Problem, Sir?"

"We were supposed to be the men that alerted the enemy to our presence. This farmer will spread the word first."

"He didn't see us, Sir, that I can swear. We heard no hooves as we approached the farm, and we did not come directly down the road but came cross country."

"Then all that they will know in Neubrandenburg is that there are raiders about."

"Yes, Sir. The pistols they heard would not sound like a battle."

I nodded. Jennings came in and I said, "Peter, we leave before dawn. Have your company eat first and then sleep. They are the priority. Do we need to remount the men?"

He rubbed his chin as Corporal Wilson came in. "Message sent, Sir, and the Foxes are just arriving. If you excuse me I will get food started."

"Be quick then, Corporal. I want a meeting as soon as possible."

"Sir."

Jennings said, "We should be alright but if we are chased back from Neubrandenburg then we will need remounts. I will go and sort out the lads."

The sergeant's words had eased my fears. It was inevitable that the presence of even just one regiment would be noticed, and the enemy alerted. The thing was not to panic. Even so I would need to make alternate plans in case this one did not succeed. It was not just the fear of failure that drove me it was the knowledge that, until we had a toehold on this land, we were vulnerable. Our numbers were still below five thousand and if the enemy mobilised quickly then we could be swept away as easily as spiders from the eaves of a house.

"I will go and make water. Sergeant, search the house."

I passed through a kitchen and saw that Wilson had men salvaging the food from the pots on the stove. Others were preparing food. We would need to eat everything that we found but it meant our precious supplies would not be devoured. We could save the salted meat, dried beans and root vegetables until we needed them. Outside I saw a hogbog. The four pigs there would be butchered and the fowl too. This had been a rich farm. I found the outhouse and made water. It did not stink as badly as one might expect and that told me that it had been emptied recently. As I emerged, I looked around. Four or five people had escaped but a farm this size had to have more workers. They would be hiding somewhere.

I went to the well and drew a pail of water. I washed my hands and face. I shouted, as I entered, "Officer's call." By the time I entered the room again it was full. My officers made it look small. I gestured behind me, "Sergeant Stirling, have a few men search for the workers. There looks to be a wood half a mile away. I think that they will be hiding there. Bring them for questioning."

"Sir."

"Wilson, the pigs and fowl outside, have them butchered and prepared."

He shook his head, "Sorry, Sir, I should have thought of that. I will see to it."

Sigismund said, "Stirling says that there is a problem."

"The garrison will soon know that we are about. We have to move sooner than was planned. I will explain all when the others return." I did not want to go over my plans twice. The two officers soon returned.

"All done, Sir."

"Good. Any casualties?" They looked at each other and shook their heads. I had not expected any but it had been as well to ask. "I still intend to take the Hunting Dogs to Neubrandenburg, but I want a contingency plan. Sergeant Dickson, I need you to take your company and the Stags down the road. I want you two miles north of Neubrandenburg. You are my back up plan. The signal for the king to launch his cavalry attack is three blasts on the horn. I want the two companies hidden along the road. If I have the horn sounded once, then you are to open fire on whoever is pursuing us."

Sigismund frowned and interrupted, "Will that not ruin the plan?"

"If I sound the horn once it will mean that the plan is ruined. A single blast means that we are pursued not by all the cavalry from Neubrandenburg but a single regiment."

Dickson said, "And if there is no horn then we wait until the enemy have passed and follow them."

His words pleased me. He showed more understanding of my mind than Sigismund. "Precisely. With luck this plan will succeed better than that of the king. It all depends upon the bait." I smiled, "The Hunting Dogs and me."

The slaughtered pigs meant we ate very well that night. Soldiers were like squirrels. They gorged when they could, knowing that they might have to endure tight bellies in the future. I spoke with Jennings, Gilmour and Murphy. They were vital to my plans. They nodded their understanding. "When

Neubrandenburg is taken then the two of you will be promoted to Corporal."

They beamed, "Thank you, Sir!"

"This regiment needs more officers. As standard bearer and trumpeter you two need to be able to command too." I did not say what was in my heart. We would lose men soon and, inevitably, some of them might be officers. I needed men who could replace them. Murphy and Gilmour were just the first. As soon as we had the chance, I would ask for more nominations for promotion. The king had promised me all the funds that I needed. He valued my regiment, even if some of his other allies did not.

I spoke to the farm workers who had been found in the woods. They confirmed what I had thought. The farmer and his family had taken the horses and fled when they heard the sound of the firing.

Before I retired, I spoke to Corporal Campbell. "We need the remounts sooner rather than later. You and the others will be waiting here for the king. Use that time to bring the herd. There is a field of oats here. It is not quite ready for harvest, but we can feed all the horses. Remount any whose animal shows signs of flagging but save ten for the Dogs. They will definitely need remounts although if our plan succeeds and we empty saddles, then the Imperial cavalry can supply them."

"I will do, Sir, but you take care. You are putting your hand in the hound's mouth and hoping he won't bite it off. The one man we can't afford to lose is you."

"I am just one man, Corporal."

"No, Sir, you are a leader. You have given this regiment something it never had before. We know who we are and, you know what, Sir? We quite like being Bretherton's Horse. We were never Deschamps' men, but we are yours." He stood, "I will go and check on Ran. You will need Marcus next time."

I was touched by the corporal's words. You can tell when a man is flattering, and Campbell was not. I had the luxury of a bed, and I enjoyed a good night of sleep. While I was away Sigismund would enjoy it. It was a privilege of rank, and my other officers made it clear to me that they expected me to take advantage of the comfort. They rifled the wardrobe. We took the women's clothes for Jane and Gertha and my officers the clothes of the farmer. The servant's clothes were shared out by the men. By the time we left the house would be a shell.

I was woken by Sigismund not long before Lauds. There were clearly still monks at the monastery close to Neubrandenburg, for while I was heating fried pork and the eggs from the fowl I heard the distant bells. When you command you have to trust your men. I did not insult them by going over my orders, I merely donned my cloak, loaded my pistols and donned my gauntlets. I used the same hat I had when we had raided Kotelow. I wanted us to be noticed.

The men were all ready and I think that they were both excited and honoured to be the ones who were initiating the King of Sweden's plan. Jennings set his four best scouts to the fore and I rode with my three officers. The flag would be furled until we spied an enemy. We rode down the road at a brisk pace. We had travelled the road before and knew that there were no villages between us and the walls of Neubrandenburg. Once we passed the crossroads, just eight miles or so from our target, I had the men halt and tighten their girths. Dawn was breaking. We would be passing through fertile and low-lying ground. There would be dykes and ditches rather than woods and hedges. We had to draw our enemy north of the crossroads to the trees and hedges where the ambush would take place.

We moved off as the sun of a new day bathed the farmland with light. It was early summer and the fields were filled with growing crops. The farmers were in for a disappointing harvest. As the army passed south then the fields would be picked clean even if they were not ready for harvesting. The horses would graze on whatever was left.

We were two miles from the walls of the town when we saw light glinting from metal. I had not yet invested in what the sailors called a 'bring 'em near' but my corporals had sharp eyes.

"Cuirassiers, Sir."

"Now it begins. Unfurl the colours. Remember, we are a rabble." I turned in the saddle, "A little less order now, eh lads? The enemy are nearby. We have to fool them into following."

They nodded and grinned. They knew my plan and would execute it well.

"Let us carry on as though we have not seen them, Corporal, recall your scouts."

Jennings put his fingers in his mouth and let out a double whistle. The two scouts wheeled around and were soon flanking the trumpeter and the standard bearer. In a few moments we had gone from being a disciplined column of twos to a motley crew who looked more like bandits than soldiers. That we had now been seen was clear for a few moments later we heard a horn from ahead and saw the glint of sunlight on metal as swords were drawn. It confirmed that they were mailed men. They each had a brace of pistols but cuirassiers preferred to close with an enemy and to use their swords. We kept on going as though we had not heard them. After ten paces or so I held up my and said, "Halt!"

We had to determine if this was one regiment or a brigade. The king's plan hinged on taking all their horsemen in one fell swoop. "Gilmour, you have good eyes, what can you see?"

"There are men behind the cuirassiers, Captain." He stood in his stirrups and shaded his eyes. "Looks like there are dragoons and harquebusiers." The former were identified by their longer weapons slung over the backs. That meant we had three regiments. It would have to be enough.

"Right lads, draw your weapons and mill around. As soon as I give the order then turn and ride as fast as you can."

"Sir." They gave a collective response.

We each drew a pistol and aimed it at the column of men heading towards us. I saw that the harquebusiers had ridden to flank the cuirassiers. The dragoons would need to halt to discharge their weapons, but the harquebusiers and cuirassiers were both capable of firing from the back of a horse. I did not think that the cuirassiers would fire.

We were all milling our horses around as though we were undecided. My men could have been actors on the stage! When the enemy horsemen were fifty paces from me, I shouted, "A ragged volley!"

I let Jennings fire and then fired mine. The seventy pistols were not fired together but the smoke rose like a veil.

"Retreat!"

Captain of Horse

The first of the harquebusiers also fired but they had no chance of hitting us for there was smoke before us. Jennings and I were at the back and the standard bearer rode at the front of our company. Next to him rode Alan Shepherd who carried the company guidon with the hound upon it. My hat would identify me as the officer, but they would see the flags at the fore and they would be the magnet that would draw them. Normally I kept my eyes to the fore but I kept turning. It would add to the belief that we were panicking. No more balls were sent in our direction, but I saw that the open fields on either side of the road had encouraged the dragoons to flank the cuirassiers as well as the harquebusiers. They were forty paces from us.

The men before me were pulling away and I shouted, "You can slow a little and spread out into the fields."

The ones before us repeated the order and we slowed and spread.

I intended to keep this lead all the way to the crossroads and beyond. Murphy was next to me, and I said, "As soon as we reach the crossroads give three blasts."

"Sir."

The sound would carry and would also mean that Sigismund did not have to worry about protecting us. They would be able to close in around the rear of the horsemen.

When I glanced around again, just half a mile from the crossroads, I saw that the cuirassiers were falling back a little. That was inevitable. Their horses, whilst they were big animals, were carrying mailed men.

Jennings and I had four pistols, and I said, "Corporal, let us turn and fire a second ball."

"Sir."

We wheeled our horses, both were better than most of the rest of our troopers, and I levelled my second pistol. This time I was steady, and I aimed. My ball struck a cuirassier's breastplate. At such a range it merely dented it. I did not see what happened to the corporal's but the two balls made the three columns of riders spread out and that suited the plan. Once they reached the road through the trees there would be confusion as the three columns rejoined. I wheeled Ran and we hurried after the rest of the company. Soon the superior legs of our horses caught up with the two scouts and the trumpeter. As we passed the crossroads the three blasts from the horn almost took me by surprise. To the enemy it must have seemed as though I had decided to give an order.

Half a mile beyond the crossroads the trees began to close with the road. I saw that the three discrete columns were now mixed. I did not doubt that the three leaders were at the fore but the colonel of the cuirassier regiment would be the senior one.

Our horses were tiring but I knew that the enemy horses would be too. I saw the Wildcat trooper hiding behind a tree. He ducked back when he caught my eye. I had been looking for the first sign of my men. He was evidence of their position. We now had the trap set. All that remained was to spring it. The balls fired from behind told me that the enemy horsemen were closer. A ball zipped by my hat, and I glanced around. They were now less than thirty paces from us. I had only been saved by the slightly uneven surface of the road.

I shouted, "Gallop!" It was just the sort of command that a panicking officer would give. In my case it was to draw the enemy deeper into a trap. We were almost at the farm when I saw the levelled muskets of the Yellow Regiment standing behind the pikes of the kneeling pikemen. The king had his ambush in place. The regiment had six years' experience and were the best of King Gustavus' army. I yelled, "Wheel!" It was like Moses parting the sea as my men spread left and right.

As soon as Jennings and I had moved then the horsemen could see the trap into which they had fallen. It was, of course, too late for them to do anything about it but they tried. The dragoons halted and dismounted. They could use their horses' backs as improvised muskettengabel. The harquebusiers halted and drew their pistols. The cuirassier charged.

It was not only the Yellow Regiment who opened fire but the Red and Green ones too. I reined in Ran at the trees and wheeled her. I drew a pistol, but I saw no target. The road was bathed in smoke. I heard the cries of pain from men and horses alike as well as the din of balls pinging from breastplates and helmets. Then I heard the distinctive sound of the wheellocks of my two companies. It was the deciding factor. I heard the enemy horns and recognised the retreat. That would be easier said than done as they were surrounded.

By the time the smoke had cleared, all that remained of the attack were the dead and dying horses and men. There were wounded horses too and they would need to be put down. The wounded men would be given medical help. King Gustavus was a Christian.

A messenger rode up, "Captain Bretherton, the king asks if you would send Captain Sigismund to pursue the enemy back to Neubrandenburg. The cavalry will follow."

"Of course, Murphy, find the captain and give him the orders. Tell him we will follow."

The messenger shook his head, "I am sorry, Captain, but the king said that you have done enough. You are to ride with him when he enters the town."

I nodded.

Corporal Campbell rode up and he was leading Marcus, "Captain, I have your horse and I shall lead my men. The remounts are behind the farm with Sinclair in charge. Some of your men will need to change horses too." He pointed to the farm, "The captain has emptied the house and all that we need is now in the wagon with the ladies." He grinned, "They are as happy as children at Christmas, Sir." I nodded and he said, "Well done, Sir."

As the army marched off down the road with muskets and pikes slung over the shoulders to follow the horsemen, I did not know what to think. I turned to Murphy and realised I had sent him off. I said to Corporal Jennings, "Corporal, recall the men."

He nodded and putting his fingers to his lips, whistled five times. The men soon appeared. They were real horsemen and were leading the horses. I said, "Those who need them, there are remounts at the farm. We are to accompany the king."

I dismounted and after stroking Ran's head said, "Well done, my beauty." I gave her reins to Gilmour and mounted Marcus.

The king and his generals appeared. The king said, "It is all very well concocting a great plan, Captain Bretherton, but without the men to complete the plan then it is an idle dream. That was magnificent and your use of two companies to close the back door was inspired. Have your men follow us but you and your standard shall ride through the gates of Neubrandenburg with me. If they try to halt us, I shall bring up our artillery and batter them into submission, but I have no doubt that they will accede to my demand for surrender. Your regiment now have their first battle honours, Colonel Bretherton!"

My men heard and cheered.

The king laughed, "It seems I have pleased your wild men. That is good."

I was in a daze as I rode down the road, passing the dead who had fallen in the flight and the fight. The promotion was just a title. My pay would not increase. I was a mercenary and had agreed a fee, but the title made me the equal of far more men. My decision to hire my sword had been a good one.

Chapter 8

When the king said I was to ride with him he did not mean actually next to him. With my standard bearer and trumpeter, we rode just behind the king and his generals. His generals seemed quite happy about my position. Gustav Horn praised my courage and the skills of my men. His words meant a great deal to me. The exception was not a general but Prince Francis Albert of Saxe-Lauenburg. He and two of his men insinuated themselves directly before me. His rank meant that the only one who could have said anything was the king and I think King Gustavus excused the faults of the young German. The comments he sent in my direction were intended to be heard by only me. They disparaged my men. Luckily neither Dermot nor John understood the German and I just let them wash over me.

The senior regiments of the army marched behind us. They regarded themselves as the king's guards. All the cavalry of course, led by General Baudissin, was far ahead of us racing to get to the gates of Neubrandenburg before they could be slammed shut in our faces. The only horsemen accompanying us would be the Hunting Dogs. I turned in the saddle to look for them, but I could not see them. I would have liked to ride at their head, but I realised that they were probably helping my horse guards to move the remounts. I confess that I was lost in my thoughts. I was still, in effect, a captain of horse for I commanded less than five hundred and ten men. However, the title of colonel had been granted and I would be addressed as such. When I returned home from this war it would be a title used to address me. It would have an effect on the men I led. I needed to reorganise them. Captain Sigismund was still my lieutenant, but I had too few other senior officers. Dickson and Stirling had shown themselves to be skilled and reliable leaders but I was aware that both Campbell and Wilson could not lead a company and do their other jobs effectively. I would have to find two replacements for them. The ambush had also shown me that we needed deputies for my company commanders. I did not know what the king had planned after Neubrandenburg, but I did not think my regiment would be used as a single body. If a company acted alone then, even though there were just sixty odd men in each company, they might need to be split and that meant appointed men who could command detachments. Paul White was the only one who was in place. He had no rank, but he was Seymour's deputy. I needed to speak to my sergeants.

As we passed along the road and through the countryside, I saw some horses wandering disconsolately through the trees. Already birds were pecking at the bodies of the men who lay there. By nightfall the foxes and other creatures of the night would take on the task of reclaiming them for the earth. There would be no one to bury them. Some of the men had been German but the cuirassiers had been Spanish. They had fallen far from home and their families would never know the fate or the resting place of their loved ones. Perhaps it was better that way. The sight sparked a tinge of regret. What if I fell? I hoped that Sigismund would tell my wife but what if he had perished too? I determined to find another who would be able to deliver the news to Charlotte.

The trees seemed to make my thoughts darker and when we emerged, after the crossroads, into the more open farmland, I found myself smiling. The signs of death were gone. Here there was little evidence of the ambush and the attack. The more open ground also enabled us to move more quickly for we were no longer bound by wood and hedge. The Imperial cavalry's pursuit of us had trampled the ground to the side of the road and the regiments behind could march eight rather than four abreast.

The flags that flew from Neubrandenburg were Swedish and Brandenburger. The town had, as the king predicted, capitulated. He halted before the gates to the town and turning, waved his hand, "Colonel Bretherton, would you and your standard accompany me through the gates? You deserve the accolade."

I smiled and bowed, "It would be an honour, King Gustavus." I turned to my two men, "Straight backs and ride proudly."

They grinned, "Aye Sir."

If Prince Francis Albert of Saxe-Lauenburg thought that he could bar our way he was in for a shock. Our three horses forced a way through him and his two bodyguards. The generals formed a guard of honour, and each one bowed his head as we passed. They were true soldiers and recognised what we had done. I put

Marcus next to the king's horse, Streiff, and my men fell in behind us with the king's standard and his trumpeter. He spurred his horse, and we moved through the gates. The walls were lined with the horsemen who had taken the town, as were the streets that lined the route to the bastion in the centre. They all cheered, and I felt myself glowing with pride. To me I had just obeyed orders, but I now knew that we had managed, through our ruse, to take a town that might have cost us many hundreds of men to take the more brutal way, an assault on the walls.

The king waved and said to me, "Come James, wave and acknowledge these cheers."

I felt self-conscious but did so. It became easier when I saw the grinning faces of some of my men. I might not know all their names yet, but I recognised faces, and that recognition made the waving easier.

The bastion was a solid building that had a single tower. I saw some of the senior colonels including Colonel Hohenlohe waiting. The king said, "Come join us. I will hold a brief meeting and then allow you to rejoin your men. I understand the need for a leader such as yourself to be close to his men. The last thing you need to do is waste your time with the generals."

As I dismounted, I reflected that the king's philosophy of war was a good one. He understood how to make war and, more importantly, how to get the best out of the limited numbers of men he had at his disposal. I dismounted and handed the reins to Dermot. "If you see Captain Friedrich find out where we are camped."

"Aye, Sir." He shook his head, "If my ma could have seen that. Her son, who those in the village said would never amount to anything, riding so close to a king that I could smell his swetebags…"

I joined the other colonels. Wolfgang clapped me about the shoulders, "You have had all the glory and made our chase little more than a fox hunt."

"You had no trouble, Count?"

He shook his head, "Your men were so close to the last of the horsemen, there were just a handful, that they made the gates easily. Once inside they held the gates." He pointed south, "The

Spanish and German cavalry we did not kill or take headed south. Tilly will know that he now has an enemy who can fight."

We were ushered into a great hall and the king went to a raised dais with two chairs. He did not sit but stood, resting his arm upon the back of one of them.

"Today we began, successfully, the retaking of Brandenburg. Our small army will soon be reinforced by more regiments who will be coming to our aid. We have just two days to wait until the men I intend to garrison this town arrive. We then head west. We have just sixty miles to ride to reach Stettin. You should know that Duke Bogislaw of Pomerania has decided that he no longer wishes to be part of the Empire. I hope that we will be greeted as liberators, but we shall march to Stettin and be prepared to fight. To that end Colonel Bretherton's regiment will scout the road and Count Hohenlohe will follow him as support. Once we have secured Pomerania, we begin to recover the rest of the elector's lands that lie to the west of us."

Men banged the tables and the count grinned as he said, "With you before us my regiment will also have a chance of glory!"

The king held up his hand, "I would urge you and your men, however, to be restrained while we operate here, in the north. We are here to relieve the oppression heaped upon the people and not add to it. We take from the enemy and not from the local populace."

Colonel von Sydow shook his head, "Easier said than done. Our soldiers need food, and our horses need grazing."

His words were prophetic.

The king smiled, "Now, rejoin your regiments and be prepared to leave as soon as the garrison arrives."

I had been at the front and when I turned, I saw a glowering German prince. He said not a word, but I saw hatred in his eyes. Sigismund's apparent insult had been the start, but our success seemed to anger him. We had an enemy. I had to trust that the king would judge me on my results and not the word of a petulant prince.

Once outside I mounted Marcus, and Murphy said, "Captain Friedrich has found us a field just south of the city. There is plenty of water and grazing." He smiled, "And, at the moment, we have no neighbours."

"Good. Let us join them."

As we passed along the streets, I saw that the king had misjudged the mood of the rest of the army. Houses were being systematically looted. It was not the senior musketeer and pike regiments that were doing so but other mercenary regiments. It was, I suppose, understandable. They had not enjoyed an opportunity to take from dead enemies, but it would anger the population, and I would not like to be the garrison that had to sit on the powder keg that would be Neubrandenburg. I knew it would not be us. Our success meant that the king would always use us as his hunters. We would find the enemy. I was just glad that I had the count's men with us. They were heavily armed harquebusiers. A mixture of German and Dutch, they had enjoyed some success in the west before joining the Swedish invasion. We had evaded the Imperial horsemen once. It was good to know that we had allies who would support us if we encountered them again.

The Tollensee was a large area of bog and lake. Sigismund had found a dry area away from the insects that infested its margins. The proximity of the water meant that the grazing was good. He knew that we had to have well fed and nourished horses. Water and grass would do that. I was taken aback when I saw the size of the horse herd. Jennings had to have had the wit to take as many horses as he could as they passed along the road through the woods. I saw the saddles stacked neatly nearby. Some of the saddles used by my regiment were not fit for purpose. The ones that had been taken were good ones with saddle holsters. The tents were being erected. In contrast to the first time I had seen the regiment, this time they were neatly ordered in company rank.

As we approached there were cheers from everyone. I saw the two women, now dressed in much better clothes and they waved and cheered as loudly as any of the men. I did not dismount as a crowd gathered around me, "We are here for a few days so make the most of it. When we leave, we head east and have a sixty-mile scout ahead of us. We have earned our first battle honour, and the king is well pleased with us."

Captain of Horse

I dismounted and one of my troopers came over, he took the reins and said, "Sir, I am Stephen of Alnmouth and Corporal Campbell has assigned me the honour of looking after your horse." He beamed, "I promise that they will be well cared for, Colonel." He emphasised the title and I knew that it meant as much to my men as to me.

"Thank, you, Stephen."

Sigismund strode over and he held out his hand, "I am so pleased with the promotion!"

I shook his hand and said, "It is a title only, but it has made me realise that we need more officers." I pointed, first to Campbell and then to Wilson. "Those two have responsibilities far above that of company commander. I would make Campbell the horse master and company commander with the rank of sergeant. Wilson can be quartermaster and sergeant. We make White a lance corporal and ask the other seven commanders to choose their deputies. In the case of Wilson, Campbell, Dickson and Stirling they will be a corporal. The others will be lance corporals."

Sigismund nodded and then, as my news sank in said, "Can we afford it?"

"From now on we keep half of the treasure we take to pay for rank and for food. I hope to take more in the future."

He brightened, "You may be right. The cuirassiers we slew yielded plate, good weapons and they had coins. It is all in the wagon."

"Good, then your task is to meet with the other officers from the regiments that use plate and sell what we have to them. We shall not need it. We keep weapons, horses and saddles that we can use. Everything else is for sale. Let the other lieutenants know this and then they can come to us."

"You said we move east. Does that mean more opportunities for us?"

"Perhaps, although the Duke of Pomerania is switching allegiance to the king. I suspect we will not have to face an army but there may be chances for us to take more horses and weapons. The king does not want us to live off the land."

Sigismund laughed, "I like the king, but he is deluded if he thinks we can manage that miracle."

I then broached what I knew would be a sensitive subject, "And once we return west, we retake Brandenburg."

He nodded, his face serious, "The Imperial Army has already raided and sacked the land. We will have to fight for it but there will be little left for us."

"And we need to let our officers know that as we will be the advanced element of this army we will take, whenever possible, from our enemies. I have a plan." I was aware of a thirst and the heat of the sun was too much, "Let us go inside and have we something to drink?"

He nodded, "Ashcroft!"

A young trooper raced up, "Captain?"

Sigismund said, "I have appointed Ashcroft as a servant when we are in camp. His parents ran an inn at Crook. He is happy to serve."

I smiled, "Then, Trooper Ashcroft, if you would find some ale, bread, ham and cheese then you will have fulfilled your duties well."

"Sir!"

He raced off.

Sigismund unfolded the two camp chairs we had acquired, and I sat. I put my hat on my cot. "The king wants us as his eyes and ears. The best way to do that is to use our companies efficiently." I splayed my hands out. "We use the eight companies to spread out before the army. We will be harder to find. You shall lead Wilson's company if he is needed at camp, and I will lead Campbell's. We delve deep into the lands held by the Imperialists and cut their supply lines. I am aware of how parlous our lines are, and they would be easy to cut. We avoid their army and seek out their isolated units. Thanks to the remounts we can ride every day without weakening our horses."

Ashcroft brought our drinks and food. He said, "I will wait close by, Colonel. Wilson has food on the go."

I glanced outside. The day was coming to a close. I had not eaten since before dawn at the farm. That seemed like a lifetime ago.

We ate well that night. We still had a butchered pig that had been cooked before we left the farm. It was summer and we knew that it would soon go off. After we had eaten Jane and

Gertha came over to thank me for the gift of clothes and shoes. I shook my head, "It was my men thought of it, but you are welcome. The wagon, it is comfortable for you?"

"Oh, yes, Captain, and my husband has found a canvas so that we are protected when it rains. The packed tents make for a soft bed. When the baby comes it will be a fine nest."

I could not imagine how they would cope on campaign with a baby. Charlotte had help, a doctor and midwives. Jane would have no one save Gertha. They lived a hard life and yet they seemed happy.

I let my men forage for Captain Sigismund and I were summoned each day to a conference of the leaders. King Gustavus had a plan, and he wanted everyone to know it. The first garrison troops arrived two days after we had. They must have left the bleak island less than two days after we had left. They were a Scottish regiment. There were even fewer of them than in my regiment. I merely had the chance to shake the hand of Colonel Munro before he was whisked off to the king's side. Two days later a larger German company arrived. I did not like the colonel who seemed to me to be an angry man. Perhaps he resented having to stay in Neubrandenburg. Even worse for Colonel Munro, he was placed in command. I did not envy either him or the citizens.

All that meant we were ready to move the day after. My men had found a wagon and it enabled us to carry more goods. The horse guards and drivers for the wagons took men from the companies. We did it equitably, but it meant we had fewer men in every company. We set off first. I ordered every trooper to carry with him a day of emergency supplies. Sergeant Wilson had turned much of the venison we had hunted into hard tack. It could be chewed or, if we had the luxury of a fire, could be made into a stew. There were always wild greens. The wagons, our supplies, tents, and remounts would be with the baggage train and a regiment of dragoons was assigned to be the rearguard and to guard the wagons. The regiment had newly arrived as well as being newly formed. They were Swedish.

The standard was not with Gilmour. The women were sewing our battle honours on the standard. It would take three days to reach Stettin and by that time we would have the standard ready to be unfurled. Jennings was ahead of the rest of the regiment. I had two companies, one on each flank sweeping to the sides. We had ambushed and I did not want to suffer the same fate although I was assured that the lands through which we passed were friendly. The Duke of Pomerania was an ally.

We were a day from Stettin when Jennings sent back Jack Armstrong. "Sir, the corporal's compliments and there is an Imperial flag flying from the ramparts at Stettin." I could see that there was more, and I waited. "He also said that there was a redoubt five miles from the city. It is defended. There look to be two large cannons, two regiments of pikes and muskets and a regiment of dragoons."

I turned to Sigismund, "The duke may be an ally, but the Imperialists hold the city. Ride back to the king and tell him. I will take the rest of the regiment to support Jennings."

"You can't take on artillery, entrenched infantry and dragoons, Sir."

"And I have no intention of doing so. The king will want to know their exact dispositions. Jennings is a scout, and I am a senior officer. My report will guide the king, now go."

"Sir."

The standard had been finished the day before and Gilmour had it with him. I turned, "I thought to unfurl it as we rode into the city but now, it seems, we need to announce to our enemies who we are."

"Sir!" His voice told me that he was happy with the command.

I turned to Murphy as the green standard fluttered in the breeze, "Sound recall." As the notes sounded for the two flank companies to return, I shouted, "Bretherton's Horse, there are enemies ahead and we must ride to meet them. Listen for your orders and obey every command."

My orders were for the newly appointed subordinate officers too. Each company commander knew my orders and how to execute them, but the new ones did not. This would be an opportunity for them to learn.

When the men joined us, I ordered the advance and we galloped, rather than trotted, to join Jennings. Stettin was close enough for the mounted elements to reach in a few hours but the wagons and infantry were still a day away. The army would camp, and we would have to forego our own camp and live off the rations we had brought while we watched the enemy.

Jennings had dismounted the men. There were horse holders and the men who had muskets were the sentries. I dismounted while the rest of the regiment organised themselves. Stephen of Alnmouth took Marcus' reins. Jennings came to me, "Sir, you can't see them from here, they are a mile away, but this is the only place with cover for horses."

"Can we get closer?"

"Yes Sir, if you take off your hat and don't mind getting your feet wet there are drainage ditches next to the road. The grass and weeds have grown and they provide cover."

I took off my hat and handed it to Ashcroft, "Sergeant Stirling, I am going to scout out the enemy. Have your company move along the ditches after us. I want a skirmish line two hundred paces from the camp. Sergeant Dickson, take command until the captain returns."

"Sir."

"Lead on, Jennings."

He went to the ditch that lay to our right and suddenly disappeared. When I saw him, he was in waist deep water. I was taller but my pistols would get wet. I took off my holsters and slung them around my neck so that they were clear of the green, scummy water. I followed him. He was right, even if someone was on the road then unless they were mounted and looked down, we would be hidden.

The road was largely straight, as was the ditch. The mile took longer to wade than it would to walk. I heard the noise from the improvised redoubt, and I tapped Jennings on the shoulder to make him stop. I moved forward and went to the grass and weeds at the roadside. I gently moved the grasses but did so very slowly. A sudden movement might be noticed. I saw the guns and the wooden barricade. They had felled trees and the two guns, they looked to be nine pounders, were ready to fire. I saw the smoking linstock. The redoubt and their preparations told me that they expected us. I knew the king would have kept that information secret so it meant we either had a spy or, more likely, a Pomeranian who could not keep his mouth shut. I could see, beyond the guns, on the far side of the road, the pikes resting but ready to be used. The musketeers had their muskettengabel planted. They were alert. I went to the other side of the ditch and saw the same. What I could not see were the horsemen. This was not the place to talk and so I headed back up the ditch.

Two hundred paces from the camp I passed Wolf Company. They were lying in the field to our left. It was a field of barley and as this was July, it was high enough to hide them. I nodded at the grinning troopers. They must have been amused at the slime covered officer wading along the ditch next to them.

When we reached the place, where we had entered, I emerged. Ashcroft had a cloth in his hand and as I spoke to sergeants Dickson and Jennings, he wiped the worst of the slime and weed from me. I saw an old stump nearby and sat on it to take off my boots. "Sergeant, I didn't see the horsemen."

Jennings was doing the same as I had done and as he poured the stinking water from his boot said, "They are about two hundred paces from the guns, Sir. My thinking is that, as they are dragoons, they can mount and flank any attacker who tries to take the guns."

"I think you are right, Jennings. Sergeant Dickson, have the men eat and then recall the Wolves. I don't think the enemy will be moving any time soon."

I left my boots off to allow my feet to dry. Ashcroft used the cloth to dry the insides.

I heard the hooves coming from behind us and knew that the enemy had to have heard our hooves. Perhaps that was why they had linstocks lit and the pikes ready to be levelled. They had heard our hooves.

It was the king along with three of his generals who rode in with Captain Sigismund. I stood and flapped my arms to make them slow and stop. I said, urgently but quietly, "Sir, the enemy are a mile up the road and they can hear you."

The king stopped and dismounted, "I am sorry, Colonel, I should have realised. Captain Friedrich tells me there is a barrier ahead."

"Yes, King Gustavus." I told him what I had seen.

He looked at the sky. "Soon it will be dark, but we still have a couple of hours to shift them."

Captain of Horse

General Horn said, "King Gustavus, if we attack the sun will be setting behind us. They will see us."

The king smiled, "And tonight we will have a beautiful sunset. The light that illuminates us will shine in their eyes. General, fetch two regiments of cavalry, the cuirassiers and the harquebusiers. Along with the colonel's regiment we should be able to surprise them. Tell the men to walk their horses for the last mile. The colonel is right. We do not want them to know we are about to attack."

I turned to Sergeant Wilson, "Light a fire, Sergeant."

He cocked his head and gave me a quizzical look, "Sir?"

"They know there are men here. Let them think we are making a camp. It will lull them."

He smiled, "Sir."

"Ashcroft, find some food for the king and his generals."

The king sat on the stump I had vacated and took off his gloves. "You are a resourceful man, Colonel."

"My lord, when I served in the lands of the Palatinate, I learned that it was always advisable to carry food with you. The extra weight was worth it."

He took the lump of unappetising looking dried venison and nodded, "A lesson learned. When we take Stettin, I will issue the order for the rest of the army to do the same." He looked up at General Banér, "Make a note, Johan."

"Sir."

"Now when the cavalry arrives, I want to strike quickly. Colonel, your men will take the right flank and the harquebusiers the left. General Wrangel you will lead the left and General Banér and I the centre." We all nodded. "The two flanks will attack first. I want the two regiments to perform the caracole. With luck the enemy will move their guns but as I will be leading the main attack, I can make that decision."

I nodded, "I will speak with my officers. We shall need to move our horses in any case for they block the space the cuirassiers will need to use." I turned, "Jennings, summon the officers."

He smiled and whistled. I saw the look on the king's face. I think the informality of it surprised him.

95

When my officers arrived, I explained what we would do. "Have the men walk their horses across the barley. Wolf, Wildcat, Badger and Hawk companies will be in the front line and the others behind. Ten men in each rank. When the first companies have fired, they will retreat behind the next four. Captain Friedrich, lead the second line."

"Sir."

I looked at each company commander in turn, "Listen for Murphy's horn. Now get the men in place."

I stayed with Ashcroft, Stephen, Gilmour and Murphy. I heard the sound of the approaching cavalry, but it was muffled. General Horn had obeyed the orders. The king had been right and it was a glorious sunset. Reds, crimson, blues, purples and oranges intermingled in shimmering layers.

King Gustavus gave his orders and then returned to me. "I will sound the horn twice and that is the signal for the caracole. When I sound it three times then we shall charge as will your men."

"Sir." That meant we would all need to have at least one reloaded pistol to fire after the muskets had their chance. I knew the reality. No matter how successful our caracole was men would be hit.

I mounted and rode over to my men. Ashcroft and Stephen rejoined their companies. I placed myself before what we thought of as the two senior companies, Wildcat and Wolf. I drew a pistol. I had six pistols, two in my saddles, two in my holsters and two in my boot tops. I should not need to reload. My job was to lead.

The horn sounded and I shouted, "Walk!" There was no need to gallop. We walked for a hundred paces and then I commanded, "Trot."

From the enemy camp I heard the beat of drums as the alarm was sounded. Pikes would be levelled, and the musketeers would blow on their fuses. The dragoons would mount. The trot took us so that we could see the regiments. One rank of pikemen was kneeling before the musketeers whilst a second line waited behind ready to level their pikes over the musketeers' heads. A solid block of pikemen guarded the flank. I could see that we had caused confusion amongst the enemy. The dragoons had two targets. There was indecision and that indecisiveness allowed us to close a little more.

Someone in the enemy ranks gave the command to open fire and it was too early. We were just out of range and the wall of smoke merely obscured us. I had a pistol levelled, "Murphy, sound the charge."

The horn sounded a heartbeat before that of the harquebusiers. I saw the musketeers frantically reloading. Cursing, no doubt, the officer who had ordered them to fire. It was now a race. I levelled my pistol and when we were forty paces away shouted, "Fire and wheel."

This manoeuvre had been well practised by my men and as we fired, they all turned to the left to head to the rear of our lines. My colour party and myself were the exception. The breeze was from the north and made our flag clearly visible to our enemy. We would be noted the next time we fought.

I holstered my first pistol and drew a second as my second ranks wheeled, and then rode to the rear. The enemy muskets were a ragged volley, but I heard cries and knew that men had been hit. By the time Captain Friedrich had fired and retreated we could see nothing of the enemy. Muskets and wheellocks had made a fog that obscured the sunset. As I glanced behind to see who the next men would be I saw that soon there would be just a sliver in the east.

It was at that moment that I heard the king's horn signal the charge. The cannons had been silent. Their commander had not made the mistake of turning his guns, but the drifting smoke meant he would not see the king and his cuirassiers until they were close. I spurred Marcus and shouted, "Murphy, the charge!"

I leaned forward as the strident notes filled the air. I saw the muzzle flashes through the fog of smoke and braced myself for the strike of ball. I prayed that the breastplate I wore would stop a ball. One ball whizzed so close to my cheek that I felt its heat. God was smiling on me. The pike that emerged gave me a target and I fired. The ball was so close that it obliterated the pikeman's head. I holstered the pistol and had drawn my sword as I neared the terrified musketeer who was busy trying to reload. As I slashed down the pikeman standing behind the musketeer lunged. I am not sure if the head would have reached me, but it was a moot point as Murphy discharged his pistol and the pikeman, who wore just a buff coat, fell back. As my men discharged their second weapons such a hole was punched in their lines that it disintegrated. The dragoons who had been using the saddles of their horses to steady their weapons, fired a ragged volley as the pikes and musketeers fled. Some clambered on to the backs of their horses and managed to escape but more were caught by my men who saw the chance of booty in the shape of muskets, horses, ball, powder and swords.

    I had the luxury of surveying the scene. The king had won. I knew that from the lack of cannon fire. The gunners had managed to send just two balls. I saw the king and his cuirassiers slashing at the gunners. On the other side of the road General Wrangel had enjoyed the same success that we had.

    I shouted, "Take prisoners!" Then added, in German, "Yield or die!" They understood for they dropped their weapons and my men showed their discipline by halting their slaughter. We had won and taken two cannons. More importantly, the road to Stettin was now open.

Chapter 9

This time we did not accompany the king into the city. In fact, we did not move from the ambush. The three regiments who charged the position had taken losses and both horses and men needed care. We had lost three men and six were wounded. The king sent his doctor to tend to them. We lost eight horses but as we captured twelve dragoon horses, not to mention two draught animals, it was a fair exchange. The king left the guns with us. He did not intend to spend long in Stettin. As he told us before he left, his purpose was to ensure that his ally, the Duke of Pomerania, was secure. The Pomeranians would not be fighting with us. The king wanted either Swedes or mercenaries.

My officers ensured that all the treasure and booty that was collected was brought to our tent and divided into two. Sigismund locked the regimental half in a chest he had acquired, and the rest was shared out. It was not a fortune, but it augmented their pay. The food, clothes, boots and weapons were also shared out. The horses, along with the ball and powder, were the most valuable commodity we gained. The greatest losses we had suffered were to the cuirassiers. The two balls they had sent had killed five men, four horses and wounded eight. However, they had taken far greater losses. Their breast plates had not helped them. I was coming to the conclusion that a breastplate was only useful against either pikes or swords and as King Gustavus had a higher proportion of musketeers, dragoons and harquebusiers then we would always have the advantage.

We spent a week at the camp by which time we had hunted every animal within fifteen miles. My men were better at hunting than either of the other two regiments. We gained skins and bones as well as the meat. The skins would make cloaks, and the bones could be made into needles and tools. We wasted nothing. We heeded the king's orders, and nothing was taken from the people. That is not to say we were above letting our horses graze on the trampled barley from the charge, but we did not go into houses and farms to loot.

The king's messengers arrived and gave us our orders. The three regiments were to head back to Neubrandenburg in preparation for the retaking of Brandenburg. Sigismund was pleased beyond words. He had hoped that once we had taken Neubrandenburg we would then head to his homeland and recover it. One good thing was that we had the horse guards, remounts and wagons with us. It pleased everyone.

We made it back to the town we had first taken in under two days. We had no foot soldiers to slow us down. We camped in the same place. It still provided the best grazing and we had privacy. The men set up our tents and Sigismund and I went into the town to see if we could pick up some more supplies. The Scottish soldiers at the gate were friendly. They knew that we were near neighbours back in England.

"How is it going, Soldier?"

The older one answered, "Not so good, Sir. The German who is running the town, von Mannheim, he has hanged four people already. He reckoned they were spies but I just think he didn't like them."

"What does your colonel say?"

"That's the trouble, Sir, Colonel Munro has gone back to Usedom to bring more of our men who have just arrived. He wouldna like what is going on. The locals are getting nasty. The last thing we need is poison in the bread and the like, eh Sir?"

I sighed and shook my head, "I will have a word, but I am afraid he may not choose to listen."

"Thank you, Colonel. I heard you were a good 'un."

I turned to Sigismund, "I will go to the headquarters. See what you can get but I don't hold out much hope."

He shook his head, "Better if you get the supplies, James. I am a German, and they may be more inclined to let an Englishman have them. Remember they all saw you with the king. It might count for something."

"Very well."

The headquarters was guarded by two huge musketeers. I said, "Colonel Bretherton come to speak to Colonel von Mannheim."

One of them gave a grin and said, "He is a busy man."

I knew that if I tried to use my rank it would not get me anywhere. Instead, I said, as I turned, "Then I will tell King Gustavus that when I return to him."

The man did not know that the king was two days away and his manner changed, "That is a different matter. Wolfgang, take him to the colonel."

The colonel was in the Great Hall, and he had clerks with him. He looked up as we entered. He frowned, "I am a busy man, Colonel Bretherton. I hope that this is important."

"Could we speak alone, Colonel?"

He put down the quill he was using, "These are my men, and I trust them. Say what you must and then begone."

I felt Sigismund stiffening next to me. I said, "Very well then. The king is on his way here."

"I knew that."

"When I tell him that you have been hanging citizens of this town, which we helped to take, he will not be happy."

He formed his hands into fists and snarled, "Who told you that?"

I smiled, "Then it is not true?"

"It is true, but they were spies."

"And they confessed all at their trial?"

"There was no trial."

"Colonel, I have come to know the king over the last months, and I have to tell you that he will not approve of such actions."

He stood and pointed at the door. His left hand came within a handspan of my nose, and I think he thought to make me flinch. I did not. "Go!"

"Colonel, you are a rude and unpleasant man. I hope that you and the men you command are good at fighting for I can see no other reason for your presence."

I turned. Sigismund shouted, as he drew a pistol, "James, behind you!"

The German was swinging his right hand to punch me in the side of my head. Had he connected then I would have been laid out. I had quick reactions and I flicked up my left hand to block it as I ducked and drew back my right hand. I did not go for his head but his belly and my blow was well struck. He doubled up, gasping for air. I used my left hand to hit him with an uppercut that made him fly backwards, knocking the papers to the ground and showering them all over the floor. He lay there, stunned and disorientated.

One of his younger officers made to draw his sword but Sigismund pointed his cocked pistol at him. He said, in German, "Go on! I would love to discharge this pistol and see what passes for your brains spread all over this floor."

I jammed my hat on my head, "Enough." I turned to the older lieutenant who had not moved, "If the colonel wants satisfaction with either sword or pistol then send word to my camp. Whatever he decides, I will still inform the king of his actions."

We backed out of the hall and into the street. We had barely walked five feet when the door opened, and the colonel appeared. He had a bloody nose and he pointed at me, "I will not forget this, Englishman. I will have my vengeance! Watch your back!"

He said it in German, and I saw some of the burghers looking shocked. As luck would have it the two sentries from the gates had been relieved and they stood there grinning. I doubted that they had understood what was said but the German's nose as well as my bloody knuckles were testament to what had taken place.

The sentry who had spoken to me said, "A man of action, let me buy you a drink, Sir."

I smiled and shook my head, "Thank you. Another time, eh? We have business to conduct, and I have caused enough trouble for one day."

The incident did us no harm and we were greeted with smiles when we went to buy the salt that we needed as well as the fresh bread. The bread would not last us more than a couple of days, but the salt was invaluable. The baker even delivered the bread to our camp. We had paid more than the locals had but that was a small price to pay for fresh bread. I made the decision that it would be unwise to return to the town for any of us. Until Colonel Munro or the king returned, I would not trust the German colonel or his men. We had no need to do so, except for the purchase of bread. It always amazed me that something as humble as a loaf of bread could satisfy soldiers. No matter what their privations on the march, as long as they could find bread they would endure it.

What we did do was to open a sort of market for the other two cavalry regiments. We had weapons, helmets and armour we did not use. The secretes had, of course, all been retained but the helmets of the pikemen were of little use to us and as we had no smithy to melt them down, whatever we could sell them for would help the regiment. That we had a surplus to sell and the others did not was a measure of both our skill and also our needs. My troopers and officers were slightly different now from the regiment I had been given. The horses that more than a third of the men rode were bigger horses than the ponies they had used. The ponies were still good for scouting but when we had to stand in the line then those with the larger horses could be in the fore. We also looked more like a regular unit. We did not have uniforms, but our weapons were more standardised as were our saddles. The green flag we had made encouraged men to choose green as the colour that they wore. It was also highly practical. As scouts the green helped to hide us when we rode in the country. The brown cloaks that men had adopted were also useful to give cover in the dark.

The impromptu market drew townsfolk. They came, not to buy but to sell. Colonel Mannheim had taken to patrolling the local market with armed men. They intimidated the locals and we were seen as a safer alternative. We were also visited by some of the Scottish soldiers billeted in the town. They came, largely, to talk and to drink in a place they were welcomed. Thanks to Colonel Mannheim they were, at best, rooked in the inns and more often than not, refused service. We still had some barrels of captured ale and Jane and Gertha proved to be good at serving ale.

Thus, it was that when the king and the army returned they passed what looked like a country fair. It intrigued the king so much that he and his generals rode up. I saw that the prince had insinuated himself once more into the king's company.

"What goes on here, Colonel? When I heard the laughter and saw the crowds, I wondered what had happened in my absence." He dismounted and held his reins out to an aide.

"I am sorry, King Gustavus, but this was not organised nor meant to offend. We just sold some of the things we had captured and did not want."

He was a shrewd man, and he saw, perhaps in my eyes, things that I was hiding. He took my arm and moved me away from the crowd. His bodyguards watched but did not follow. "Come Colonel, tell me."

I told him all, including the fight.

He sighed, "You and your men are most useful to me, but it seems to me that you and your captain often rile my German allies."

"It is not deliberate, King Gustavus."

He smiled, "I realise that. I know little of Colonel Mannheim except that he has a strong company. I will speak with him. However, it would be wise if you spent as little time as possible in the town." He began to lead me back to his horse. I was coming to know the king a little better and I knew that his silence merely marked his thought process. When we reached the aide he said, "Colonel, this aide is Cornet Charles Larsson."

I had not marked him before for he was one of many aides to the king. I saw that he was young, he looked to be in his late teens, and he was smartly dressed. He had a good sword and there were two pistols in the saddle of his horse whose reins he also held alongside those of Streiff. He bobbed his head, "I am honoured, Colonel Bretherton. You and your men have a fine reputation."

The king said, "Charles' father, Thomas Larsson, was the man who saved me when I was a young officer, learning my trade. A wound from the Polish wars means that he was forced to retire but I promised him that I would help further Charles' career." He smiled, "So far that has involved little more than holding the reins of my horse and fetching me beakers of ale. I wish to change that now." He leaned in and spoke quietly so that the cornet and I had to come closer to the king to hear his words. "Charles, you will bring my orders directly to Colonel Bretherton and when I send him off you will ride with him as my liaison officer. I trust you, Charles, and I know that if you return with a message from the colonel then it can be trusted. What say you?"

He grinned and showed his youth, "It would be perfect, King Gustavus. I crave the chance for adventure."

The king sighed and shook his head, "If you view this as an adventure then you are not the man for the job. The colonel and I need a level head and not some Swedish berserker."

He became serious, "I am sorry, King Gustavus. I will try to be a better officer."

Seemingly satisfied the king said, "Good." He took Streiff's reins and mounted. "Colonel, the cornet will bring your orders by this time tomorrow. You can leave your camp here, but I need you and your regiment to scout the lands we shall retake."

"We will be ready." I hesitated and then, as the cornet mounted, said, "Cornet, we live rough when we patrol. Find yourself a good cloak, a hat and a blanket. You will endear yourself to my men if you try to have some supplies to put into the communal pot. Our camp is not the camp of the King of Sweden. We are scouts who live off the land and our wits."

"Thank you, Colonel, I will heed your advice. I wish to learn, and I will do all that you command."

When the king and his army had passed within the town those who had visited also left. It gave me the chance to gather my officers, "The king has told me that we will be leaving in the next few days. The camp stays here. The wounded men can replace the horse guards and drivers. They can have more time to heal. Go and prepare the men."

Ashcroft came over to the captain and I when the others had gone, "I have some cheese to go with the last of the bread, Sir, if you would like it."

"Cheese?"

He grinned, "A young lass came from the town, Sir. She seemed to take a fancy to me." I cocked an eye, and he added hurriedly, "I paid her, Sir. I got the coins from Sergeant Wilson."

I smiled, "Very enterprising, Ashcroft, and that sounds delightful. We will enjoy both in the shade of our tent."

It was pleasant to eat fresh bread and a good cheese. The ale was delicious, and we enjoyed the afternoon sun for a while then I said, "Brandenburg, what can you tell me, Sigismund? It is your homeland after all."

He nodded, "It is the Margravate of Brandenburg and is part of the Holy Roman Empire. It is ruled by John Sigismund, Elector of Brandenburg. Thanks to his marriage he also rules the Duchy of Prussia and, as you know, is the king's father-in-law." He smiled, "Prussia is not in the Empire but, sadly, Poland lies between the two countries. The capital used to be the city of Brandenburg but it was moved to Berlin."

"But why does Brandenburg not fight with the Empire?"

He shook his head, "That is the problem, James, the land is divided between Catholics and Protestants. Our elector does not seem to know which side to support despite his relationship with the king. I am Protestant as is our first minister, von Winterfeld."

"Then there is no army of Brandeburg?"

He downed his ale and shook his head, "Unless King Gustavus Adolphus succeeds in defeating the Empire then there is no Brandenburg. I fear that we will have to be ruthless and destroy our enemies. There will be much death before there is rebirth."

He filled up his beaker once more. I did not know how I would deal with such a situation. He would have to fight and kill many of his own people to secure his homeland. I had thought we would just be fighting the Spanish and Austrians of the Hapsburgs. Now I knew differently.

The cornet arrived at noon the next day. He had a horse that was laden. I would need to pare down what he had brought. It had been my fault, of course, I had not been clear enough the previous day. He did not seem to know what to do with his horse. I waved over Stephen of Alnmouth, "Stephen, take the cornet's horse and put him with mine."

"And his gear, Colonel?"

"Just leave it here. We will sort it later." When the groom had gone and Sigismund, having spoken to all my officers, had returned I said, "You have orders?"

He nodded, "The king did not commit them to paper. They are spoken." He closed his eyes and when he opened them, he spoke in a rush, "You are to scout, first south towards Fontanestraße and then north and west towards Mecklenburg. He wants the land east towards Berlin to be scouted too. Magdeburg is now an ally of the King of Sweden, and we need to ensure that the lands to the east of it are not a threat. You have a week to scout out the two places and then return to the king with your news." He stopped and smiled.

I turned to Sigismund, "We will divide the command. This is your land, which one would you like?"

"Berlin."

"Good. You will take Wolf Company, along with Fox and Badger. I will take Wildcat Company, the Hunting Dogs and the Stags. The other two can stay here. Go and tell the officers. We leave at dawn. Have Sergeant Wilson sort out the supplies."

"Sir."

After he left, I said, "Tonight you can share a tent with the captain and me but first we sort out this gear. There is too much."

"Sir."

We pared it down and made a pile that he would leave at the camp. I pointed to the camp chairs, "Now sit and I will explain how we work."

"Sir."

"The king needs intelligence and we are to gather it. You can write?"

"Of course, Sir. I spent a year at a German university, and I can speak a little English."

"Good, then when we can, use English. The officers can speak German and a little Swedish but for clarity then English is best, eh?"

"Sir."

"Keep a diary of what we encounter. When I am done then return to the town and equip yourself with what you need." He nodded. "I know I told you to bring powder and ball but if you have to use it then it means things have gone awry. We are like ghosts. I want us to slip through Brandenburg unnoticed if we can. We will not use towns and villages but sleep and camp where we can. An isolated farm will be the only shelter we might expect. The captain is our German expert, and he will not be with us. I shall have to rely on you to help me gauge who is a friend and who is an enemy." That was the point at which his expression changed. His smile disappeared and he became serious. I suppose I had been the same when I first went to war. You think it is all going to be glory and battles, but the reality is far removed from that.

"Sir."

I smiled, "Right, go and sort yourself out and then, when you return, we shall enjoy a luxury that will be increasingly rare, a hot meal!"

Chapter 10

I rode with my scouts. I left Gilmour and the standard at the camp. He was not happy, but we did not need the colours and I knew that the rest would do his horse good. I took Murphy as I needed his horn. Ashcroft and Stephen of Alnmouth acted as my aides along with the cornet. I had decided that Jennings deserved to be a sergeant. He was a modest man and seemed inordinately pleased at the promotion. He had earned the promotion. The first fifty miles, which took us more than a day to cover, were in heavily forested land. My scouts reported more animals than people. There were charcoal burners who lived in the forest but that was all. The trees afforded relief from the late August sun. We were still in the forest when we camped. We were confident that there were no enemies nearby and so we lit a fire while our better hunters went to forage for food. I sat with the cornet and Sergeant Jennings to add detail to the map. We marked the houses with an X. They were there as way points.

It was a successful hunt, and the fillet of venison was cooked to be eaten immediately. The rest was put into a pot where it would simmer all night, supervised by the night watch so that we would have a good breakfast. The hide would be tanned by the men making water on it as we travelled. We had one spare sumpter to carry the supplies and pots we would need. The skin could be carried there.

After we had eaten, I spoke with my officers. I included the cornet in the discussion. He was an integral part of the company. He had been briefed by the king. I had devised a plan to help us move invisibly through the land. Seth Johnson had proved to be good with languages and he was the best German speaker of my troopers. "I want you, Charles, to go first into each of the towns we pass through. I am not worried about the villages, but we need to know the allegiances of the towns. If they are Catholic, we skirt them and if they are Protestant we ask them for information." I saw the fear on his face, and I smiled, "You say you went to University in Germany?"

"Heidelberg. It is far to the south of here."

"Perfect, then you are a Swedish scholar returning to your university. Seth can play your servant, and you explain your weapons as being a necessity in these troubled times." He seemed relieved at that. "Now the first town we should encounter will be Fontanestraße. We should reach it tomorrow, just after twelve. Seek food and do not be obvious about your questions. You will know the signs that it is Catholic. Listen for bells. Sniff for incense as you pass the churches. Feign a total lack of interest in their religion. You are a scholar and studying…make something up."

"I enjoyed philosophy, Sir. I can talk about Aristotle and Plato."

Sergeant Dickson laughed, "Aye, that will send them to sleep."

Ignoring him I said, "If it is Catholic then you carry on through the town when you have eaten. Sergeant Jennings will have men watching you. If it is Catholic, we will rejoin you."

"And if it is Lutheran?"

"Then stay there when you have eaten." He nodded, "You have that? Catholic, leave as soon as you have eaten or if you discover it quickly then do not eat. If it is not Catholic, then order more wine."

"Thank you, Sir. I am clear about my orders."

I rode with the Hunting Dogs, and we followed the two men. Murphy came with me. Once we neared the small town, Jennings and I went with the two men until we could see the town but remained hidden and out of sight in the trees. The other two companies would join the Hunting Dogs and wait. Just as we could see the two scouts so the rest could see us. They rode in and I saw that there was a problem from the off. Four men appeared from the side of a building, and they were armed with swords and what looked like ancient muskets. As I did not see a linstock they did not worry me, but their movements did. They surrounded the two men and while I could not hear the words, I heard raised voices, and it was neither the cornet nor Seth who was doing the shouting. When the cornet was dragged from the saddle I reacted instantly, "Murphy, sound the charge! Jennings, draw pistols."

I drew a wheellock and cocked it. I spurred Marcus and he leapt forward. The horn and the sound of our hooves froze the townsfolk. The crowd that was gathering turned to stare at us and the man who had raised his musket to club the cornet halted. I did not hesitate. I fired the wheellock. The ball struck the man with the clubbing musket in the shoulder. He dropped the musket which struck the cornet on the head. The others raised their muskets and then realised that they could not be fired yet. They were brave men, and they drew their swords. Seeing but three of us, the three companies were still masked by the trees, the townsfolk drew weapons. Seth had a pistol, and he fired it at one of the swordsmen. It was point-blank range and the man's head disappeared showering the other two and those around them with brains and bones. It takes a strong man not to react and they did. Jenning's wheellock fired and another of the swordsmen fell. Murphy's pistol was the last of ours to fire and the sound, along with the thundering hooves of three companies decided the townsfolk. They ran.

Seth had dismounted and was tending to the cornet. His head had been gashed by the falling musket, but his eyes were open. He would survive.

I turned, "Sergeant, have your men secure the town."

"Should we pursue the townsfolk?"

I shook my head, "There is no need. We have a town to search and when they return, they will find that we have taken their food, animals and any coins that they have. We wanted to know if this town was Catholic, and it is. Had they not attacked our men they would not have been raided. This is the price that they pay."

The cornet was more embarrassed than anything, "I am sorry, Sir, my first task and I failed you."

Before I could answer Johnson leapt to his defence, "It wasn't his fault, Colonel. They would have done this with anyone who came to their town from the north. They know that we have taken Neubrandenburg."

I nodded, "Then we need to be doubly wary on our ride east. We will sack this town and then move on east towards the old capital, Brandenburg. I will not risk entering that town but we will look, instead, for evidence of Imperial troops. The king is keen that Magdeburg is kept safe. It is our only ally at the moment."

Being as close to Berlin as it was the town was prosperous. There were few farms and the only animals to be had were fowl. We took them and the eggs. There had to have been pig farmers close by, for in the butchers shops we found four cured hams and two butchered pigs. We happily took them. The bakery had been abandoned and the fresh bread we took was more than welcome. The men systematically searched every house. They did so carefully, and we were rewarded with chests of coins. We found a wagon and draught horses, and they were secured.

The cornet pointed to the church, "There should be rich pickings there, Colonel Bretherton."

I shook my head, "It may sound perverse in a war that is caused by religion, but in my experience, the sacking of churches, whilst it brings financial reward, hurts our cause more. Let us leave their church."

We left in the middle of the afternoon. We made a bonfire of the old weapons we had found but we left the bodies of the dead where they had fallen. Their families could bury them.

We headed back to the forest. Better a secluded bower in the forest than a roof and the risk of a blade in the back. We set sentries and ate well. I sat with my officers on logs that had been hewn by charcoal burners. I pointed, on the map, to the next city, Brandenburg, "The odds are that this one will also be a Catholic stronghold, and it will have defences. It was the capital of the Margravate. My aim is to see if it is defended. It is only fifty miles from Magdeburg. We then head north to Mecklenburg."

Charles said, "Is that not where General Wallenstein comes from?"

"He does and for that reason we are there to discover just what enemies we face."

When we reached Brandenburg, we did not need to approach closer than half a mile. We could see, from the eaves of a wood we found, that Imperial standards were flying, and the walls were guarded by musketeers. When I saw the company of horsemen leave the city to head west it confirmed that there was a strong presence there. It was not an army, but it did threaten Magdeburg. We headed due north and did not use the roads. It meant another night in the woods. The cornet was struggling with the rigours of such a life. You learn to sleep on the ground. You make a bed with whatever is to hand, normally grass or leaves and the blanket from your horse. You use your cloak and your blanket. An oiled cloak is invaluable when it rains. We had been lucky for the nights were dry and warm. That could change.

We saw no large settlements until we neared Temnitztal. We saw an old keep. There was a castle and, from its walls flew an Imperial standard. The difference with Brandenburg was that we saw no cavalry and just a handful of soldiers.

"We will skirt this town." I pointed to the tower, "That might have been useful in the days of knights, but King Gustavus' artillery will have that down in the blink of an eye. Sergeant Jennings, find us a route around the town."

He led us through the forest that surrounded the isolated town. Jennings, like all good scouts, had an internal compass. We were looking for something to take us north. It did not matter if it was northeast or northwest. Mecklenburg lay to the northwest and Neubrandenburg to the northeast. The road we found went due north. I was with the other companies and did not see the Hunting Dogs as they discovered it. I knew from having travelled with them what they would do. They would ensure that the road was clear both ways before sending a handful of men in both directions. When it was clear they would move on. I reached them just as Sergeant Jennings shouted, "The road is clear, Sir."

He led his company up the road, and I waited at the side while the other two companies and the small wagon we had found negotiated the track. The Wildcats were bringing up the rear and I waited to speak to Sergeant Dickson. It was as I was speaking to him that the regiment of harquebusiers trotted up the road from the south. I knew it was a regiment for they had their colours at the fore as well as guidons. They had turned a corner and were just fifty paces from us. The noise of the wagon masked their hooves for they were not galloping but walking. I think we saw each other simultaneously.

It was Murphy who shouted, "Sir! Horsemen." He drew his pistol as he pointed. He fired. The ball was wasted but the sound would alert the Stags and the Hunting Dogs.

Captain of Horse

I shouted, "Skirmish line! Murphy, sound the recall!" The strident notes would summon my two companies.

I drew a brace of pistols. My men all drew a single one. It all depended now on what the enemy would do. They saw a single company and an irregular one at that. The horn sounded and they charged. They had been in a column of eight and that number filled the road. They rode horses that were big and would simply bowl into us.

"Present!" Our one advantage was that we were still, and my men were spread in a line which was twenty men wide. Many were in the eaves of the forest, but we had a solid platform. The Austrian horsemen were moving, and their aim would not be the best. I levelled my pistols, "Fire!" We fired at a range of forty paces. The wall of smoke stopped us from seeing if we had hurt them, but I heard screams. I holstered my pistols and drew two more. My men would be drawing their second. "Fire!" Sergeant Dickson also had two pistols and between us we could do much damage. This time our volley was more ragged but there were cries and screams. Holstering my pistols I drew my sword. I was just in time for two harquebusiers emerged from the smoke. One fired at me and the ball took the feather from my hat. I was suddenly aware of men on my left heading towards the harquebusiers. It was the Hunting Dogs, and they were in their natural element. As I slashed across the neck of the harquebusier who had fired at me, Sergeant Jenning's men fired. The sound of pistols to my right told me that Summerville and his men had also arrived. The colour party at the fore of the enemy regiment had survived and with their leader they came like angry dogs for vengeance. I still had two pistols, and I drew one and fired it. The standard bearer used his flag like a lance and charged at me. I had to lean to the side to avoid being thrown from Marcus' back. I hacked at the standard and I struck both the standard bearer's gauntleted hand and the standard.

At the same time the cornet slew the man next to the trumpeter. Sergeant Dickson's sword sliced across the shoulder of the officer's horse. It screamed and reared. The officer was the leader and a good rider. He steadied the horse, but the attack had shaken him. He saw the dropping standard and shouted, "Retreat!"

The Austrian horn sounded, and men began to disengage. It was easier said than done. They probably outnumbered us, but we had surrounded them, and men attacked on three sides are more likely to flee than stand. As the smoke cleared and my men cheered, I shouted, "Hold!"

I looked and saw that the Wildcat Company had two dead men. Others were wounded. We had slain twelve men; I saw their bodies and eight horses stood disconsolately in the road.

I shouted, "Put the dead in the wagon. Take the horses and the weapons. Have the men's wounds tended to. Sergeant Jennings, send four men to follow the harquebusiers. I need to know if they are going to follow us."

I nodded to the cornet, "Well done, Charles. That was more like it, eh?"

His hand was shaking, "I killed a man."

Sergeant Dickson nodded, "Who would have killed you if he had the chance. You did alright, Sir." He did not know it, but the cornet had just been given the greatest compliment.

We were not pursued, and we rode north as fast as we could. We found a farm that had been deserted. It looked to have been recently abandoned for although there were no animals in the farm, there was a pot bubbling on the fire. The crucifix in the alcove confirmed that they were Catholics. We set sentries and tended to the wounds. The dead were laid out ready for burial. The two men were wrapped in sheets taken from the house and we found a secluded part of the forest. I hoped that their bodies would not be despoiled but we could not take them with us. The sentries apart, all three companies were there to hear my words as they were interred. Stones were found to cover them and when we laid soil upon them, we all walked over the soil before returning the turf. It was all that we could do. They would be remembered around campfires and when tales were told of past battles, but they were gone.

It was a lesson to us all.

Mecklenburg had an Imperial presence and mindful of our encounter on the road we scouted from a distance. The road to Neubrandenburg was one which passed through a land of lakes and forests. Whilst there were few towns the villages we passed through, all of them Catholic, were places that could hold up an army. We did not stay in Müritz on Lake Müritz for there was an ancient castle. There was no Imperial standard flying from its tower, but we skirted the town to the north and camped in the forest. There was still daylight, and I took a decision. "Cornet, I want you and Johnson to leave now and report to the king. We are close enough to Neubrandenburg for you to do it before dark and the sooner he is apprised of the situation the better."

He looked surprised, "Am I ready?"

"You are ready, and Johnson is an old hand. Give the king your papers and tell him that we will arrive tomorrow." He and Johnson set off immediately. I then spoke to my officers. "If the king comes west then this is the land through which he will pass. I want to split us into three columns tomorrow. Each one will take a different route to reach Neubrandenburg." I pointed south. The small town and castle were beyond the trees. "If our enemy gets wind of an advance then they can fortify Müritz. We could take it but that would slow us up and show the direction we were taking. Let us see if there is another route that has fewer obstacles." They understood and they nodded. "The king will be taking artillery, and we have the wagons. For that reason, I want you, Sergeant Dickson, to take the small wagon we captured." I held the map up and pointed, "I think that this route that passes through Varchentin looks the best one. Summerville you will take this southern route, the one through Plasten and I will see if there is a way through the forest, to the south. The Hunting Dogs and I will explore that possibility."

"Is it wise, Sir, to split us up?"

I nodded, "You are thinking about the encounter with the harquebusiers?" He nodded. "We are close enough to our army that we could run for home. If you have to abandon the wagon, Sergeant, then do so."

I would not be dissuaded and the next morning we took our separate journeys. Jennings and his scouts found a well used trail that passed through the forest. We found old charcoal burner camps and hides that had been used by hunters to hunt the animals who lived there. We found plenty of spoor. It was a dark path with only occasional clearings where the sun could shine. When we stopped at what I took to be noon it was clear that the army could not use this route but a smaller element, such as my regiment, could.

The forest ended just a few miles from the southern shores of the Tollensee. We could see, in the distance, the walls of Neubrandenburg. It was late in the afternoon. By the time we reached the walls of the town it was almost evening. "Sergeant Jennings, take the company back to the camp. I will report to the king."

"Sir."

The Scottish regiment was on duty and I asked, as I walked a weary Marcus into the town, "Has Colonel Munro returned?"

"Oh yes, Sir." He pointed to the land to the east, "And another ten thousand soldiers too."

I had not noticed the tents but now I did.

"Thank you."

We would be moving soon.

I did not have to wait long for an audience with the king. His usual generals were with him. I did not see the unpleasant prince. Cornet Larsson was beaming as he hovered in the background amongst the other aides.

The king smiled as he nodded towards him, "The cornet told me of your adventures. He is in awe of you, Colonel."

I nodded, "He has the makings of a good officer. He acquitted himself well. Has Captain Friedrich returned?"

"He has but he encountered more problems than you did. He lost ten men." He shook his head, "Still, we have learned where we can go. First, is there a route to Mecklenburg?"

"I will have to speak to Sergeant Dickson first, but I think so. Müritz looks to be the only obstacle. At the moment there is no garrison there, but our presence must alert the enemy."

"Just so. By the time we move we will have eighteen thousand men, Captain. If we can secure the land of Mecklenburg, then Magdeburg has protection from the north. Tilly, zu Pappenheim and Wallenstein are still in Saxony. I do not have enough men yet to face them and my plan is to make the lands to the east of Berlin, Protestant once more. By spring we will have enough men to face the Imperial Army in open battle. Until then we make whatever gains we can."

I nodded, "Thank you for your honesty, King Gustavus. It is refreshing to be taken into your confidence."

He shrugged, "You are an intelligent officer, and you have shown you know how to use your mind. If we think along the same lines, then we have more chance of success. We will leave this camp sometime in October. I will send Cornet Larsson to you as soon I have my order of battle sorted."

I left and headed back to the camp. I was anxious to discover what had caused Sigismund's losses. We had lost a dozen men in a short time. We could ill afford such losses.

When I arrived back at the camp, I was relieved that Dickson and Summerville had both returned unscathed. Sergeant Dickson told me that the wagon had negotiated the road easily. I nodded, "Tomorrow is a rest day. Let the men enjoy some relief from the saddle. We will be leaving once more in October."

"Righto, Sir, I will tell the lads."

I was left alone with Ashcroft and Sigismund, "Bring our food to the tent, Ashcroft, and then you can join your tent mates."

"Are you sure, Sir? I don't mind hanging around."

"No, the captain and I can cope."

I needed to be alone so that I could find out the details of his scouting expedition. He was silent as we ate and when Ashcroft disappeared to join his friends I said, "Sigismund, just tell me what happened. Your moodiness does not suit you."

He shook his head and, before he spoke, downed half a beaker of ale, "I let my feelings get in the way of the job, James. We passed through a village that had been Protestant. It was surrounded by Catholic communities and the people had been massacred and their bodies left to rot. There were only twenty or so, but it made me angry. I had the men bury them and we continued east."

As he drank again, I asked, "Was this east or west of Berlin?"

"East. We were almost at Frankfurt an der Oder. When I saw the Croatian horsemen, I ordered the attack. It was anger that made me do so. What I did not realise was that there was another regiment of cavalry. Even as the Croats fled from us, we were attacked in the flank by some hussars armed with harquebuses. I had to order the retreat."

I nodded, "And that was when you lost the men."

"Yes. Seven were left on the field but three others died of their wounds."

I drank my own beer. Croatian light cavalrymen were like us, mercenaries. They were also renowned for their depraved behaviour. Rape and pillage were second nature to them. Sigismund had made a mistake, and his moodiness was a sign that he knew he had made a mistake.

"Have you learned from this, Sigismund?"

"What?"

"You made a mistake, and men died. If you have learned from this then good will come of it but if you descend into a melancholy world of self-doubt and morbid thoughts, then you are no good to me."

He sighed, "When I was sent to find you and bring you to the king, I wondered why I had not been given the command. If I had then I doubt if the regiment would have lasted this long. Perhaps I should retire."

"And that would be a shame. You are a good officer, and the one mistake does not change that. You need to become like ice. When I served in the Palatinate, I saw atrocities that turned my stomach. Men can turn into animals if not well led. We cannot change human nature, but we can control our own. I need you, Sigismund. Stirling and Dickson are good company commanders, but they cannot lead like you and I."

He smiled, "If you think I can be salvaged then I will do my best. You are right and when I chased after the Croats, I was like a wild beast myself. I will try to be more like you."

"Good. Then tomorrow we start anew and put the past behind us.

Chapter 11

Men arrived at Neubrandenburg every day. They came mainly as companies and regiments, but there were men who came alone. A week after our return half a dozen men wandered up to our camp. Alexander Stirling brought them to our tent, "Sir, these men have made their way here and wish to fight against the Catholics. General Horn said that we might be able to use them." He leaned in, "They are Englishmen, Sir."

I looked at them. They looked thin, almost emaciated. They had leather jacks and soft hats. None of them were musketeers. Their hands did not have the distinctive patina of powder. Each had a hangar on his belt. Their ages ranged from one who looked to be barely eighteen to a greybeard with a balding pate.

"You are soldiers?"

The greybeard stood a little straighter, "Yes, Colonel. I am Bill Burton, and I served in King James' army. More recently we were mercenaries fighting for King Christian of Denmark."

That explained much. When Count Tilly had trounced the Danes it had temporarily given the Imperialists the upper hand. The Danes had been forced into a peace and the mercenaries they had used were discarded.

"These are your only weapons?" I pointed at the hangars. A short sword, they were more of a tool than a weapon.

"It is all that we were allowed to keep, Colonel. We can fight." He added defiantly.

"Can you ride?"

"I can."

"And the rest of you?"

Half nodded and half were silent. I sighed, "Sergeant, what are your thoughts?"

Stirling was surprised to be asked but he nodded, "We need men, Sir, and if these lads are willing to learn then we could whip them into shape." His voice became sterner, "And if they are willing to take orders."

"That goes without saying." I stood and walked over to them. "We are a small regiment, but we have earned a reputation that has brought us to the attention of the king. Heed the words of the sergeant and you will all do well. Captain Friedrich, as adjutant can you and the sergeant allocate these new men to their new companies?"

Bill Burton said, "If it is all the same to you, Sir, we would like to stay together."

I frowned, "Making demands already, Burton, that does not bode well."

"Sir, we have been through much already. There were another six when we set off walking from Denmark. We are tent mates."

I looked at Stirling who shrugged, "I lost six men when we were attacked. They can join Wolf Company. That might make training them easier."

Over the next fortnight another eight volunteers arrived. All had come to fight as mercenaries but, unlike Burton and his men, arrived as individuals. We took them on. It meant we had fewer remounts but thanks to our success we were able to furnish them with weapons, boots and, in some cases, clothes.

I knew that I needed to spend more time with my officers. If nothing else the attack we had endured on the road had shown me that we needed to act as one. Jennings, Dickson and Summerville had responded well but I knew Jennings better than any other officer and I wanted that relationship with all of them. I took to spending each day with a different company. It was as I worked with the Wolf Company and their six new men that I was able to talk to my Scottish sergeant.

"How are the new men?"

"They will be fine. Bill Burton was a corporal, and he is a natural leader."

"I saw that when he faced up to me. I shall bear him in mind when we need to promote someone."

"They were badly handled in their previous contract. Their officer was killed, and the Danes just abandoned them."

"It was a major defeat, Sergeant."

"I know but it is worrying. I like the king, and he is a good leader. Would he stand by us?"

"I like to think he would, but you never know these things until the matter is put to the test."

We watched the men as the Lance Corporal took them through their drills. Sergeant Stirling told me that they had used a variety of ancient weapons. We had acquired good ones. It was the sergeant who brought up Captain Friedrich, "Sir, if you don't mind me asking, how is the captain?" I did not answer but looked to see if he was stepping over the invisible line between commanding officer and subordinate. "It's just that he was quite shaken by that village we found. We all were. I think we would have happily slaughtered those Croats when we found them if we hadn't been surprised by the hussars. The captain took the loss of the seven men we left on the field badly. It couldn't be helped, Sir. If we had tried to fetch their bodies, we would have lost more men."

I understood now. The captain felt he had let down the dead men. I nodded, "He was shaken but he will come through this. You and I know, Sergeant Stirling, that such things either destroy a man or make him stronger. He is throwing himself into his work. Thank you for letting me know. It has helped."

He shrugged, "We are a good regiment, Sir. We weren't at Christmas, I know that. It was not the fault of the men but Deschamps and the other Froggies. We have, now that we are well led, begun to show what we can do. I think our enemies are in for a shock when we meet on the field of battle."

I learned more in that morning than when I met with the others, but I still felt I was closer to my officers by the end of the week and therefore closer to the men.

Cornet Larsson came for Sigismund and me towards the end of September. "You are both invited to a conference. The king is about to announce his plans."

He waited and so we prepared. The clothes we wore about camp were rough and ready. A conference necessitated our best clothes, boots and hats. As we changed, I said, "How is life at headquarters, Charles?"

"I prefer being with you, Colonel. The king says that I am to be attached to your regiment when the advance begins. I will learn what it is to be a soldier."

"And what kind of soldier will that be?"

"Why a horseman, of course."

He led us through the town gates to the hall the king used. This time there were many more officers present. We had more reinforcements who had arrived in the last week. It explained the conference. Count Wolfgang saw me and came over to give me his normal effusive greeting. "Are you still living in a tent, Colonel?" I nodded, "The rest of the senior officers are enjoying the pleasures of an inn."

"I am happy to share the camp with my men."

He shook his head, "One of the pleasures of being a colonel is enjoying the money that it brings."

Sigismund said, "The colonel sends all his money to his wife and son."

He looked surprised, "Really?"

"Unlike you, Count, I have no lands. This is my profession."

The conversation was ended when Gustav Horn announced the arrival of the king. We sat and I found myself flanked by Sigismund and the cornet.

"We leave next week to bring hope to the Protestants of Mecklenburg. We will head west. As the city has walls that may need to be reduced, we will have to take siege guns and that will slow us down. The cavalry will be the vanguard, and we will take the main road through Plasten and Müritz. Our left flank will be guarded by Colonel Bretherton's regiment. I hope to have the city under our control by Christmas. We shall spend much of the winter there before we head east."

Count Wolfgang said, "King Gustavus, Tilly is in Saxony, should we not take the war to him?"

"He is too strong at the moment. I intend to weaken other parts of the Empire." He smiled, "I have plans afoot, Count, but I will have to keep them private. I do not wish to jeopardise the negotiations."

Once again, the remounts and our ladies would travel with the wagons. We now had two of them. They had been useful in a summer campaign. In a winter one they would be vital. They offered shelter at night as well as the means to carry supplies. Of course, Jane's child did not cooperate. Paul White's son was born early, the day before we were due to leave. Our camp was still isolated and there were no other camp followers to help. We had no doctor and it was left to the two women, along with White himself, who had to deliver the baby. I was touched that the whole regiment seemed worried by the birth. Although the men continued to pack and prepare, they all kept an ear cocked for the sound of a baby.

The wail came when the camp would normally have been asleep. I could do little to help for I was the colonel and the regiment was my responsibility but I felt I ought to show support. I went with Sigismund to the wagon they were using as an improvised birthing bed.

Jane looked tired, the bloody sheets were being carried by a beaming Gertha who said, "He is a healthy boy, Colonel."

I smiled, "Good and you, Jane, are you well?"

"I am, Colonel. Thank you for asking."

I hesitated for my next question needed to be delicately phrased, "And when can you travel I…"

Paul White answered, "Sir, Jane and Davy," he grinned, "that is the bairn's name, can travel in the wagon. Sergeant Dickson has put me in command of the wagons, supplies and remounts. I can keep an eye on them. We won't slow you down."

I looked down at Jane and thought back to Charlotte after she had given birth. My wife had had medical help, servants and a warm bed. She had been given time to recover. Jane and the baby would have to endure the wagon for a week at least.

She looked up and said, "Colonel, all will be well. Other women have had to give birth and then march with the baggage. My mother bore three children that way. I was the youngest. I have the luxury of a wagon."

I looked at White, "Then I leave you with your first command, White."

As I turned away to head back to my tent I saw a slightly shamefaced Sergeant Dickson. He straightened his shoulders and marched over to me, "I am sorry about the presumption, Sir, but Alex and I thought it was for the best to have White in charge of the wagons."

I nodded, "It was and is a good decision but next time, Sergeant, come to me first. After all this is my regiment."

For some reason, the birth put a spring in the step of my men. There were smiles and laughter as we prepared to leave the camp. White and his men would take down and pack the tents while we headed west. Jennings and his Hunting Dogs led and I travelled with the colour party, Charles, Sigismund, Stephen of

Alnmouth and Ashcroft. Thanks to our recent fights all of them had two pistols each as well as good swords. The colours could be defended. Stephen of Alnmouth also led Ran and Sigismund's spare horse. We had learned from the earlier expeditions.

We travelled along the track we had used when we scouted. It was just a couple of miles south of the road that the main column would use. Jennings' men were spread out, not only ahead but half a mile from the road too. While the other companies rode in a column of fours, they were in single file with gaps before them. It made them almost impossible to see. The men had learned on the job and Jennings had honed the skills they had. He was a good teacher and an excellent officer. Dickson and Stirling were wild men in battle who were at the fore. Jennings was not cut from the same cloth. He fought well but almost coldly, and he was able to detach himself from the action and make decisions. He had shown those skills in every action thus far and I could not fault his decision making.

The camp Jennings found for us was an old charcoal burners' clearing. There was a hovel and the remains of their fires. He and his men had already lit the fire when we arrived.

"So far the road is clear, Colonel, and there is no sign of recent activity. We were the last men to ride along here. There may have been hunters since we were last here, but I guarantee not a horse has stepped on the track."

"Thank you, Jennings. Well done."

Charles, Sigismund and I sat on three stumps that Jennings' men had found. "The one aspect of this campaign I do not like is that we left at the same time as the main column."

Charles frowned, "Surely it makes sense to keep you close to the main body, Sir."

"We should have left a day earlier than the army and by now we would be at Müritz. Jennings might be right and there might not have been horsemen on this trail but I guarantee the enemy would have men watching Neubrandenburg. There could have been spies in the town and once the enemy know that King Gustavus is bringing his tiny army west then they could make their plans. It is too far for Count Tilly to intervene but there are other leaders. Until we reach Mecklenburg then the enemy have the advantage."

Captain of Horse

Charles shook his head. He still did not understand. Sigismund said, "There is one road for us to take so the enemy knows our line of march. They could stop us, attack the flanks, attack the baggage train. They know where we are, and they have the freedom to attack when and where they will." He laughed and held out his beaker for Ashcroft to fill, "It is why we are so successful. We are small enough to attack where we will, and we have the speed to escape."

I did not sleep well that night. It was not just the rough ground but also Sigismund's words. He had spoken of the baggage train. I had not thought of an attack there but as they would have the artillery for the attack on Mecklenburg then it was an obvious place to try to hurt us.

I woke before dawn and, after making water, roused Sigismund and Charles. "Charles, I want you and Johnson to ride to the main column. Speak to the king and say that Colonel Bretherton is worried about an attack by the enemy on our baggage."

"Surely he will have thought of that, Sir."

I shook my head, "Until Sigismund mentioned it I had not, but I think it is our weak spot. If we lose the artillery, then we cannot assault Mecklenburg and we have to endure a winter siege."

He and Johnson rode off and I felt better.

It was close to noon when McBride rode in, "Sir, we have found the enemy. They are just five miles from Müritz and they have two artillery pieces in a redoubt on the road and they have musketeers and pikemen on the south side of the road hidden in the trees."

"No cavalry?"

He hesitated, "We didn't cross the road, Sir, so if there were any they would be on the north side of the road."

That would make sense. I nodded, "Return and tell Sergeant Jennings that I will be bringing the regiment."

"Sir."

I could not use the horn and so I whistled a summons along with the waving of my hat to call for my officers. They galloped up, "We have found the enemy. They are north of us. We will turn and head north. It will mean leaving the trail and negotiating the trees. When we see the ambushers, I want half of the men to dismount. They can tie their reins to the trees. We will walk to within fifty paces before we open fire with pistols. The signal will be a single blast on the horn. When I have the charge sounded then I want the rest of the regiment to charge with their horses. I will lead the men on foot and Captain Friedrich the horsemen. Ashcroft, ride to Sergeant Jennings and tell him that he and his men are to take the artillery pieces when they hear the single horn."

"Sir."

"Do you all understand?"

"Yes, Sir."

I turned to Gilmour, "You will wait with Stephen and the horses. You come with the horsemen. Murphy, you will be with me."

They all nodded.

I mounted Ran for she was the better horse to pick her way through the trees. Stephen could lead Marcus.

It was a stray shaft of sunlight catching the backplate of an officer that told us where the enemy waited. I held up my hand and the line stopped. I dismounted and prepared my two pistols. I slipped the lanyards over my head and then replaced my hat. I had no secrete but I did wear my breast plate beneath my jacket. My riding boots were not the best footwear for walking through the forest but that could not be helped. Stephen held Ran and I looked down the line. The officers who would lead the attack on foot all waved that they were ready. With Murphy at my shoulder, we picked our way over the pine needles that had fallen and lay undisturbed. Within a few paces we saw, more clearly, the ambush. Muskettengabel were in position, and the linstocks glowed. The pikes were stacked against the trees. The main column was not yet in sight. Even as we took another four steps, I saw frantic activity and heard orders issued. When the pikemen grabbed their pikes, and the musketeers blew on their serpentines then I knew that the ambush was about to be sprung. It was as I took another three steps that I noticed that there were men armed with swords, axes and spears intermingled with the others. These were citizens, no doubt from Müritz and the surrounding villages.

Captain of Horse

The king would be riding at the fore, with his generals. That was his way. The ambush would be sprung when the king was seen by the artillery pieces. The cannons would blast down the length of the column. Even as we moved another couple of paces, I heard the sound of horses' hooves on the cobbles of the road.

One of my men must have stepped on a branch which cracked. Even though there was the sound of distant hooves the forest was silent and a man turned. He saw us and even as he started to cry out the warning I was shouting, "Murphy, the horn!"

We did not need a volley and I raised my two pistols and fired them both even as the single blast from the horn shattered the silence. There was a ragged series of pops and bangs and then the smoke filled the space between us. I dropped the two pistols, they hung from their lanyards, and drew another two. I took two steps forward and fired again.

Murphy had fired his weapons, and I said, "Sound the charge!"

I holstered my pistols and drew my sword. The three notes sounded above the cacophony of noise. Pistols popped and men screamed. There were flashes in the fog of smoke as muskets were fired at us. I heard the sound of Swedish horns as the king reacted to the skirmish in the forest.

The men with the spears and swords who loomed out of the smoke almost took me by surprise. They should not have done. I used my gauntleted hand to grab one spear as I deflected the sword with my own weapon. The third man thought he had an easy kill. He lunged at my chest. The spear head knocked me back a pace or two, but the hidden breastplate had saved me. Murphy's sword, an old-fashioned two-handed claymore, hacked through the swordsman's arm. It was then that my horsemen galloped through the gaps. They had been hidden by the smoke and the pine needles had deadened the sound of their approach. They were not galloping but that did not matter for they towered above the ambushers. The forest prevented the pikemen from forming solid ranks and as my men fired their wheellocks and harquebuses at point blank range the enemy were slaughtered.

Captain of Horse

Stephen appeared with my horse, Marcus, and Murphy's mount. We mounted and as I rose above the smoke, I saw the Swedish cuirassiers, led by General Baudissin, hurtling down the road in pursuit of the fleeing ambushers. As I reached the road, I saw that there were enemy horsemen in the trees north of the road but King Gustavus himself had led horsemen to engage them.

I reined in next to General Horn, who saluted with his sword and said, "Well done, Colonel. You sprang the trap well."

I pointed west, "And they had artillery at the far end."

"Then take your regiment and chase them back to Müritz."

"Sir!"

"Murphy, sound the recall."

As he did so Cornet Larsson and Trooper Johnson rode up, "The king put a company, the Yellow Regiment, to guard the wagons. They are safe."

"Good." I shouted, "Bretherton's Horse, column of fours!"

It was a ragged column we formed for the road was littered with bodies, but it was easier than picking our way through the forest. When we reached the artillery pieces, I saw that Sergeant Jennings had captured them intact. I had not heard their boom.

"We chase the enemy to Müritz. Follow us."

"Sir."

The men who had fled were on foot. At our approach many took to the trees, and I sent the Stag Company to capture them. The gates of Müritz were still open as we neared them. There were forty or so men racing for their safety, and I saw our chance. Marcus was relatively fresh and I slapped his rump with my hat. He leapt forward. My men would struggle to keep up with me. I glanced behind me and saw that Cornet Larsson, who was also well mounted, was the only one within ten paces of me. As we ploughed through the back of the men racing to get inside the gates, I thought we had failed for the gates began to close. It was the officer in the breastplate and helmet who saved the day for us. He managed to get himself between the gates and his armour made it hard for the men holding the gates to close them. I pulled back on Marcus' reins and his mighty hooves smashed into one of the gates. That and the wedged man was all it took, and the cornet and I were inside the open gates.

Captain of Horse

I drew my sword and whirled Marcus shouting, "Keep the gates open, Cornet."

It takes a brave man to approach the snapping jaws of a war horse and that added to my sword seemed to keep the men trying to get at us at bay. So long as Larsson and I were in the gateway then they could not be closed and my men were rapidly approaching. The musketeer on the walls who aimed at me thought he had me. I saw the flash, the puff of smoke and then heard the pop as he fired at me. He was fifty paces from me. Had the ball been just a little higher then it would have struck me in the face and I would be dead or, at best, disfigured for life. As it was the ball hit my jacket and then my breastplate. I felt as though I had been punched but the ball did not penetrate.

Sergeant Stirling and his Wolf Company galloped through the gates and the defenders fled for the castle. I croaked, "After them. Do not let them get inside the castle."

"Sir."

The cornet said, "Are you hurt?" He was looking at the smoking hole in my jacket.

I smiled, "My breastplate and luck saved me, Cornet Larsson, but I think I have used all the luck I have this day."

I waited until my whole regiment had entered the town before I dismounted. I had meant what I had said to the cornet, I had been more than lucky. Perhaps I needed a helmet too.

Sergeant Stirling had managed to take the castle keep easily. There was just a handful of men left to defend it. I was lauded once more by the king and his generals for we had managed to trigger the trap and had also been in a position to take the town. When a chest of coins was found in the hall of the castle my regiment was given half. There were silver Reichsthalers and all of my men benefitted. We had taken the risks and been rewarded.

We spent a week at the town on the lake while more men arrived to garrison it. The week at Müritz had helped Jane and her baby. There were other camp followers with the army and they had rallied around to help her. The result was that when we left Müritz she was able to sit up and, wrapped against the cold and nursing her son, watch the land as we headed west.

The road to Mecklenburg was more open and through farmland. We resumed our normal role as scouts and the vanguard. Mecklenburg, so we were told, was largely Protestant, hence the king's decision to secure it, but there was a large Catholic element who supported the Imperial cause. The Duke of Mecklenburg was an advocate for Emperor Ferdinand. The king moved cautiously through the land. This was a land of farms that raised animals. Part of our job was to ascertain which were Protestant and which supported the Catholic and Imperial cause. Most purported to be Protestant. However, we found enough enemies to provide the army with fresh meat right up to the gates of Mecklenburg. That meat would prove useful for the gates were closed and we found ourselves in a siege.

I was resigned to a cold November and December until I was summoned, by Cornet Larsson, to the king's headquarters. I saw that just two of his generals were there, Gustav Horn and Johan Banér. There was another man I did not recognise. The king smiled, "You and your men have done well, Colonel. The siege is a time where you and your men can rest. They need not take part in the assault on the walls which will inevitably follow. In any case, such an assault will not happen until the defenders are weakened." He nodded to his two generals, "I spoke of plans that were afoot and you are to be part of them. You are to be part of the group that will go to Bärwalde. It is two hundred miles away. Cardinal Richelieu has offered to negotiate a treaty. As the Elector of Saxony, John George of Saxony, is there too, it was deemed a good place to hold the talks." He waved over the other man, "This is Jakob Kohler, he is my new ambassador to King Charles in London. When you reach Bärwalde you will escort Jakob and his men to Rotterdam and then London. You know the land, I believe?"

I nodded, "I travelled it when we retreated."

"Good. Once at London your work is done. You have given great service to the cause and you deserve a reward. You need not return to Mecklenburg until February. You have time to visit your family. You were promised, I believe, a month of leave each year. That is now due."

I was taken aback and did not know what to say. It was so unexpected that I felt there had to be a catch.

Gustav Horn said, "We leave in an hour, Colonel. It goes without saying that while you must delegate your responsibilities you cannot tell your men what we plan. It would jeopardise not only the plan but our lives." I nodded. "Tell Captain Friedrich that the king has granted you a leave. You will need a companion."

Cornet Larsson piped up, "I should like to volunteer."

The king shook his head, "You will be needed here."

I had recovered enough to find my voice, "I will take Stephen of Alnmouth."

Gustav nodded, "There will be funds made available for the passages that you will need to take. I will deal with that."

The king stood, "Good luck, Colonel."

Chapter 12

Stephen of Alnmouth was delighted to be going with me not least because he would have the chance to visit, albeit briefly, his home.

My parting was brief for we had to hasten. Winter was not the time to be travelling in the Palatinate although the dead months did mean that war had, generally, ceased. Sigismund was happy to be left in command. The year had seen a great change in the regiment and this Christmas celebration would be more civilised than the last. It became clear, as we travelled south, that I was not really needed as an escort. The king was a kind king. Rather than have me cool my heels for two months he was giving me the opportunity to see my family. I was just grateful.

I got to know my two companions quite well. I learned that Johan Banér, like Jakob, was more of a diplomat than a general. He would take on most of the negotiations. However, all of my companions were good riders and we rode as hard as if we were hastening to war. We made the journey far quicker than I had thought we would. The French delegation was there already and Gustav Horn and Johan Banér asked Jakob and I to wait until the negotiations were well under way as it could affect what Jakob needed to know for his new role. For the first two days Stephen and I waited in an antechamber. By the third day the general said we were not needed. I went to the market with Stephen. It would be our best, perhaps, our only opportunity to buy gifts for home. The market was a good one and we bought well. We enjoyed some food and wine. A waiter had spilled some wine on my jacket, and I stank of drink. He was most apologetic. We were just on our way back to our lodgings when Stephen, uncharacteristically, grabbed my arm.

"Colonel," he hissed. He pulled me into the shelter of a door. "Over there, those three cloaked and hooded men."

I looked and saw the men he meant. They had just emerged from a down at heel inn and had pulled up the cowls of their cloaks. They were soldiers but that was all. Soldiers were not an uncommon sight.

"What of them?"

"That is Captain Deschamps and with him is Sergeant Lavalle."

"So, they are mercenaries and must serve in a company here. Perhaps a French one."

He shook his head and spoke earnestly. Both his words and manner told me he was not making this up, "No, Sir, when they left, we heard that they were joining the Imperialists. The captain was a Catholic."

I looked again at the three men. "Do you recognise the third?"

He shook his head, "No, Sir."

I made a decision and handed my purchases to Stephen. "Stay here, the captain does not know me."

I strode over and effected a slight sway as though I had been drinking. The illusion was aided by the spilt wine. I lurched into the three men and spoke in English, "Oh, my dear fellows. I am so sorry."

I noticed that their hands all went to their weapons. I feigned a smile as though I had not seen the movement. "Could you direct me to an inn. I need food to soak up the wine I have just enjoyed."

I knew that both the captain and the sergeant had to understand English. The third one, however, was the one who spoke and he spoke English with a Spanish accent. He also had the olive skin of one from the Iberian Peninsula. He reminded me of Don Alvarado, the man who had hunted me in England and tried to kill me. He pushed me away, "Begone drunken Englishman. If you cannot handle your wine, go back to England."

I adopted an indignant pose, "Sir, I am an officer and a gentleman. I resent your words."

The next words were spoken not in English but French. I could speak French well. It was Captain Deschamps. I recognised him as an officer for the sergeant was, as had been described to me, an older, cruel looking fellow, "Don Alessandro, let us leave. We are attracting attention; this man is a drunk and we have work to do."

The sergeant put his hand to his dagger, "Should I slit his throat, Captain?"

"No, let us just leave."

I pretended I had not understood a word, "What are you jabbering about? Speak English or German."

The sergeant pushed me hard. If I had been drunk, I might have tumbled and cracked my head. As it was, I reeled and slapped my hands against the wall of the inn they had just used. It would make them think that I had hit my head. When I turned, they had gone. I ignored the bystanders who stared at me and staggered back to the doorway.

Stephen was concerned when he came over, "Are your hurt, Sir?"

I smiled, "Perhaps I should take to the stage. No, I am well, but you were right. There is something odd here."

We hurried back to our lodgings. The others were waiting for us to dine with them. I turned to Stephen and handed him a thaler, "Have food and then retire to our room."

"Sir."

The three Swedes looked surprised at my manner. I sat and leaned in. I quickly told them what had occurred.

Johan Banér smiled, "So, it is nothing. There are many mercenaries here and two French ones when there is a French delegation should not be surprising."

"Stephen of Alnmouth said that the captain and sergeant had joined the Imperialists and the man they were with was Spanish."

"It can have nothing to do with us."

Gustav shook his head, "The colonel has good instincts, Johan. What do you suggest, James?"

"Stephen and I will watch the back of the house. The front faces the streets. If there is malicious intent then it will come from the rear."

General Horn nodded but Johan snorted, "And why should we be in danger?"

I shrugged, "Oh, I don't know, perhaps because you are about to negotiate a treaty with France which will give the might of the French treasury to aid the Protestant cause. That is why we are here, are we not? I am not asking you to lose sleep, General. Stephen and I will do that. You said that by tomorrow you will have the agreement drawn up?"

General Gustav nodded, "There will need to be a treaty written up and agreements made but yes, we believe that today's negotiations went well and I see no reason to think that our business will not be concluded soon."

"And that news will be readily available to Spanish spies." I saw their faces take in that news and they nodded. "When I have eaten, I will disappear, and Stephen and I will watch."

I ordered and devoured my food as quickly as I could. Stephen was in the room we shared already. I told him my plans. He nodded his agreement, "I know nothing of this Spaniard but the two Frenchmen…"

"I will sleep now. Wake me at midnight and I will take over. Wear your leather jack and have two loaded pistols. Take no chances and if you hear anything untoward then wake me." I nodded to the door, "There is an alcove close to the rooms occupied by the others. Secrete yourself there."

"Yes, Colonel."

I slept remarkably well considering my mind was filled with thoughts of treachery. When Stephen shook me awake, I was ready in an instant and felt refreshed. He yawned, "I heard nothing, Colonel. The other gentlemen went to bed a couple of hours ago. They have locked their doors."

I nodded and said nothing. I knew that a lock could be picked. If I wanted to bar entry, I would lock the door and then jam a chair against it. "Go to bed. I will wake you when I am tired."

I loaded my pistols and then went to the alcove. It had a couple of steps and led to a cupboard in which was kept linen. I placed my pistols on the ground and leaned my sword against the corner of the cupboard. With my back against it and wearing dark clothes, I was almost invisible.

I remained still. I had been trained well to be a sentry and I had not forgotten what was needed. The noise, when it came, was barely discernible but I heard it. Whoever was climbing the steps was walking at the sides to avoid the creak I knew was there. I moved my hand to grip my sword. Knowing that someone was climbing the stairs made me more alert and my nose detected the smell of the men coming closer to me. I even heard the breathing of one of them. I suspected it was the sergeant. I caught the whiff of tobacco too. Stephen had told me that the sergeant smoked. I stood, using the tip of my sword to help to do so silently. I drew my dagger, and I waited in the shadows. There was a distinct creak as one of them put a boot on the top step. Silence fell and I knew that they were waiting to see if they had been heard. The two men moved into view and I saw that it was the sergeant and the French captain. The sergeant held a brace of pistols. The captain held one and he used his spare hand to slowly lift the latch on the room occupied by the three diplomats. He pushed against it. There was the slightest of noises. It confirmed that it was locked. The captain laid down his pistol and then took a set of lockpicks from his pouch. If the key was in the lock, then it would avail him nothing. However, this was my chance for the captain was kneeling. The sergeant's attention was on the captain and I stepped out and I put my sword to the sergeant's ear, "Put down your pistols, sergeant and you, Captain Deschamps, rise slowly and with your hands before you."

The sergeant signed his own death warrant when he pointed his pistols at me. I lunged and my sword's tip went into his eye. He screamed, the noise sounding like a vixen in the night and he fell backwards down the stairs. The French captain grabbed and raised his pistol in one movement. He had quick hands. I swept my dagger in an arc and caught the end of the barrel just as the pistol fired and smoke and the crack filled the air. He barrelled into me and I found myself falling backwards down the stairs. I kept hold of my weapons. I was saved by the body of the moaning sergeant. The captain fell on top of me, and I was pinned by the weight of his body. His right hand drew his dagger. My left hand held my dagger, and I began to raise it. Beneath me the sergeant thrashed. He was not yet dead. His movement unbalanced me, and my dagger did not meet the captain's blade. I would have died if Gustav Horn had not stabbed the would-be assassin in the back. I threw his body from me as I felt a prick in my back. The sergeant had managed to draw his own dagger and was stabbing me. I moved and slashed. This time there was no mistake and my blade ripped across his throat.

Stephen and the others stood at the top of the stairs while, at the bottom our French host stood looking shocked. Gustav Horn came towards me and kicked the bodies. "They are dead and you are wounded."

I put my hand to my back, and it came away bloody, "A scratch."

"Nonetheless it needs to be tended." He waved to Stephen, "Tend to Colonel Bretherton."

A shocked Johan and Jakob had their weapons out and Johan said, "Our men were guarding the back door."

Just then a groom raced in and said to our French host, "Master, the three guards and Hans the ostler are dead. Their throats are cut."

Gustav nodded, "Now we know. Your instincts saved us, Colonel. We will end the negotiations tomorrow."

The wound did not need stitches. Stephen cleaned it with vinegar and then used the old soldier's remedy of smearing honey on the wound before binding it in a bandage. It would heal. The bodies were searched and Spanish gold found in their purses. It proved my point. The Spanish were behind it. Gustav tossed the purses to me. "And take their weapons and horses. They are yours by right."

The French host pointed to the two dead men, "And the bodies?"

Gustav Horn took charge of the situation, "Throw them in the river. Let this Don Alessandro wonder what has happened to his killers and you, Colonel, can watch for him."

I had no sleep that night and the next day Stephen and I went with the negotiators to the meeting.

The French negotiator, de Charnacé, was told of the attack and I was brought out as evidence. He was shocked. By the end of the day an agreement had been reached. Cardinal Richelieu would need to be informed of the details before it was ratified but it was in place. The French were guaranteed trading privileges in the Øresund Strait. Sweden agreed to maintain an army of 36,000 in Germany, of which 6,000 would be cavalry. To support this force, the French negotiator agreed to pay 400,000 Reichsthaler or one million livres per year, plus an additional 120,000 Reichsthalers for the current year. This was a fortune for King Gustavus and for the Protestant cause. He would be able to hire more mercenaries.

That night, as we celebrated, Gustav said, "You had better leave on the morrow for England. I believe we are safe now for the agreement is signed, but Jakob needs to get to London. We do not need King Charles to feel threatened by this alliance."

Jakob asked, "Are you fit to travel, Colonel?"

I smiled, "When you are safely delivered, then I can go home. Believe me, I am fit."

With Jakob and his three servants and the two spare horses gained from the dead assassins, we made good time. We reached London in the second week of December. Stephen and I had been more than vigilant on the road, but we knew we were not followed and were largely ignored. Jakob had coins and we paid well for our food and accommodation. We reached the home of the king, St James' Palace, and, my work done, I left Jakob there. We had a long journey home.

I did not relish the long ride and so we headed to the Pool of London. There we found a collier which had unloaded its cargo. London in winter was desperate for coal from Newcastle. The captain had an almost empty hold for his return voyage north and, although we had four horses to load, he was happy to take our money. The voyage to the Tyne would take five days and that was about the same length of time it would take to ride hard. The advantage was that we would be under shelter, as would our horses. I paid the captain, and we sailed.

Once we reached Newcastle, I let Stephen go home. We agreed that he would meet me in Hartlepool at the end of January. That would give me time to find us passage back to the Baltic. We parted and I rode hard to reach my home in one day. I had two horses and I stopped merely to water them and change my mounts. I cared not if I was saddle sore for I wanted every moment I could with my family.

The doors in the village were all closed and not a chink of light could be seen. There was a heavy frost and not only did my breath appear before me but the heat from the horses rose like steam. I banged on the door. Inside I heard Margaret's voice. "Who is it calling at this ungodly hour?"

She opened the door, and I put my finger to my lips. Her mouth opened in astonishment and, slipping a cloak around herself she went to take the reins of my horses.

Captain of Horse

Charlotte called from the living room, "Margaret, who is it? I pray you close the door for there is an icy draught here."

I went to the living room door and opening it, stood there.

Charlotte stood and, most uncharacteristically, burst into tears. She ran to me and threw herself in my arms. "I should have warned you but…"

She reached up and, to silence me, kissed me full on the lips. Elizabeth the cook appeared in a dressing gown and, seeing me there, she too burst into tears.

I laughed, "Had I known I would cause such distress I might have stayed away."

Elizabeth recovered herself, "Captain, God has sent you and we shall have the most wondrous celebration this Christmas. I have soup and it will take but a moment to heat it." She put her hand on my shoulder, almost as though she wanted to make sure that I was not an apparition. "It is good to see you home and whole, Captain."

Margaret came in. I saw that she was shivering, "I have given the horses to Alan, Captain. He will tend to them."

"Alan?"

Charlotte had also recovered herself, "I hired a stable hand. We needed someone to look after the horses and work outside. When your pay came last month, I spent some. I hope you do not mind."

I laughed, "I am delighted, and the money is yours to use as you see fit, my sweet."

She linked my arm and took me to a two-seater couch close to the fire. It was new. "Come sit here and let me drink you in while you tell me what brings you home."

During the ride from Newcastle, I had run through all the things I could and would tell her and that which I would keep hidden. I would need to tell her that I had been wounded but I would leave the details vague. I had barely explained the reason for my return from the wars when Elizabeth brought in a bowl of steaming soup and home-made bread. Margaret poured me some wine and they hovered. I smiled, "Thank you, ladies. You need not stay up on my account. I will see to the pots."

"We do not mind, Captain."

I nodded, "And now I am a colonel. I hope that does not cause confusion."

Their eyes widened. Elizabeth beamed, "A colonel, how wonderful. We will leave you. Mistress, ring the bell when you need us."

The door closed and Charlotte said, "Colonel Bretherton? I hope you did not put your life in jeopardy to be so rewarded."

I knew when to lie and this was one such occasion. I ate and spoke of my time in Pomerania and Germany. I ended by telling her that I had been on a diplomatic mission and that seemed to please her.

"And I hate to bring it up, but when do you return?"

"I have until February, but I will need to see the Swedish agent in Hartlepool to arrange a passage. My groom will meet me in Hartlepool at the end of January. We have more than a month."

"And when you see William, what a change you shall see. Why he can almost toddle now and he makes the most delightful sounds. I swear he will be speaking soon."

I put the tray on the table and slipped my arm around her. I kissed the top of her head, "I am not sure if I will be granted another leave any time soon but I have hopes that King Gustavus will have the beating of our enemies. When this war is over, I shall come home a rich man. I have more gold for you in my bags."

"The greatest riches, Husband, are that you are whole and alive. I shall examine your wound on the morrow and see how well this Stephen of Alnmouth tended to you."

She was pleased with the healing that had taken place. Honey and vinegar were always effective, and the scar would be just a thin white line by the time I returned to the wars.

William took a day or so to get used to me. I was upset at first, but Charlotte explained that the only men he had seen had been Roger and Peter and that was just once every two months or so. Alan the groom was a recent addition to the household. I could not complain. It was my own fault that I was away.

Roger and his son heard of my return and two days after I had walked through the door they came to speak to me. Roger was as proud of my promotion as if I was his son. "Your father would be proud."

"And my mother?"

"You know that you were her raison d'être. You could never do wrong, but I know that she would be delighted in your success and your choice of bride."

As much as I resented any time away from my wife and son, I knew I had to arrange a passage before Christmas. George Smith, the agent, would need time to arrange a ship. I rose before dawn and was in Hartlepool even as the bells from St Hilda's chimed twelve. I told him that Stephen would be arriving and he assured me that he would accommodate my trooper. I slipped him some silver to ensure that he did all that he promised. He also had news for me. The city the king had besieged had fallen within a few days. According to George, who had heard the news from a sea captain, a handful of men had been lost in the assault. My mission completed I rode back and reached home just as darkness fell. I had been away a day but it felt like a lifetime.

We were then able to prepare and to enjoy Christmas. I think Elizabeth and Margaret were more excited than even my wife and me. They saw the whole family together. When Charlotte and I insisted that the three servants all join us for the meal I was sure that they were going to burst.

Roger and Peter had wanted us to dine with them but I wanted the time with my family. However, the day after Christmas Charlotte and I accepted an invitation for lunch. Theirs was a house of men and they fussed over Charlotte. William had stayed in our home with Margaret, and it was good to see Charlotte as a lady rather than a mother. After a fine lunch and a delicious port Charlotte said she had to return home and see to William but that I should stay. The port was a good one and the thought of another glass persuaded me to remain.

I was able to tell them the story of the war. The one extra glass turned into a second. Roger had enjoyed the wine too and when I had finished, he told me of the politics of the new king. "We hear things later up here in the north but the king has angered the Protestants. He leans towards Catholicism and Arminianism. Worse, he has suspended Parliament and has made peace with Spain. He has angered the Scottish lords with taxes upon their titles. I fear we have a king who does not listen and that does not bode well."

"If Parliament is suspended then what can they do?"

"A king needs money. Every king does and without Parliament he has to rely on his own resources. The king has expensive tastes."

When I left, I was more depressed than when I had entered. Conflict in Germany was one thing but what I did not need was a religious war in my own land. When King Gustavus won the war against the emperor, I might be needed back in England.

Time, as it always does when it is the most precious commodity in the world, flew and soon it was time for me to leave. What made it even more galling was that my son had so warmed to me that he giggled and laughed when he saw me. I had learned that I had the ability to pull funny faces, make silly voices and generally make my son happy. So it was that when I left and he sobbed his heart out, I felt mine breaking and the ride to Hartlepool was both long and lonely.

George had done well and found Stephen and I berths on a ship sailing to Peenemünde. The ship was carrying ball for King Gustavus. He was spending his French subsidy already. The ship would be sailing the next day on the last tide. Even that annoyed me. It meant I could have spent an extra day at home. Stephen was also somewhat morose. To take my mind off my problems I asked him why he was unhappy. It seemed he had met a girl or, rather, rekindled affection for a girl he had known all his life. When he had left to go to war, she had been courted by another. That young man had fallen ill and died of the plague whilst visiting London. He and Emma, the young woman, had grown close in the village by the sea and were now both smitten with one another.

"I think, Colonel, that when I have enough money, I shall return home and marry Emma. Neither of us are getting any younger and I am the only man in the family. I have sisters. I should like the name to carry on and I no longer have an itch to travel."

I nodded, "If you wish to stay now, you can."

He shook his head, "Thanks to those killers I have some silver but not enough and, besides, I will need to say goodbye to my tent mates. They looked after me." He smiled, "I know that with you and the king as our leaders we will win more than we will lose. I told Emma to look for me next year."

"Good."

My worries disappeared for I knew how dangerous our world could be and I now had to worry that Stephen would survive and return to his Emma.

Chapter 13

Neubrandenburg February 1631

When I reached our camp by the city taken in my absence, I discovered that we had not endured any desertions and even attracted another six volunteers. The regiment was in good heart and the winter spent at Mecklenburg had seen horses grazed and bellies filled thanks to the French subsidy. The king had left garrisons in the captured towns, and we still had an army of eighteen thousand. As well as Swedish soldiers there were many Scottish regiments. They were musket and pike. There were three colonels, all Scottish, John Leslie, John Hepburn and Robert Munro who now commanded a large force of mercenary soldiers. I liked them all from the moment we met although I knew Robert Munro already. The king was keen for us to get on and he held a feast when the two new colonels arrived with their troops. The three had already been told of my exploits and the reputation of my border horse. They were keen to know what to expect. My English was easier to understand than either the Swedish or German that was generally used.

When the king held his meeting with his generals the three stayed close to me, as I was able to translate some of the words that they did not understand. It made a bond that would help us in the days to come.

"My fellow warriors, we begin the next part of our crusade soon. Elector George William of Brandenburg still courts the favour of the emperor. We have concocted a cunning plan to make him change his allegiance. We will march one hundred and ten miles to the eastern side of Brandenburg and take the fortress of Frankfurt an der Oder." There was a buzz of conversation as the plan was discussed. I had to explain to the three Scotsmen where Frankfurt an der Oder lay. Captain Friedrich had scouted it out already. The king allowed the conversation to continue for a short while and then held up his hands for silence, "Once we have that eastern bastion in our hands then we can move west through Brandenburg and bring succour to those who have endured the tyranny of Emperor Ferdinand. I hope that by recovering the lands of my father-in-law, those within

Brandenburg who favour the emperor will switch their allegiance."

After the meeting had ended, I was summoned to King Gustavus, "You and your regiment will have the honour of being the vanguard. We need to be as hidden as an army of eighteen thousand can be. When we reach Frankfurt an der Oder your task will be to collect supplies and give us a warning if the Imperialists attempt to reinforce the garrison. To that end I am assigning an extra wagon. I know that you have two, but I want your men to have enough powder and ball."

"Thank you, King Gustavus."

"I will provide drivers for your wagons too. It seems to me a waste to have horsemen of the calibre of your men seated on a wagon when they could be put to better use. I have six Germans I will attach to your regiment. They will be paid for directly, but you will need to feed them."

"Of course." I smiled but the order was a worry. We had women with the regiment and my men could be precious about strangers being in such close proximity. I would need to ensure that all was well. The strangers could be like a stone in a boot, a minor distraction but it could cause problems if not dealt with.

I held my own meeting with my officers. All my company commanders were now sergeants, and I had decided to make Stirling and Dickson into lieutenants. They would still lead their companies, but their promotions allowed me to be more flexible. I told them of the plan and then the news of the drivers. As I had expected, Sergeant Seymour and Corporal White frowned when told the news. The others saw no problem. After I had finished the briefing, I kept the two officers and Sigismund for a private meeting. Ashcroft and Stephen of Alnmouth kept watch for I wanted the meeting to be without eavesdroppers.

I decided to be blunt, "I saw from your faces that you were both less than happy about the new drivers." They looked at each other and said nothing. I sighed, "Come, you should know me by now. I like things in the open and that way we can find solutions to problems and not let them fester and poison us."

"Sir, it is just that, well we have families. Gertha is with child and my bairn, well, you know…"

White added, "And there are two more women now, Sir. Their men might not be happy about strangers and German ones at that."

My voice hardened, "Let me be blunt. All of you chose to take women and put them in this position. I am married and my wife is many leagues from here." I was aware that Stephen was outside and could hear my words. "There are other men who have left sweethearts at home. I will speak to these drivers and if any are unsuitable then *I* will deal with it." I emphasised the word. "The king wants this regiment to do what it does best and that means I need every trooper and officer to have his mind on the task in hand and not worrying about his woman. If you are that worried, then leave your families here. God knows that it will be much easier for all if that were to happen."

Sergeant Seymour shook his head, "No, Colonel Bretherton, you are right, and you have been more than fair. You have never let us down and we trust you. Sorry about…"

I smiled, "It is forgotten, now go and explain to your families about the arrangements."

When the German drivers arrived then all fears were allayed. The king had found us six of the oldest men I had ever seen in an army. All of them had to be grandfathers. With either grey hair or no hair they would not be a threat to anyone. Their stories were all remarkably similar. They had served in the Protestant armies or the Swedish army when it had retaken Poland. All had lost their families while they had campaigned. They each hated Catholics with a passion I found hard to equate with the grey hairs. They took to the women and especially the infant, Davy, and when I saw smiles from Sergeant Seymour and Corporal White then I was relieved. We made sure that they were armed. They would be the only protection for the women. Not all the drivers in the baggage train were as trustworthy.

We left the city in March and headed south and east. It seemed such a long time since we had done this and yet we all moved seamlessly into our roles. Stephen, Ashcroft, Gilmour and Murphy rode behind Sigismund and me. Jennings and his Hunting Dogs were almost invisible as they filtered across the land ahead of us. With a company to our left and one to our right we were able to deal with any threat as well as being able to capture any spies. That first week we captured six. The enemy had planted spies close by Neubrandenburg. We knew that they were spies for what other reason would a man hide in woods with a horse to hand and weapons to defend himself? I say captured but only four were prisoners, the other two tried to fight my troopers. They died. We retained the horses while Gustav Horn had interrogators discover the enemy organisation. It became clear that these men were sent by the Spanish and the one name we discovered was Don Alessandro. The man who had sent Deschamps to kill our generals was a spymaster. It was useful information especially as I had seen him. I doubted that I would ever be in a position to identify him, but I would still watch for him.

We found opposition, for the first time, at the small town of Quilitz. It had a wooden wall around it but that would not have stood much chance against even the regimental artillery, but it was my men who were fired upon and we dealt with the situation.

I sent Wolf Company along with the Hunting Dogs to get to the far side of the town and then dismounted the Wildcat and Hawk companies. With Gilmour carrying the standard and Murphy the trumpet, protected by Ashcroft and Stephen of Alnmouth, Sigismund and I led our first assault on foot. We ran at the walls. The smoke from the ancient weapons fired from the low ramparts merely obscured our charge. They were, in any case, fired too early. When I saw the walls through the smoke, I halted our two companies and then ordered them to open fire. More than a hundred pistols, harquebuses and muskets blasted both the defenders and the wooden walls. I had four men with axes who ran at the wooden gates while my other men boosted troopers over the walls. By the time the main army had arrived, alerted by the gunfire, the town was ours. We had suffered a dozen minor wounds and killed twenty men. We relieved the houses of treasure, food and anything else of value. The other towns through which we had passed had not been raided by my men. I did not know what the rest of the army did, but I wanted Bretherton's regiment to have the reputation of only taking from enemies.

Captain of Horse

Quilitz was just thirty-five miles from Frankfurt an der Oder. By now the enemy would know we were coming. They would lay in supplies. It also meant that the towns through which we next passed, while they did not oppose us, hid everything of value. King Gustavus was ruthless and whatever could be found was taken. These Brandenburgers were relying on the hope that we would be defeated, and they would be able to resume their lives.

The enemy scouts tried to halt us just three miles from the fortress. They waited in ambush hidden in the woods that flanked the road. Sergeant Jennings was wise to such ruses, and he sent a rider back to tell me that there were half a dozen companies of dragoons hiding in the woods. After informing the king of the ambush I led the Otter Company to the southern side of the wood and Sigismund led the Badger Company to the north. We filtered through the trees and when I saw the backs of the dragoons, I ordered Murphy to sound the charge. The effect was astounding. Jennings and his men had been waiting for the horn and they galloped up the road. Sigismund led the Badger Company to charge the other side. The attacks totally confused the dragoons. Had they concentrated their fire on any one of us then they might have enjoyed a little success. As it was their balls were wasted. Twelve were killed and the rest were taken prisoner. We had purses, horses, weapons, ball and powder. I saw the smile on Stephen of Alnmouth's face. Every purse he took meant a day closer to the time he would be home and married. None of my men saw the suffering our attacks were causing. They were fighting for a cause. That they were profiting from that cause was incidental. Sigismund and I knew that the king was hurting Brandenburg much as a surgeon would cut out a canker. There would be pain but Brandenburg would be free once it was over.

The crossing over the Oder was guarded by a small fort and a bridge that led to the barbican at the Lebus gate. The small fort would have to be taken first. While the king had his engineers build a redoubt from where they could bombard the barbican and the walls, we were sent to scout the lands to the north and south of the fortress. My new organisation came to the fore and with my captain and lieutenants we each led two companies. We were strong enough to take on a patrol of anything less than a regiment and yet the four elements could cover a large area. This was Catholic country and close to the border with Poland. Anyone we found would be an enemy. Our job was to eliminate enemies and to take any animals and supplies that could feed the army. We were more than a hundred miles from our base. Either we took food, or we would all die.

By the end of the first day, we had cleared every village, farm and house for a distance of fifteen miles. The next day I planned to patrol further afield. As we made our weary way back to the siegeworks we heard the sound of cannons as the defenders tried to disrupt the work of the engineers. General Lennart Tortennson was in his element. He was a supreme gunner, and the Imperial guns did not cause him one moment of trouble. What they did do was to make a thick fog of smoke that encircled the river, barbican and the walls. They were wasting both powder and ball.

Our new carters proved their value for by the time we reached our camp they had made the three wagons into an enclosure. Within it Sergeant Wilson's cooks, aided by the women, had food already cooking. Animals hunted in the forests, dried beans and now the freshly plundered vegetables ensured that we would eat well, at least for a while. We needed to take the city quickly.

The next day we went deeper into enemy lands and enjoyed a similar success. As we rode back Stephen of Alnmouth had a grin as wide as a full moon. I knew why but Corporal Murphy did not, "What makes you smile so much?"

He shook his head, "I did not know that I was, but I am happy." He patted his pouch. "We took more silver today and with what I have collected already I will have enough by autumn to return to Alnmouth and marry."

Murphy shook his head, "I was married once." He shook his head, "God's blood, she was pretty but had a tongue like an adder and a temper like a shrew. I was glad when she ran off with a butcher. I am well rid of her."

Stephen's face fell and I said, "Take no notice, Stephen. There are others like Seymour and White who are happily wed, as am I."

The Irishman smiled, "No offence, Colonel. I was just saying how marriage is not for me. My money goes on ale and women. I will start to save when I get hairs like our German drivers."

That set all my men talking about their futures and their plans. Being a mercenary was not a vocation. It was a means to an end. They were all good soldiers, and this was a way to benefit from those skills. Stephen also had skills with horses, and he planned to breed hardy horses in the borders. He would never be rich but so long as a man did what he enjoyed and had a family who supported him then all would be well.

Once the redoubt was built, and the larger artillery pieces placed there then the assault began. The general was methodical. He had the guns concentrate their fire on one target. Once that target was destroyed they moved on. It gave the defenders no chance to repair damage. By the end of the first day the bastion at the end of the bridge was ready to fall and the Lebus Gate no longer had guns to fire at an attacker.

Our camp was close to the bastion and as we ate and watched the enemy attempt to repair the damage, Sigismund and I discussed the siege. "I can see that the enemy artillery is destroyed, Sigismund, but men still have to cross that narrow bridge and then try to break in. They will lose men."

He nodded, "You are right, James, but remember the incentive for the first men to break in. They have the first choice of treasure. We have done well by being the first into villages and towns. The dangers here are greater than we endured but so will be the rewards. This is a rich city and the plunder will be great."

I glanced to the two large Scottish camps just behind the redoubt. The Scottish regiments were ready to assault. They were, as yet, untried. They had not lost a man but that would change when the breaches were made and the assaults began. I knew that we had the easiest task. Light horsemen could not assault walls. Cavalry could not assault walls. That was a job for musketeers and pikemen. I had noticed that the new men had a higher proportion of musketeers than the Imperial Army. That gave us an advantage but only so long as we were well supplied with powder and ball. At the moment we were just a relatively short way from our supply base but if we enjoyed the success that the king planned then we would be stretched.

By the end of the next day, it was clear that an assault would be made. We had spent the day searching the countryside for food and when we returned, we saw the officers leaving the king's tent. He had given his orders. Cornet Larsson came for me not long after I had taken off my breastplate and holsters.

"Colonel, the king would speak to you."

The young Swede had changed since I had first met him. He now looked like a seasoned warrior. He was festooned with weapons, and I saw that he had a breastplate too. He saw me looking at him and he smiled, self-consciously, "My time with you, Colonel, showed me that I was woefully unprepared for war. I had a view in my head of a noble knight charging his enemies. I saw the reality and I have tried to emulate you and your men."

I nodded, "Good, you are becoming a soldier then. You like your new role?"

He lowered his voice, "I like most of it, but I am afraid that being the king's aide brings me into contact with some officers who are eminently unpleasant." Just at that moment we both heard a laugh and looked over to see Prince Francis Albert of Saxe-Lauenburg with two other officers. The prince saw me and made a comment to the two officers who both laughed. Cornet Larsson said, "A case in point, Colonel."

I smiled back at the prince. I had learned that was the best way to deal with his insults and said, quietly, "He has little influence, and the king only needs him as an ally. You know the king by now and you must realise that he values military skill above all else. The prince will not have an important role to play."

Gustav Horn was with the king, and he smiled when we entered, "It is good to see you again, Colonel. I trust that the leave you enjoyed refreshed you?"

"I did and relieved that you and the others had a safe return to the camp."

"Aye, they thought their assassins would succeed."

The king said, "Let us deal with the here and now and not the past, gentlemen." He pointed to a map of the city. "Tomorrow we will assault Frankfurt an der Oder. I am confident that thanks to our artillery the assault will succeed. When it does, Colonel, I want you to head north and east towards the Warte River. Landsberg guards the river. I would have it scouted out.

According to the maps it is just fifty miles away. You can be there in a day while it will take us some time to reach it. We can do so more quickly if we know if our guns are needed. Do you understand?"

"Yes, King Gustavus."

"Cornet Larsson will accompany you and he can report back. He seems to grow in your company. Who knows, perhaps when he returns this time there will be promotion, eh, Cornet?"

"I hope so, my lord."

"And then, King Gustavus?"

"And then, Colonel, we can seek out Count Tilly. We have more troops on their way from Sweden and more mercenaries from Scotland. With Brandenburg secure we can strike into the lands they took after the Dutch and Danish collapse." He jabbed a finger at the map, "I think that the count has two choices, take Magdeburg or move east and face us."

Gustav Horn nodded, "Magdeburg is the jewel he will seek, King Gustavus. It is a stronger fortress and city than this one. Twenty-five thousand people live there."

The king shrugged, "We shall see. We deal with each problem as it occurs and then plan. I do not look beyond the end of the month. Things can easily change." He hesitated and then looked at me with a sad look on his face, "Count Tilly has taken advantage of our departure from Neubrandenburg. He made a surprise assault and has taken and sacked the city. The garrison are either all dead or prisoners. We now have to fend for ourselves. You and your men must take as many supplies as you can. Frankfurt an der Oder is now vital to us."

A disaster. If we had not been given the drivers then our tross would be destroyed and as for the women…

When I returned to our camp, I summoned my officers and told them of the loss of the city. "It means that our baggage becomes even more vital. We must protect what we have and take as much as possible for our enemies. We will not take the whole regiment. I want Otter Company to stay with the baggage. We need them to be protected. I want at least one of our companies to have fresh horses."

Sergeant Jennings was the brightest of my officers and he said, "You think we will be moving soon?"

I nodded, "We will have taken the most powerful city in this part of Brandenburg. My guess is that we will secure the rest of it before the king faces Tilly."

"Where is Count Tilly, Colonel?"

"Anyone's guess but General Horn seems to think he is closer to Magdeburg. That is why I want at least one company that is well rested. While you wait, Sergeant Wilson, get as many supplies from the town as you can."

Lieutenant Dickson snorted, "We have yet to take it, Colonel."

Lieutenant Stirling smiled, "I was speaking to the Scottish lads who are going to lead the assault. They are confident enough and the defenders didn't fire a single cannon today. The new lads want success and I think they will get it."

I enjoyed a good view of the assault. I went to the redoubt with Sigismund. We watched the cannons fire their last salvoes at the wooden Lebus Gate. When the smoke cleared, I saw the two Scottish generals, Munro and Hepburn as they led their men through the wreckage of the bridge fort and over the bridge to the gate. The damage to the bridge meant that they were unable to charge in a solid phalanx. That helped them as the defenders with muskets, and there seemed few of those, did less damage to the attackers than I had expected. We heard the roar and crash as they struck the men in the wrecked gateway. Stirling had been right; the Scots were eager for a fight and when the long metal snake entered the gate then the king was able to order supporting regiments to follow.

I turned to Sigismund, "Assemble the men."

He looked surprised, "But the assault has barely begun."

"If Lieutenant Stirling is right then it will not be long."

As if to confirm my words, when we reached our camp Cornet Larsson was there already, mounted and armed and with two young Swedish horsemen with him. He smiled, "The king has given me my own command. There are only two of them, but it is a start. The king says that when the standard falls from the citadel you are to pass through the city and complete your task."

I nodded, "Stephen, I will take Marcus." I had used Ran for the last few days. Captain Deschamps' horse, I had named him

Fiery, for his angry eyes, had yet to be ridden to war. Marcus was the better choice.

We mounted and with flags and guidons unfurled we waited. We had just an hour to wait. The flag fell from the citadel, and we picked our way gingerly across the bridge. Whoever commanded the city for the king would have to make many repairs. There were piles of bodies at the gates and Swedish soldiers were already shifting them. There would be too many to burn, and I did not envy the men the task of digging graves for so many. The Scottish soldiers had cleared the main throughfare and as we passed the citadel, we could still hear the fighting as groups of defenders fought on.

Colonel Munro himself was at the gate that led from the city. He pointed north and east, "There, Colonel, you will find those who fled before we reached the gates. There are soldiers, although the majority of those who evaded us were women, children and merchants."

I saluted the general, "You did well, Colonel."

He grinned, "Aye, well the lads were eager. There will be purses to be lifted and drink to be had. We have made a good start."

I nodded, "Sergeant Jennings."

"Sir! Hunting Dogs, with me."

Our scout company galloped past us and, as they headed up the road, I waved forward the rest of my regiment.

Chapter 14

Landsberg 1631

The king's order for us to pursue so quickly had taken those who had fled the city by surprise. As people fled, they heard our hooves and panicked. Much of the treasure they had taken was discarded as they took to the woods and fields to try to escape us. We found small chests, purses, food and animals. It did not slow us much for we had seven companies, and one company could easily be spared to gather the detritus of the retreat. We found discarded muskets and knew that the soldiers who had fled were not a threat.

We rode hard and saw the last bastion of Brandenburg in the distance. Sergeant Jennings had found a good place to view the town. He pointed, "There is a bridge over the river, and it is defended but," he grinned, "my lads found a place over there," he pointed east, "where the river is just ninety paces wide."

Cornet Larsson had been listening and he frowned, "How do you know, Sergeant?"

Jennings pointed to two troopers who were emptying the water from their boots, "I had two of my lads swim it."

I nodded, "Well done. Officer's call!" As Murphy raised the horn I shook my head, "Just fetch them, Murphy. We will keep our presence here a surprise, at least for a short time."

When the officers were gathered, I said, "Captain Friedrich, take Lieutenant Stirling, with Wolf, Fox and Stag companies. Ford the river and cut them off from the north."

He nodded, "Do we attack, Sir?"

"No, just stop them from leaving and warn us of any reinforcements."

"Sir."

"The rest of you, as soon as it is dark we close with the walls. Sergeant Jennings, is there any cover close to the bridge?"

"There are a couple of houses and a farmhouse."

"Lieutenant Dickson, have your men take those houses and the farm. Secure the people but make sure that they are unharmed."

"Sir."

"Cornet Larsson, I am afraid there will be neither rest nor food for you. Return to the king and tell him what we have found." He nodded, "Do you need it to be written?"

"No, Sir."

"Then God speed."

Lieutenant Dickson and his men took the houses and the farm without a sound. I was confident that the people of Landsberg would have no idea that a regiment of mercenaries was camped on their doorstep. The houses and farm we occupied hid our horses and we used the fires in the dwellings to cook our food. Sigismund and the men on the other side of the river might not be so comfortable but I knew that my men would make themselves invisible.

I rose before dawn and walked with my officers to view the town. There was a bridge and the gatehouse looked to be defended, but there was no fort guarding our end of the bridge. In any case I knew from Sergeant Jennings that the river could be crossed by horsemen.

"When the men have eaten then have the Wildcats mount. Let us see how they react. Have the other two companies take cover and be prepared to fire their weapons."

"Sir."

I was in the farm, and we enjoyed a fine breakfast. We had taken all the houses without loss and before food and treasure could be hidden. The farmer and his family had glared at us, but they were not so foolish as to try anything. They would be just hoping that their home would be intact when we left.

I left Jennings in command of the defences along with my standard bearer. "Have the men make a skirmish line and have their weapons ready but keep them hidden."

"Sir."

I rode with the Wildcat company as well as Murphy, Stephen and Ashcroft. We had primed pistols at the ready. As we neared the bridgehead, we heard the sound of a horn and then the tolling of bells. We had been seen.

"This is close enough, Lieutenant."

"Sir."

We halted a hundred paces from the bridgehead. As the river was almost ninety paces wide, we were safe from muskets. If I

Captain of Horse

thought that we were in danger from artillery, then I would retreat. I doubted that they would waste powder and ball on us as we were spread out in a thin line. Cannonballs were saved for masses of men. Soldiers appeared on the battlements. I saw light reflecting from helmets. At one point I watched a huddle of men gather. They were debating our presence. When I heard firing from the north then I knew that the other half of our regiment had been seen. This was a different regiment from the one I had first encountered more than sixteen months earlier. I knew that they could deal with whatever problems faced them. Since his minor aberration Sigismund had been as solid an officer as one could wish for.

The horsemen who flooded from the fortress were a mixture of regiments. I did not see metal glinting and knew that they had no cuirassiers with them, but they did have dragoons, harquebusiers and swordsmen. The bridge narrowed them but once they were clear they spread into a rough line.

"Be ready to fire when I give the command."

I heard the creak of leather and the sound of wheellocks and harquebusiers being prepared. My men still had a variety of weapons. I took out two wheellocks. Marcus was a steady horse and I had a good platform from which to fire. My plumed hat and the trumpeter next to me made me a target. The ones at the fore who raced across the open ground were drawn to me like moths to a flame. They sought the glory. As I was in the middle of the road that meant the ones coming at me had the faster road. When they were fifty paces I shouted, "Fire!" Even as the flames belched and the smoke filled the air I shouted, "Murphy, sound the retreat!" I holstered my pistols and drew a third. As soon as the last note sounded and my men turned, I prepared to wheel Marcus. The horseman who emerged through the fog had a sword pointed at me and he was just ten paces from me. I fired and wheeled. The shout from behind me told me that the glory hunting horseman had been downed.

My men were well trained, and they looked for the gaps ahead where the other companies waited, weapons resting on whatever was to hand. With Jennings in command, I was confident in order prevailing. He had a cool head. I passed close to the standard. The breeze made it flutter above my tall standard bearer's head. The first horsemen who reached our defences would see it and any survivors be able to tell the rest of our enemies that Bretherton's Horse was the regiment that they faced.

Jennings shouted, "Fire!" The two companies' combined firepower sent more than a hundred balls at the enemy.

I wheeled Marcus and holstered my fired wheellock. I peered at the smoke, ready to draw and fire a fourth weapon. All that came through the smoke were the horses of the men we had hit. Horses are, in the main, sensible creatures and seeing a barrier both human and man-made, they stopped.

"Reload!"

Jennings was too good an officer to take anything for granted. However, as the breeze which fluttered the flag cleared the fog, we saw that the attempt to dislodge us had failed and the survivors were flooding back over the bridge.

"Sergeant Seymour, take your men and bring back any prisoners and weapons."

"Sir!"

"Right lads, you heard the colonel."

The dozen horses were brought back first. They had saddles, holsters and weapons. There were no prisoners. The wounded men had made it back to the city and all that remained were the fifteen men we had hit. Weapons, purses, and helmets were brought back. The booty would be equitably distributed.

"Lieutenant Dickson, set sentries and light fires for the food."

It had been a successful day. When the king did arrive, he found a crossing that could be taken. His invasion of Brandenburg had begun well. We were reunited with the rest of our men and our baggage. We now had ten women who followed the regiment, and their safe arrival always put my men in better heart.

We took the city on St George's Day. My English contingent took that as a good sign. The city yielded after the king's artillery had destroyed their gates. We did not enter the city but stayed in our commandeered farm. Cornet Larsson, now newly promoted to Lieutenant brought the king's congratulations to us. He was eager to tell all.

"General Leslie is in command at Frankfurt an der Oder. His most difficult task will be to bury the three thousand dead who fell. We lost but eight hundred. It was a great victory and thanks to you and Captain Friedrich, we lost barely a handful in this assault. You and your men will receive your fair share of the booty."

I nodded, "It is all good news then."

Larsson frowned and shook his head, "We have heard that our ally, Magdeburg, is under siege. Count Tilly has more than thirty thousand troops there and if it falls then Saxony is lost."

I shook my head, "Then all that we have done here will be wasted."

"The king hopes that it will hold out. There are strong defences with redoubts and forts all around."

"Then he plans to leave soon?"

"I do not know."

It was early May when I was summoned to headquarters. The king had dallied. I knew that there had to be reasons but my regiment had been tasked with ensuring that we had all the supplies we would need for our march to Magdeburg. Our supply lines were stretched. We had not lost a great number of men but with the garrisons we had to supply we still did not have enough men to face Count Tilly. That became clear when I met with the king and his cavalry commander, General Wolf Heinrich von Baudissin. I knew the general from my time fighting for the Dutch and the Danish. He had been with Count von Mansfield.

"Colonel, we are about to move from the town you helped us to secure. My aim is to move south and west. Frankfurt an der Oder is secure. With Landsberg in our hands we can reclaim the rest of Brandenburg."

"Magdeburg, King Gustavus, I have heard it is besieged."

"It is and I have had many missives pleading for our help." He waved a hand as though the army was all around him, "we have just fifteen thousand men. The last message I had was that General Graf zu Pappenheim was about to assault the city with forty thousand men."

My heart sank for I knew what would happen to the people who had defied the emperor. "Then it is lost and as we have lost Neubrandenburg we are cut off."

He nodded, "To the rest of the army it still holds out but here, in this room, you deserve to know the truth. We are too far away and have too few men to take on zu Pappenheim and Count Tilly. We will head south and west. The general here will lead the cavalry and you shall be our eyes and ears."

General von Baudissin was a good leader and I liked him. "You have a good reputation, Colonel and, more than that, they say you are lucky. I am not one of those who despise luck. You have it and I shall use it. There will be a difference from the way you have operated hitherto. You will still scout but if we have an enemy to face, I will need your horsemen in the line."

"But, General, they are not line cavalry."

He smiled, "You have made them a better regiment than any could have hoped. When Prince Francis Albert of Saxe-Lauenburg disparaged you on your arrival there were some who listened to him. Now his words fall on deaf ears for the green flag and the arrival of Bretherton's Horse heralds victory." I took the compliment, but I was not sure we could do as he asked. "When we fight, your regiment will guard the two flanks. Your Captain Friedrich showed that he is more than capable of leading half of the regiment. With four companies of your regiment on each flank then my cavalry will be able to act effectively." He smiled, "We will always have fewer cavalry than the Imperialists. We need to use them wisely and well. We will leave in a week. I trust your horses and men will be ready."

"We will."

The king said, "We must head back to the west and our base in the Baltic. We need to be reinforced. We have made a start, Colonel, but that is all."

As I made my way back to our temporary home, I was not sure if I liked the new arrangement. We had enjoyed a great deal of freedom as the scouts of the army, now we had some of that licence taken from us, and we were also tied to the cavalry.

We left and headed west. We had taken supplies from the eastern part of Brandenburg, and we moved at the pace of the wagons. One advantage we did enjoy was the ability to summon cavalry to support us. That became increasingly necessary when we heard the tragic news that not only had Magdeburg been sacked, only three thousand of the twenty-five thousand inhabitants had escaped. The rest had been massacred on the orders of Emperor Ferdinand. It was a disaster. We had lost our only ally.

Johan Banér had been missing since before the taking of Frankfurt an der Oder. It was Jennings who found him and his escort as we headed for Werben on the Elbe. Zu Pappenheim held the city but we had heard that he did not have the support yet of Count Tilly. Gustavus Adolphus was planning a bold strike. The diplomat was relieved to see us, "I am glad you found me, Colonel. We have spent the last week avoiding Imperial patrols." He leaned over so that only I could hear his words, "After the fall of Magdeburg and Neubrandenburg it will be good to give the king some good news."

"Good news, Sir?"

"Aye, our successes have persuaded the Elector of Brandenburg to be our ally. He has agreed to subsidise our efforts. If we can only bring the Saxons to help us, then we have a chance." He pointed behind him, "There are Imperial horsemen at Burgstall."

"Thank you."

Burgstall was not on our line of march, but I warned Sergeant Jennings.

The good news prompted the king to be bold and he sent General von Baudissin with a strong force of cavalry to scout out Werben. We discovered that zu Pappenheim had troops between Havel and Werben. We skirmished with them and unloaded our weapons, but it came to nothing. We returned to the king who had been discussing his plans with Generals Horn and Banér.

I was there with General von Baudissin when he outlined his plans. "Count Tilly has been reinforced with troops from Italy and is ravaging Thuringia. He has thirty thousand men. Until we have more troops, I cannot face such a force. However, we have more than enough men to deal with the thirteen thousand men commanded by zu Pappenheim. I intend to do so with cavalry while he has his men spread out. I intend to drive a wedge between the two Imperial commanders, and we will take the bridgehead at Tangermünde. While you, General von Baudissin achieve this I will build a fortified camp at Werben. With luck, by the end of the month we shall have doubled the troops available to us."

The general took me into his confidence as we left, "Colonel, you and your men are, in my view, unique. If this was a battlefield then I would have every confidence in my ability to win the day but taking a bridgehead with cavalry is out of my compass. You have done this before, what do you suggest?"

"I do not know the place, what do you know of it, General?"

"I know that more than a dozen years ago a woman set fire to the town and it has been rebuilt since then. There is a castle, but the walls are not as important as they once were thanks to the fire. There is a bridge across the Elbe but thanks to the fire there are no longer any buildings upon it."

"And the river, can it be forded?"

"I believe so, by horsemen who do not wear plate."

"Then get close to the town and I will devise a way in."

We left the baggage with the rest of the army. It would be safer that way. We also left our remounts. What we did take was every weapon. I did not know how we would manage to make an entry into the town but I knew that we needed as wide a variety of weapons as possible.

The rest of the cavalry was assigned the task of occupying zu Pappenheim and making him withdraw. Such a movement would distract the enemy who with luck would not expect us to be operating so far behind enemy lines. We reached the village of Schönhausen just two miles from the bridge and, more importantly, hidden from the river by a forest. While the general secured the town I went with Jennings and my three senior officers to the river. Night would soon be upon us and we had the chance to spy out the land.

We watched from the shelter of the trees. The town and bridge were to the west of us and we would be hidden from all but the most intense scrutiny. We saw men on the walls and in the castle. The sun was still high enough to illuminate them. The bridge had two guards at each end. Even as we watched we heard the bell and then saw the gates to the town close.

I turned to the others, "The gates will be opened at dawn. If we could take out the guards at the end of the bridge and replace them with our men, then we could swim the river during the night. If we use one company, then when the gates open we can rush the gate, and the rest of the regiment can pour over the bridge."

"You need men who can speak German and can swim, Sir."

"Yes, Stirling, and men who can slit a throat silently."

He nodded, "I have half a dozen we can use."

"It will have to be the Hunting Dogs who swim the river and hide, Sir."

I nodded, "I know, Jennings. I will lead this attack. Captain Friedrich, you will bring over the regiment."

He was resolute as he nodded, "I will not let you down, Sir."

"Then let us return to the general. Dickson, have a dozen of your men return here with a good officer and keep watch."

"Sir."

The general was surprised that I had come up with a plan so quickly. "The thing is, General, that the longer we delay the more chance the enemy has of discovering we are here. My plan only works if they think that the rest of the army is the threat. I am confident that my men can take the gate but even a regiment will struggle to hold it. We need your dragoons and cuirassiers."

"And you shall have them."

After eating I went with the Hunting Dogs and the killers selected by Lieutenant Stirling. Their part was crucial, and I made it clear what they would have to do. "You will split into two groups of three. The ones who are swimming across the river need to slip into the water unseen." They all nodded.

Angus McBride said, "I am a strong swimmer, Sir."

"Me too," volunteered Walter Smith.

"And I am as good as these two, Colonel." Graham Turner was the smallest of the men, but he looked to have the broadest shoulders.

"Then you three swim over and when you are in position signal the other three. All four bridge guards must die immediately and be replaced instantly by four of you in their clothes." They nodded. I turned to Sergeant Jennings. "We move once we have the bridge. There is no moon tonight and the clouds beginning to come from the west means that there might be rain and, in any case, they will help to hide us."

We could see across the river and there were shadows close to the wall where horses could be hidden. We had to have silent horses and that was another reason I had chosen the Hunting Dogs. They had trained their animals to be as quiet as they were.

That done, we moved into position. This was always the hardest part, the waiting. When I saw the six shadows slip towards the river I could feel my heart racing. If they were seen or heard, then the jig would be up. It was with some relief that I saw them merge into the shadows by the river. If I had not known where to look, I would have missed the three men as they swam, across the river. I saw that two of them were completely naked. They were the two taller ones who would wear the clothes of the men that they slew. I did not see the other three but knew they would have eyes on the ones swimming across the river. As the two naked men stepped from the river my fears rose once more. Surely, they would be seen. It was when they moved closer to the bridge that I realised they had used the piers of the bridge to hide them from view. We had an unobstructed view but the men on the walls, if they were looking, would not. I did not see the signal that they gave but saw the result as the three men closer to us rose like wraiths and in sudden, quick and savage movements slit the throats of the two guards. It was too far to see the far side but when there was no cry, I assumed all had gone well.

The leader of the three on our side of the river, Hamish Hamilton, stretched. That was the signal and Jennings and I led our horses and men down to the river. The trees and bushes gave us total cover until we reached the water. I peered at the sky. Dark clouds hinted at rain. What was more important was that the river was plunged into darkness. We stepped into the black waters and let our horses move across the bed. We held onto the pommels. I had two pistols hung around my neck although it was highly likely that they would be too damp to fire. The Hunting Dogs would need to use cold steel. The water was cold but not icy. It was summer. Ran, I had chosen my steadier horse, was a good swimmer and she moved purposefully towards the other shore. Once she had purchase, I walked her as close as I could to the walls. I kept my eyes, not on the ground, but on the walls just twenty feet above me. I heard, rather than saw, the sentry who

Captain of Horse

marched from the gate towards the far tower. We had watched them while there was still light, and we waited for our men to cross. They looked to have a duty that took them from tower to tower but only once every fifteen minutes. For the rest of the time, they must have been in the guardhouse. There had been no fighting at this crossing since the war began and I suspected that complacency had set in. I reached the wall and breathed a sigh of relief. The only way we could be seen would be if a man peered over the side. That was unlikely. The rest of our men arrived. Jennings and I took our positions on either side of the gate and the rest spread out from us. Now we had to wait.

My scouts knew how to be silent, but the sentries did not and they spoke as they met in the gatehouse above me. The talk was reassuringly mundane. They spoke of which of their brothers in arms were enjoying the amorous advances of a couple of local whores. Another conversation was about the increases in the price of beer since the war had started. Another was a mocking conversation about the bridge guards. The two sentry boxes at each end were not the same as the comfortable guard house they enjoyed. When the rain began the mocking became louder. One of the men at the bridge made an obscene gesture in reply. It was the perfect thing to do and brought more derisory comments. It also drove the sentries within doors and that suited us. My wide brimmed hat helped but it did not take long for my shoulders to become soaked. It guaranteed that our powder would be too wet to fire. It also meant the defenders might be in the same position. I saw the sky lighten to the east and knew that dawn would soon be upon us.

The bell that sounded within the walls was not one of alarm but merely the indication that the gates were about to be opened. We had heard it the previous night just before the gates were closed. It was the signal for us to mount. There was a collective creak as slick, wet boots slid over equally slippery saddles. It could not be helped but as there was now more noise from the town that was waking up it did not matter. I drew my sword and waited. I heard the bar as it was lifted. The gates would swing inwards and so Jennings and I moved our horses closer to the middle.

One of the horses snorted and I heard a voice from within, "Someone is eager to get in."

Another voice shouted, "Could be a message from the general. The constable said we were due one."

As the doors began to open, I urged Ran on. He and Jennings' horse pushed against the doors and their weight made them spring open. We had to make all speed. Jennings and I slashed with our swords as shouts went up. At first they were shouts of surprise, but as more horsemen with swashing swords galloped through, they became shouts of alarm. From across the river, I heard our horn sound as the rest of the regiment galloped over the wooden planks of the bridge. Their hooves sounded like thunder. As it was still raining that seemed appropriate.

The men on the bridge had also raced to join us and they were the ones who, while we took the roads close to the gate, grabbed muskets and guarded the gates.

In the end we did not need the rest of the cavalry to take the town. The arrival of my regiment ensured that it capitulated. However, the castle showed signs of wishing to hold out until General von Baudissin's arrival made the constable surrender. His regiments of dragoons and cuirassiers were a mighty show of force and he knew he could not hold out. We spent three days emptying the town of everything of value. The powder and ball were particularly useful and then we spiked their guns. We could have slighted the walls but a messenger from the king demanded our return. He sent a regiment of musketeers to hold the town, and we handed the defences over to them. He had word that Count Tilly was on his way. We hurried back to Werben, just twenty-two miles away.

Chapter 15

Burgstall and Werben July and August 1631
King Gustavus had made a solid camp. It was fortified and we had more cannons than I had seen before. The powder and ball we had taken were invaluable. We had little time for rest as we were given the task of searching for the enemy. Once more we split into eight companies, the better to search a larger area. It was the Hawk company, with me leading them, that found the four cavalry regiments bivouacked at Burgstall just a few miles south of Tangermünde. I saw the potential immediately. It was not a fortified camp. Perhaps they had not realised that Tangermünde had fallen. I sent a messenger back to Werben and we camped and waited.

Colonel Axelsson Silfversparre and his Uppland Horse arrived along with my other companies. I recognised not only the red standard they used but their horses and uniforms. I liked the Swede and his men for they were the Swedish equivalent of my regiment. They had more than five hundred men but used just four companies. He spoke English as well as German and we were able to converse easily.

"What have you found for us, Colonel?"

I pointed to the small village, "There are four regiments of Imperial horsemen there. They have a loose camp and have not fortified it. If you listen, you can hear them carousing."

We were both silent and the sound of songs and laughter drifted over to us.

He grinned, "Then it would be rude not to visit with them." He rubbed his beard, "You take the left and we take the right?"

I nodded, "I will sound my horn when we are ready to charge."

"And mine."

The Hawk company had enjoyed the longest rest and so we would be the ones who charged. I gave them my orders, "We charge, fire and wheel to the left. The Uppland regiment is to our right and I am guessing that they will ride to the right. We do not pursue. Our aim is to take their camp and to kill as many of them as we can. There is a battle coming and the fewer men we have to fight the better."

We would charge in company order. Each line would have fifteen troopers and there would be three lines for each company. The campaign had taken its toll and with wounds and illness, until we had time to rest and recover, we would not be at full strength. The exception was the front rank of the Hawk Company which had four extra men, me, Murphy, Ashcroft and Stephen of Alnmouth. We walked forward through the dark until we saw the fires and heard the men. The obstacles to our charge were natural rather than man made. My regiment were all good riders and any impairment to our charge would be avoided. I looked down the line to see that we were ready. The standard was behind me.

I drew my pistol and said, "Sound the charge!"

I spurred Marcus and we began to trot towards the fire. Normally we would halt and fire but we wanted confusion amongst the enemy. The noise of our weapons would be enough. I intended to draw my sword as soon as I had discharged my weapon. I said, "Sound the charge." I heard the horn of the Uppland regiment. The two horns would tell the cavalrymen that there were two regiments attacking them.

The horns had alerted the enemy, and the drumming hooves told them the direction we were taking. There were sentries and the half dozen harquebuses that opened fire merely added smoke and noise. They were hurriedly fired and, so far as I could tell, had no effect. I waited until I was ten paces from the nearest cavalryman before I opened fire. The officer wore a breastplate and was levelling a wheellock at me. My finger fired first and the ball struck him just below the chin, throwing him to the ground. Marcus' hooves ensured that he was dead. My weapon was the signal for the rest of the front line to fire. I holstered my pistol and, drawing my sword, pointed to the left. As we headed for that, as yet undisturbed part of the camp, the second line opened fire and followed us. It meant we had an increasingly long line charging through the camp. I slashed at faces, backs and arms as men emerged from their shelters or stood to wonder at the horror that had so rudely awoken them. When I heard the Imperial horn, I recognised the call to retreat. In hindsight it was the only order that could have been given but it caused panic as men ran for their horses, abandoning equipment on the way. My regiment was now a long line sweeping through the camp and we found an increasing barrier of tents, fires, cooking pots and bodies. By the time we reached the horse lines more than half of the horses had gone. Some had been taken and others had come loose.

"Sergeant Longstaff, secure the horses."

Horses were like gold, and these were good horses. The Imperial Army had fine horse herds.

"Sir! You heard the colonel."

"Murphy, sound recall."

There was no point in having my men chase the fleeing men. Their horses were fresher, and I wanted to lose not a man.

By the time dawn had broken we had the camp, and no Imperial soldiers remained. We hitched some of the horses to wagons and loaded the food, weapons and equipment we had found. The men had profited from the dead, but our army would benefit from the encounter. King Gustavus would be able to feed and arm more men. That was the reality of these raids.

It took all day to reach the camp at Werben. Even if we had wanted to patrol the next day it would be out of the question. As it turned out the king now knew where Tilly was to be found. He was marching to Werben. We had pricked him enough and now he had reacted. He was bringing the war to us. King Gustavus would finally meet a general who had the skill to test him.

The general reported to the king, and we found our camp. The king had garrisoned the town, and every musketeer and pike regiment were camped close to the artillery which ringed the camp. With a good ditch and a hedgehog palisade it would take every one of Count Tilly's thirty-five thousand strong army to dislodge us. Our wagons and horses were towards the centre of the camp with the other cavalry regiments.

I was weary. We had been constantly in the saddle, and I was looking forward to some time in camp. Thanks to our success we had plenty of food. Even if Tilly besieged us, we could last for at least a week with little distress. As we had discovered, the only way for an army such as ours to survive was to take from the local populace and we had already done so. With an army twice the size of ours, Count Tilly and his men would go hungry unless they attacked and defeated us quickly. I went straight to bed after I had eaten and slept the sleep of the righteous.

I woke not long after dawn refreshed. Sergeant Wilson's cooks, aided by an increasing number of women, had food already being prepared. When they saw that I was awake they brought me food. It was Jane and Gertha who did so. They had been with the regiment the longest and they ran the rest of the women as strictly as any commanding officer.

"Morning, Colonel."

"Good morning, ladies. How are the children?"

Jane gave a wry smile, "They are both a handful, but we have the measure of them eh, Gertha?"

The young girl nodded, "We have indeed, Colonel." Her English was now perfect and the trace of an accent merely made her sound adorable.

I took the bowl of food and the beaker of ale, "The wagons are comfortable?"

"They are perfect, Colonel. We travel as well as the Queen of England." Jane looked at my tray of food, "If you need anything else, Colonel, you know where we are."

"This feast will suffice."

I knew that we were lucky. On our travels we had witnessed distressing scenes of abandoned families. We had heard the discord in other camps as disagreements flared into violence. Perhaps we had needed the violence at the start of my command to cauterise the wounds. Whatever the reason I would try to maintain the equilibrium. A regiment that was happy was usually successful. Sigismund awoke just as I was finishing my food. He said, "I will take a walk and look at our defences."

I nodded, "I will visit the officers when I have eaten."

There was no sign of the Imperial Army but it was only a matter of time. The gunners were all camped by their pieces. Lennart Torstensson was a good general, but he was a real master of the artillery. We had more than forty pieces ranging from the regimental pieces to much larger guns. I went to one of the bronze cannons to stroke its polished barrel.

The gunner rose and smiled, "Bettina will soon sweep all before her, Colonel."

"Bettina?"

"You are a horseman, Colonel, and may not understand that our guns are like your horses. We cosset and care for them. Bettina has as much attention as the queen herself."

I nodded. "What size is she?"

"She fires a twelve-pound charge, Colonel." He picked one up and handed it to me, "They are cleverly designed. See how the powder charge and the ball are fastened together. It means that we can fire three balls to every ball sent by enemy musketeers."

"What about enemy artillery?"

He snorted in derision, "The Papists have good horsemen, no offence to your men, Colonel, but they have few guns, and their gunners do not know what they are doing. You have been with the army a long time, Colonel, has Imperial artillery ever hurt us?"

He was right. "You have a good field of fire here."

"Aye, we do. General Torstensson himself placed every gun. I hope that the enemy do make the mistake of attacking us. If they do, then the whole army will see that it is we gunners who will save Germany."

I smiled and headed back to our camp. Whilst he was right that our guns were a powerful weapon it would be cavalry who would win the war for the king.

The Imperial scouts appeared on the fourth of August and on the fifth Count Tilly arrived with his army. It was a powerful one and I saw regiment after regiment march and camp beyond the range of our guns. They had many more men than we did. I was standing by the old gunner and Bettina as the enemy began to array their army. He chuckled, "Less than two dozen guns. They will do nothing, Colonel, mark my words."

I had little chance to debate with the gunner for the horn sounded for an officers' call. There was no tent large enough to accommodate us all and the king stood on a wagon bed to address us, "Count Tilly, it seems has come to drive us from the borders of Saxony. My orders to every man are simple ones, we hold our ground and fight off every attack."

I saw nods of agreements from his generals. The exception was Prince Francis Albert of Saxe-Lauenburg who said, incredulously, "We simply stand and wait, King Gustavus? We have enough men to drive them from the field and avenge the butchery of Magdeburg."

"Prince Francis, believe me Magdeburg will be avenged as will Neubrandenburg."

We had heard that the garrison had been butchered. The Scottish soldiers had escaped the slaughter as they had been brought to augment the army. Colonel von Mannheim had paid the price for his high-handed actions.

"However, we have just sixteen thousand men and until we can be reinforced then our war is a defensive one. We will use our cavalry to hurt the enemy as General von Baudissin demonstrated but it will be hit and run. This is not a war for glory, Prince Francis, it is a war to end the tyranny of the empire."

Men had moved away from the prince, and he realised he was a lone voice. He said no more.

"Be vigilant and listen for the horn."

"What is the password, King Gustavus?"

He smiled, "As it always is, '*Gott mit uns*'!"

The king had not done as the Imperials had done and assign a coloured scarf for each man. It was too expensive. The enemy wore red sashes and so the best way to identify an ally was to use a password.

We waited all day for an attack that didn't come. We saw Count Tilly, wearing cuirassier armour as he rode along our defences looking for weaknesses. There were none to be found for it had been constructed well. When I woke early the next morning to make water, I left my tent to find I was in a sea of fog. This was real fog and not the fog of battle. I went back in and said, "Sigismund, wake the officers. There is fog."

I armed myself and hurried to the guns at the perimeter. Already someone had told the king for a horn sounded and the army was woken. The old gunner was dressed and ready. I walked before his cannon and made water. He chuckled, "Aye, Colonel, my lads have been using the ground before Bettina for the last few days. I doubt that an enemy will get close but if they do…"

Over the next half hour regiments arrived to take up their allotted places. Sigismund brought my regiment even though we had not been ordered to do so. We placed them behind the artillery pieces. We could hear, through the fog, the sound of men advancing. Count Tilly was taking advantage of the weather. We could have fired but that would have wasted ball and powder. We stood with weapons at the ready. King Gustavus and his senior officers rode to the guns. We only saw them at the last moment such was the thickness of the fog. As he passed, I saw the concern on his face.

Stephen of Alnmouth and Ashcroft appeared next to me. They had some bread and a beaker of ale. "We thought you might need some food, Colonel. The captain said you had not breakfasted."

"Thank you, Stephen." I bit into the bread which had been toasted on the fire and smeared with butter. It was the best way to make stale bread more palatable. I had just downed the ale and handed the beaker to Ashcroft when I realised I could make out shapes advancing towards us. Either the enemy was closer than I thought, or the fog was thinning. Suddenly the sun burned off the last of the fog and revealed the enemy less than two hundred paces from us.

General Torstensson himself shouted the order to open fire and our guns all fired at the same time, replacing natural fog with gunpowder smoke. Every musketeer and harquebusier readied his weapon. I held my two pistols. The range was too far for such weapons, but the attack was being pressed home with relentless courage. The pikes and muskets came on even though the cannonballs were decimating their ranks. They halted forty paces from us and levelled their muskets.

I shouted, "Fire!" I discharged my weapons and then shouted, "Drop!" The smoke from the guns meant that we disappeared so that when the muskets fired, they did no harm. The gunners were protected by the wooden embrasure and gabions placed before them and my men were crouched. The cannons cracked again and even as we rose and reloaded, they fired a second time. The gunner had been right. The guns were faster to reload than our weapons. As we levelled our weapons to fire a second time the cannons roared once more.

The pikes came on while the musketeers reloaded. I knew, from my conversations with the other colonels, that few men in the Swedish army adhered to the pike. They were heavy to carry and, in battle, cumbersome. Many retained their armour but used swords. The Imperial tercios still clung to their weapons. We fired and dropped again, and a ragged volley came from the enemy muskets. As we rose and the cannons blasted once more, I saw that the pikes were getting closer. I holstered my weapons and drew my sword. The pikes had been thinned too but such were their numbers that the ranks had been filled from the rear. The pikes charged and rammed their long weapons at us. There were officers with swords and bucklers as well as corporals with halberds. I grabbed the head of the pike that was closest to me and hacked off the end of the one next to it. My men were all doing the same. We could use powder weapons but my men all preferred cold steel and the blades were razor sharp. Pikes were useful for holding off horses, but men had hands and so long as you did not touch the actual head you were safe from harm. I had heard that the Scottish army had suffered in the same way at Flodden where the shorter billhook had proved decisive. The pikemen whose weapons had been rendered useless dropped the long and now defunct piece of matchwood and drew their swords. That was when they were dangerous, for the ones we faced wore breastplates. It would take skill to kill.

The officer who came at me had a Spanish morion with a red plume while holding a polished metal shield. He punched at me with the shield. I took the blow on my right hand, and it hurt. The gunners' toilet came to my aid when he swung his sword. He slightly lost his footing, and I was able to block the blow with my sword. I drew, unseen, my dagger. His eyes were on my sword. He tried the same combination of moves. He punched with the shield but he made sure of his footing and when he swung his sword it was both a truer strike and one with more power. When my left hand whipped out and deflected the sword his eyes widened in surprise. Bettina belched again and was so close to the swordsman that he took a step back. I lunged, not at his chest which was encased in metal but at his thigh which had no protection. The tip sank into flesh and I turned the blade as I stabbed. I did the same when I withdrew the sword, and the result was a wide wound that would bleed heavily. I pulled back and repeated the move to the other leg. He roared in anger. I recognised the words as Italian. When Bettina fired again, he

Captain of Horse

flinched and I was able to end the duel with a sudden stab to the face. He sank at my feet.

There was less smoke now as it was only the artillery that was firing. I saw the enemy begin to fall back. Just at that moment I heard the horn sound for cavalry to mount. I shouted, "Bretherton's Horse!" and sheathed my sword. Nodding to the old gunner, I ran through the men who were having their wounds treated and hurried to our horses. Stephen of Alnmouth was faster than I was and by the time I reached the horse lines he had saddled Marcus. I mounted and looked for my officers. They were busy saddling their own horses. Murphy and Gilmour had already done so and they mounted and rode next to me.

"Unfurl the colours. Let our enemies know who chases them this day."

Stephen had saddled Sigismund's horse and Ashcroft had also saddled and mounted. Lieutenant Larsson galloped up, "General von Baudissin wishes you to join in the pursuit of the enemy, Colonel."

I nodded, "Just as soon as we are ready we will follow."

He shook his head, "His men are mailed, Colonel, it will take some time. He asks for you to close with the enemy horsemen. I am to ride with you and keep the general informed." The Imperial cavalry had not been engaged and the general wished to hurt them.

"Very well." I turned. More than three quarters of my men were mounted. "Murphy, sound the advance." As he sounded the horn I shouted, "Column of fours." That formation would allow us to negotiate the guns, and we could spread out once we closed with the enemy.

I headed for the gap created where Imperial pikeman had managed to take out a three-pounder gun. It lay on its side with the bodies of the gunners and the pikemen littered around it. We then had to pick our way through the bodies of the dead. A horse could be hurt if it slipped on a metal breastplate and there were still blades that might incapacitate a horse. It was only when we had passed the last body that I was able to order the gallop. We ignored the men who were surrendering. The infantry and artillerymen could take them prisoner. We were hunting horsemen.

Captain of Horse

I heard a cry of *'hakkaa päälle'* to our right and turned to see the famous Finnish light horsemen called Hakkapeliitta. These were fierce warriors who took no prisoners and their battle cry, I had learned, meant, *'hack 'em down'*. If the Imperialist cavalry saw and heard them, they would surrender to us. They rode smaller horses than most cavalry, but their mounts were very fast, and they gradually overtook us. I saw their leader, Torsten Stålhandske with his distinctive metal gauntlets, his name meant 'steel glove', exhorting his men to close with the fleeing cuirassiers. He grinned at me as he passed me. They would catch up with their enemies first. I saw that some of his men had deadly war hammers. Steel backplates and helmets would not protect the metal clad horsemen.

My two pistols in my saddle holsters were ready to fire and I drew one. I could ride easily with my left hand and I rested the wheellock on my saddle as we closed with the fleeing horsemen. I saw the men at the rear turn and when they saw it was the Finns who followed they whipped their horses even harder. The sight of the Finns made them veer more to their left and that brought them closer to us. I waited until I was just ten paces from the nearest cuirassier, and I fired my pistol. I could not expect accuracy, but the ball hit the man on his right shoulder. His left hand held a whip, and it made his horse veer to the right as he dropped the reins. He was a doomed man for his horse would take him closer to the Finns.

I holstered my wheellock and drew a second. The doomed cuirassier had opened a gap, and I urged Marcus to close with the Imperial horsemen. This time I waited until I was almost abreast of the nearest man to my left and I fired at his side. It was a lucky shot for it found the gap between breast and back plate. The balls I used were large and it tore a hole in his side and carried on through his body. It threw him from his horse. His dying hand dragged the reins with him and his horse crashed to the ground. Murphy was a good horseman, and he managed to jump the fallen animal.

To my right I heard the screams and cries as the Finns used war hammers, small axes and swords to butcher the horsemen. They were killing more men than we were. I saw Sigismund slash with his sword at a cuirassier, but the blade merely screeched and scratched off the backplate. The only effective weapons we had were the pistols and they had been discharged. I managed to wound one man by slashing at his unprotected thigh. I chose his left side. He screamed in pain but carried on riding.

The chase ended for us when we neared the village of Burg where there was a bridge over the stream. The Imperialists had placed a small gun there and left a company of musketeers. We were lucky in that they opened fire at the Finns and eight of them fell. We wheeled to the left to take shelter in the trees there, "Dismount and fight on foot."

Stephen took my reins and that left me free to run with men to the stream. The Finns were butchering the gunners and musketeers, but the reputation of the Finns, who never took prisoners, meant that the Italian soldiers fought to the death. By the time I reached the scene the Finns had finished and were continuing their chase. Looking down the road I saw General von Baudissin leading the rest of our horsemen. He saluted as he passed, "Take the gun and weapons!"

"Yes, Sir."

I waited until the four regiments had passed us and then ordered my men to find horses to pull the small piece of ordnance. My men collected the weapons and the purses. One of the horses they found had belonged to a cornet who had also been the standard bearer. The standard had gone but there was a stirrup bucket. All we needed was an arm strap and our standard bearer would be able to use both hands rather than holding on to the standard. We were ready to move by noon. Our journey back was halted frequently as we moved the dead and took their weapons. It slowed us down, but the men were all richer by the time we reached our camp. We delivered the gun to the gunners and then returned to our camp. Two men had been lost in the chase and four wounded in the battle but that was as nothing compared with the mounds of Imperial dead. Tilly had met the king in battle, and the victor was clear.

Chapter 16

When the general returned it was with the news that Tilly had halted his retreat and formed up for battle. I was not privy to the discussion, but I heard later that the prince wanted us to fight a battle. King Gustavus declined. We had killed enough men and Tilly, even though he had lost more than five thousand men still enjoyed superiority of numbers. Count Tilly, no doubt running out of supplies, retreated south on August the 8th.

We spent the next weeks building up our army. We were bolstered with the news of a new ally. Elector George of Saxony was forced to choose between the Empire and the Protestant alliance. He chose the latter and we now had the Saxon army as well as the Swedish soldiers who were sent from Sweden. The French subsidy was being put to good use as was the money coming from Brandenburg. For me it meant more money being paid to Charlotte. I was now paid as a colonel and the subsidies allowed back pay. It was good to know.

Our new ally and the fact that Count Tilly headed south determined our next course of action. Gustavus Adolphus built up his army. More artillery pieces were procured, and wagon loads of powder and ball arrived. We had the luxury of being able to fatten up our horses and graze them on good grass. The ones who suffered were the Brandenburgers. Our army needed feeding. They had been freed from the yoke of the emperor, but it was at a price.

We also had more allies. The Hanseatic city of Bremen chose to support King Adolphus with money and troops. That was not a surprise. The Swedish navy was now the most powerful one in the Baltic and Bremen was a trading city. William of Hesse-Kassel also joined the alliance. With Brandenburg and Saxony as allies many smaller duchies saw the chance to free themselves from the Imperial yoke.

We moved west to Düben to meet with our allies. What surprised me, especially after our victory at Werben, were the numbers of Swedes who deserted on the road south. When I spoke with Lieutenant Larsson at one of the meetings he told me that one in twenty Swedes had deserted. Allied to our sick and wounded we were a tenth down on the army that had been at Werben even as we gathered for the march to Leipzig.

Once more we were to be with the scouts but as one of the enemy leaders was the impetuous Graf zu Pappenheim, a noted cavalryman, King Gustavus and General Horn had decided to make our scouts a more powerful force. It would not be the cuirassiers of General von Baudissin but us, the Finns, the Uppland regiment and a regiment of Swedish dragoons who would be the bait to tempt the impetuous German. I was summoned to meet with other senior leaders. At the meeting where the plans were drawn up, I knew that men like Lieutenant Larsson, General von Baudissin and General Munro, all expected me to be placed in command of this large brigade of cavalry. They were surprised, although I was not for I knew that while I had enjoyed success I was not yet experienced enough to lead such a vanguard. However, I was surprised when the commander was appointed; Sir James Ramsay, called 'the Black' to distinguish him from a second Sir James Ramsay who was called 'the Fair', was an infantryman. I said nothing but I saw the look of confusion on General von Baudissin's face.

After the meeting the king and General Horn asked me to stay behind. The king said, "Were you, like some of the others, disappointed that I did not give you the command of the cavalry scouts?"

I smiled, "No, King Gustavus. I was not."

"I feel I owe you an explanation. As you know there are many Scottish soldiers in my army. The Marquess of Hamilton is the most senior. It was his suggestion that I appoint this colonel of musketeers." He shrugged, "It also helps that his brother served King James and is a courtier at King Charles' court. Colonel Ramsay will be guided by you. Advise him and teach him. He is an older man, and the wild Finns are more likely to heed his orders. Your chase after Werben led Colonel Stålhandske to see you as a leader like him. I know that you are not. Your men are brave and fight well but they also obey orders and that is what is needed. I need you and the other regiments to keep our numbers hidden. Count Tilly has a large Imperial Army and he is awaiting reinforcements from the Catholic League. General Egon of Fürstenberg-Heiligenberg is leading an army of eighteen thousand men. We will be outnumbered but I want doubt in Tilly's mind as to how many men we actually have. You will confuse him. There are four small regiments but if you can keep the enemy at bay then that can only help us. Sir James will command the three regiments of musketeers who form my vanguard. Your men will be the screen."

I was honoured in his confidence. When I met Sir James, who awaited me outside the headquarters, I was pleasantly surprised.

"Colonel Bretherton, might I walk with you? Perhaps we could enjoy a mug of ale."

"Of course, my lord."

"I will be honest with you; I can ride but I am not a cavalryman. I am more used to standing in line and awaiting cavalry to attack me." He stopped and smiled, "Perhaps that is why the king uses me this way so that I can better understand our enemies. The Imperial Army outnumbers us in horsemen."

"That they do, my lord and they are good soldiers."

"Yet you and your border horse," he smiled, "aye, I remember their reputation from home, have managed to best them at every turn. When other regiments lose men, yours remain loyal. I have heard that you attract recruits while others see them desert. I can see lessons to be learned."

He gestured at the door of an inn and we entered. It was busy but not crowded. Some junior officers vacated a table for us to use and I nodded our thanks. A man approached and asked for our order. We ordered ale and a local delicacy, a bowl of hot, fried, pigskin crackling. It would be heavily salted and go well with the ale. We waited to continue our talk until the ale and crackling had arrived.

"I will lead but I want you close at my side. I have a couple of lads from home who will ride with me but the banner that flies over our heads will be yours. I want advice. I am not too old to learn, and I know from Colonel Munro that you have an old head on your relatively young shoulders. So, talk to me while I enjoy this wheat beer and delicious crackling."

"Hitherto, my lord, we have used my scouting company to range ahead. I like to use two companies, one on each flank to prevent us from being surprised. With your permission we shall continue to do so. I know a little of the other regiments. The dragoons will be solid enough and will give us the ability to use their firepower to take any smaller group we find. My men and the Uppland regiment are light horsemen. We move quickly and can fire our weapons to deter an enemy. The Finns, however, will chase after any enemy."

He wiped his hands on a cloth and nodded, "We will be close enough to my three regiments of musketeers so that we have support. I am not a foolish old man who thinks that a glorious charge of cavalry can win the day. If we find a large number of the enemy, then I am quite happy to order a retreat to my musketeers."

I smiled and raised my beaker of ale, "Then we are of one mind, my lord, for while I know the skills of my men, I know that if we meet enemy cuirassiers we will be outmatched."

He touched my beaker with his, "Good, then let us two foreigners see if we can win this Swedish king a victory over the Catholics."

Back at our camp I gathered my officers. "We will lead the scouting horsemen, but we will move at the pace of the musketeers. Sergeant Jennings, that means you can move further ahead than normal. One lone company might remain hidden where a regiment would be seen. We will keep sixty remounts with the main body." I turned to Sergeant Campbell, "You can split them between the other companies." I smiled, "We have Finns with us, and I would not like to lose our remounts to our allies."

Campbell nodded, "Aye, Colonel, we know the Finns."

"Colonel Ramsay is leading the vanguard, but he will ride with us. The musketeers of the vanguard are our security. I am quite happy to take shelter behind them should danger come."

Captain Sigismund had regained all of his confidence. We had now his homeland as allies and he said, "There will be a battle, Colonel?"

I nodded, "Even if we are outnumbered there will be a battle and this time King Gustavus will not have the luxury of a defended camp. Make sure we have enough weapons, powder and ball. The enemy have many thousands of cuirassiers. As we learned after Werben, the only way to defeat them is with a heavy ball fired at close range. Tell the men that the best place to aim their weapons is at the unprotected legs or the horses. I know it goes against the grain for horsemen to kill horses but this is war."

That night I wrote a letter to Charlotte. I had spoken to Stephen of Alnmouth. Our success had finally allowed him to collect enough money to return home and marry his sweetheart. While I was loath to lose him, for he was a good soldier and an excellent groom, I had promised him the chance to return home and I would rather he left with permission rather than, as so many others had done, desert. He would deliver the letter. I slept better that night than I had for a long time. I think it was the knowledge that if something happened to me then at least Charlotte would have heard from me.

The next day the first thing I did was to give the sealed letter to my groom. "I know that you will not leave until the situation here is resolved but as you will be with the remounts I thought it better to give it to you now."

He frowned, "I should be at your side, Colonel, with Ashcroft and the colour party."

I shook my head, "I will be riding Ran and you will need to teach Williams, Marcus' ways. I am grateful that you have been at my side, but you are my groom and soon you will be going to England and your bride-to-be. I will rest easier knowing that you are as safe as can be." I smiled, "Besides, when we win, and win we will, then you will have an easier journey back to England."

He nodded. I knew that he would not be alone. If we were to face Tilly in battle, then I knew we would have losses. Some men would be so badly wounded that they would not be able to continue as soldiers. They would return with Stephen.

Colonel Ramsay brought with him two men. Both looked uncomfortable on horses, and each had, not a harquebus, but a musket. Their swords were also the heavy claymore favoured by Scottish foot soldiers. They wore the faded but distinctive blue Monmouth caps and had a grey uniform. They were the colonel's bodyguards but if we fought on horseback, they would be a hindrance rather than a help.

The colonel nodded, "Your men look keen, Bretherton, but why are they not in the same uniform? As you can see my men, like the rest of the Marquess of Hamilton's men are all dressed the same."

I shrugged, "We are a unique regiment, my lord. Their weapons are also not the same but one thing they have in common is the ability to follow my orders. I am content with them."

"Aye, well, they are your men. Let us ride."

As we passed the four musketeer regiments, they all cheered. The colonel was popular. He shook his head as we headed down the road to Leipzig. "When we arrived at Stettin, a year ago, there were six thousand of us. Now we are just four regiments, and they are all understrength. We have lost more to disease and desertion than war. How is it that you still have a full regiment?"

"We are lucky, my lord. We have been able to take from the enemy. My men have full bellies and purses. They may look like a ragged warband of bandits, but they know that they will profit from the war. When they go home it will be by mutual choice and not because they are sick of it."

"It will be interesting to see how you operate then."

I shouted, "Hunting Dogs!"

Jennings led his company, and they galloped off. Sir James asked, "Hunting Dogs?"

"Numbers seemed to be impersonal, and we named each of the companies after an animal. You can see from their guidons the creature."

He looked behind and saw the emblems sewn by the women.

"The Hunting Dogs are my scouts. The names seem to work."

"Indeed, they do, and you have organised well. I can learn much from you."

The journey was slow and, until we reached the crossroads close to Bad Düben, uneventful. Jennings and his men had found a few enemy scouts and disposed of them but other than that it had been a quiet journey. I had got to know Sir James better and my men had taught the two bodyguards how to ride. It had taken almost three days to cover the fifty odd miles from Düben. It was not long after one in the afternoon when we had heard distant bells at a church that my scouts rode in.

Jennings looked at Sir James when he gave his report. The other colonels had joined us for they knew the galloping horsemen brought news. "Sir James, General zu Pappenheim is leading two thousand Imperial cuirassiers up the road. They are a mile away."

Sir James knew his business. He turned to me, "Colonel, let us fall back to the musketeers. I will ride back and prepare the vanguard."

Even as I acknowledged the command, I heard the cry, '*Hakkaa päälle*'. To my horror I saw the Finns, led by their colonel, gallop down the road. The Hunting Dogs had to clear the road to avoid being ridden down by our allies.

Sir James shook his head. I said, "We can do nothing about them. The rest of the brigade will fall back in good order to the musketeers."

Sir James and his two bodyguards whipped their horses as we all turned. The scouts were now the rearguard. A few minutes later we heard the crack of pistols and harquebuses followed by the cries of men as the Finns struck the cuirassiers. Perhaps their success after Werben had given them a false idea of their abilities. Whatever the reason we now had just three regiments of cavalry to guard the flanks of the musketeers.

Sigismund said, "Two thousand cuirassiers is a strong force, Colonel."

"I know." I shouted to the colonel of the Uppland regiment, "Colonel, take your men and guard the left flank of the musketeers. No heroics!"

The Swede gave me an indignant look, "We are not wild Finns, Colonel!"

"Captain take our men to the right flank."

"Sir."

"Colonel." I turned to the colonel of dragoons.

"Yes, Colonel?"

"Have your dragoons support the two regiments of horse. Dismount your men."

He looked relieved. "I will, Colonel." Dragoons were really musketeers who were able to ride to war. Supporting us meant that if we charged the enemy, they would be able to give the musketeers added firepower.

Sir James and his bodyguards were in place when we reached the musketeers. They had their muskettengabel planted and were spread out in three blocks. As I led my men to the right flank, I hoped that we, in turn, would not be outflanked.

I turned to Ashcroft, "Ride to the king and tell him we are being attacked by two thousand cuirassiers."

"Sir."

Forewarned, the king could ensure that if the horsemen did break through they would get a warm welcome.

As I prepared my wheellocks and watched my men do the same I wondered at the wisdom of Tilly's plan. Did he think we were just a detachment from the main army? Perhaps my scouts had made the enemy think we were doing as we had so many times, raiding and taking supplies. I did not understand the move, for two thousand cuirassiers represented a large proportion of the Imperial cavalry. Whoever led them was gambling.

The arrival of the Finnish survivors was the first warning we had of the approach of the enemy. If nothing else they had drawn the advance elements of zu Pappenheim's men closer to us. The Finns did not stop but kept going to the rear. They had been badly mauled. I saw many empty saddles and there were wounded men amongst the survivors.

The horsemen who were at the fore of the chase rode to within a hundred paces of the waiting muskets before they halted. We were a solid wall. I recognised General zu Pappenheim, I had seen him before. He and his senior officers gathered to view our lines. The main body would still be a mile behind the vanguard. King Gustavus had anticipated problems. Zu Pappenheim must have thought he had the beating of us. His vaunted cuirassiers normally swept all before them. The Scottish musketeers were something he had not yet encountered. When the horns sounded and they formed lines then I knew what was coming. They would charge and perform a caracole. It would be a test of the musketeers' nerve. It took time to reload a musket, and I wondered what Sir James' plan was.

The first regiments sent their men to charge towards us. I was in command of my men and they would listen for my orders, "Bretherton's Horse prepare and listen for my command."

I knew, as did Sir James, that the cuirassiers would halt before they opened fire. Timing would be vital. They halted forty paces away surprised, no doubt, that the musketeers had yet to fire. I waited until Sir James gave the command to fire before I ordered my men to do the same. I heard the dragoons as their longer ranged weapons added to the wall of ball that hurtled towards the enemy. As I expected, the collective gunfire produced a cloud of smoke as thick as the fog had been at Werben. I heard the sound of men crying as they were hit. Both sides suffered casualties. I also heard the distinctive ping as balls struck the metal of plate. I heard the cuirassiers wheel as I holstered my pistols and drew a second pair. My men would be reloading. As the smoke cleared I saw the next squadrons approach. They were emboldened, no doubt, and thought that the musketeers were still reloading. Sir James had a surprise for them. As soon as the cuirassiers halted, he ordered the second rank to open fire. I fired my second pair. As most of my men did not fire again, I had a better view this time. I saw men falling from horses as they were hit. One horse was struck and, in its falling, threw its rider. He quickly grabbed the reins of a loose horse and mounted. He was a lucky man.

  The third charge was half hearted. I think the colonel of that regiment just wanted his men to discharge their weapons. It proved disastrous for both the dragoons and my men had reloaded and Sir James' third line was ready. More men were dropped, and the horn sounded for the retreat. The Scots and the two cavalry regiments cheered but we did not move until the enemy was out of sight. As soon as they were Sir James gave the command to clear the field. Five regiments flooded over the field to take weapons, purses, breastplates, helmets and hunks of horsemeat. By the time the king and the main body had arrived the bodies were all piled at the side and the road was clear.

  King Gustavus and General Horn halted next to Sir James and me, "Colonel Bretherton, have your scouts follow the enemy and see where they go."

  "Sir. Jennings, remount your men and follow the cuirassiers." I did not insult him by saying discreetly. He would know.

  Sir James said, "Sorry about the Finns, Your Majesty, they just…"

  The king held up his hand, "I know all about the Finns, Sir James. They are what they are but now we know that the enemy is not falling all the way back to Southern Germany. We may well have a battle, the question is, where?

Chapter 17

Podelwitz 1631

My scouts came back but it was a day later, and we were ten miles closer to Leipzig at the village of Wölchau. As soon as Jennings returned, I went directly to the king taking my sergeant with me. All the generals were gathered and this time we had the Saxon elector and his generals too. I hoped that Jennings would not be intimidated by the august body. He could speak a little German but not well enough to speak to them all and so I translated.

"Zu Pappenheim has united with Count Tilly and General von Fürstenberg. We waited until we were sure that they had gathered, and my rough count is that the enemy has thirty-two thousand men."

The king nodded and asked, in English, "And where are they, Sergeant?"

He pointed south, "Breitenfeld, just a few miles north of Leipzig." He answered in English.

The king nodded and took twenty-five silver thalers from his purse, "For you and your men, Sergeant. I know that I can rely on your reports."

"Thank you, King Gustavus."

"Rejoin the regiment, Jennings. Tell Captain Sigismund I will return when time allows."

"So, gentlemen, what do we do?"

General Horn smiled, "This is too good a chance to miss, King Gustavus. With our allies we have more than parity of numbers. We may well outnumber them."

That was true but the Saxons were untried and as the Finns had shown not all of our troops were as disciplined as they should have been. The desertions and losses to disease had cost us and there were few regiments up to full strength.

"I agree but I am aware that Tilly has rarely been beaten and his men are confident. Werben was a single mistake. I do not expect him to make a second. However, if we are to avoid more desertions we must march to face him. Colonel Bretherton, your scouts have done fine work already, but I wish you to take a company and scout out the road ahead. You know the enemy and, as good as your officers are, you are better. I need your eyes and your nose."

"Sir."

He looked at a map and jabbed a finger, "Podelwitz is just a couple of miles from Breitenfeld. We will gather there and await your news." He turned to his generals, "And we will march in battle order. I shall be on the right wing, General Horn in the centre and our Saxon allies to our left. If Tilly chooses to advance and to take us on then we will be ready to fight."

I knew that while Jennings and his men were tired they would be happy with the rewards from the king. We had remounts and they would be able to ride fresh horses. I gathered all my officers and told them of the plan. "Jennings and I will leave before dawn. The company is there as an escort for us. Sergeant Jennings and I will be the ones to get as close to the enemy as we can. Captain Friedrich, you will command in my absence."

"Sir."

After they had been dismissed, I sat with Sigismund and Sergeant Jennings. "You and I will wear simple brown cloaks. You have a good corporal you can leave in command?"

"Yes, Sir, Robbie is as solid as they come." He hesitated and then said, "What exactly are we going to do, Colonel?"

"The king has a map but that does not tell him of the terrain. We need to walk the land."

Sigismund shook his head, "What a risk! There will be sentries and piquets."

I suddenly said, "The red sashes we took from the cuirassiers, what happened to them?"

"We gave them to the women to use."

"Get us two and a couple of cuirassier helmets."

Sigismund smiled, "Yes, Colonel."

When he had gone, I said, "Find Campbell. I want two of the cuirassier horses we took. If we encounter an enemy, we tell them we are stragglers from the fight on the road. While we wait for the captain I will give you a quick lesson in German."

I knew that all we needed to do was to rehearse a conversation and that might buy us enough time to escape if we were apprehended.

We wore the sashes but carried the helmets. They had even found a pair of cuirassier swords that two of the men had taken. We had their scabbards and they, being a longer weapon, would mark us as cuirassiers. The rest of our equipment would look similar enough to that of the enemy. The cloaks hid the breastplates. We slipped away from the camp before dawn. We gave the password and disappeared south. We did not take the road for I knew it would be watched. This was hilly country, and the roads would be, for the army, the fastest way of moving. Deploying such a large army would take time. The land to the right of the road led to the village the king had chosen as his gathering point and it would give us the best chance of cover.

We soon found the first obstacle. The Loberbach stream was narrow and could be crossed but the ground was so boggy on both sides as to both slow down an army considerably and make deployment impossible. "Sergeant, send a man back to the regiment. Tell Captain Sigismund that he will need time to cross the Loberbach. If the enemy are quick enough and close enough, they could attack while the army is disordered."

"Sir. Grayson, come here."

While the sergeant issued his orders I studied the ground. I saw, as the sun rose a little higher in the east, the hamlet of Göbschelwitz. Like Podelwitz it lay to the south of the boggy ground and on slightly higher ground. The rider sent, we moved towards the village. We halted in the village. It was a small one, but the buildings would hide my company from view. I made an instant decision.

"Sergeant, the company will remain here and fortify the village. You and I will go on alone."

If he thought me reckless, he said nothing. I was being calculating. If the Imperialists saw such a large number of men, then they would send riders to disrupt them. Two riders might escape observation.

I dismounted, "We will lead our horses as weary men might do. I intend to approach the camp from the west. If we see cuirassiers then my plan fails and we will have to flee north with whatever scant information we can gather but I am hopeful that the cuirassiers, having fought already, will be resting." My

Captain of Horse

sergeant nodded and dismounted. His corporal, Robbie Simpson said, "Good luck, sirs. I shall keep the lads alert."

We walked back along the stream and the depression kept us hidden from view. When I had deemed we had travelled enough I turned south. I noticed immediately that not only did the land rise but it appeared to lead to a long, low pair of ridges. As yet unoccupied any general worth his salt would use them. They would make a killing ground of the land before them. I could have turned and rejoined the king with that valuable information, but I knew the king needed as much detail as I could gather. I saw a road ahead, leading south to a village. From the map the king had shown me it had to be the village of Breitenfeld and, after we had trekked a few hundred paces, I was able to make out the Imperial standards fluttering from the top of the church. It was where the Imperial headquarters lay. I saw camps before the village. What I did not see were horses. We might be safe.

We halted just four hundred paces from the village and the ridge. I feigned adjusting my girth. We could be seen by any sentries to the north of the village, and I knew that there would be some. "I am wearing the officer's helmet and sword. You are dressed like a trooper. I will do all the talking. We only use German. Be ready to mount and ride. One of us must get back with whatever news we discover. You are a clever man, Jennings, if I fall you will know what to tell the king."

"Sir, but let us be positive, eh? This plan is a good one. Let us just throw the dice and see what falls. As you say, we both have enough wits to make a good attempt at escape if there are problems."

I led the large horse and adopted a trudging gait. The two men who stepped from the trees were irregulars. They were calivermen. They were soldiers who carried a smaller weapon than the musketeers, it was called a caliver, and the advantage it had was that it did not need a stand. They were used by light infantry and skirmishers. More importantly, they would be unlikely to question a cuirassier officer. When the man spoke, it was in heavily accented German. He too was a mercenary. I guessed he would be either Hungarian or Croat. That gave me an advantage for he would be unlikely to recognise my accent.

"Password!"

I was prepared for this and replied, "Jesu, Maria." Some of the enemy wounded had been questioned whilst they were being tended and they had revealed this valuable information. It was enough to make the men relax and to lower their calivers. "Where have you come from?"

I knew that the men we had fought had been from the Imperial cuirassier regiments. We had the name of one colonel, and I used that, "We were in the charge that almost won us the day against the Swedes. We are two soldiers from Colonel Jean de Merode-Waroux's Imperial Cuirassier Regiment and who are you?"

The senior of the two stood a little straighter, "We are Hayduk." I frowned, "From Hungary." He patted his curved sword. "When these Protestants come, I shall collect their balls as trophies." He pointed to the south and east, "Others, like you, have been returning but you are, I think, the last. Your regiments are on the far side of Breitenfeld where the grazing is better."

His companion laughed. "And the wind takes the smell of their shit away from our camp."

"Keep a good watch, their army is just a few miles up the road." My words drew their attention north as I had intended and allowed us to mount our horses and move down the road a little way and out of sight. My plan was simple and relied on what I had observed of large armies. When they were billeted, they rarely noticed other soldiers. It was like hiding a tree in a forest. So long as we could avoid cuirassiers and senior officers then we would be fine. As we neared the village, I saw that there were other mounted men, but they were mainly more Croat and Hungarian light horsemen. We passed through the village, but I took us around the smaller road and away from the front of the headquarters. I paused at the corner of the building for I saw a face I recognised as the men went into the headquarters. It was Don Alessandro. The Spanish spymaster was here. What did that mean for us?

When we emerged on the other side, I saw a vast army laid out before us. We halted beneath the shade of a tree, and we dismounted. I drank some water from my canteen as I studied the camp. You can work out the number of men by counting fires. There were usually ten or twelve men for each fire. I saw before us the infantry and artillery. The cavalry camp was on the far side, as the Hungarian had told us. I could only count twenty-six artillery pieces. General Torstenson had almost double that number. It took some time, but I estimated that there were about twenty-one thousand regular troops and a thousand or so irregulars. I knew that my estimate of the irregulars might be wrong as there would be many used as sentries.

We mounted and we headed through the camp towards the cavalry camp. This would be the riskiest and most dangerous part. Some of the officers waved as we passed and I waved back. Jennings was following me and all that they saw was an officer and a trooper heading to the cavalry camp. I saw the cavalry standards on the slightly higher ground when we neared the stream. I took the opportunity to let our horses drink while I studied the tents and standards. I was still counting when Jennings grabbed my arm. He did not point but nodded with his head. Eight cuirassiers were moving towards us from their camp. We could fool musketeers, pikemen and irregulars but not cuirassiers.

I mounted and said, "The jig is up, Jennings. Let us ride. Slowly at first. Let us follow the stream a little way." We rode along the north bank of the stream. There was boggy ground to our right and ahead the road to Podelwitz.

The cuirassiers saw us mount and spurred their horses. They were racing to get to us. I jerked my reins around and headed up the bank. Jennings was alongside me almost instantly. He glanced under his arm and shouted, "They have drawn weapons, Sir."

"Then let us hope the crossing of the stream slows them down."

I was gambling that with a couple of hundred paces start we might outrun them. Podelwitz lay two miles up the road. We would be aided, as would our pursuers, by the descending ground but when we neared Podelwitz it would rise again, and our animals would slow. I risked a look behind and saw that while the stream and boggy ground had, indeed, slowed them, another ten had left the camp and they were coming not through the boggy ground but up the road that was to the east of us and ran parallel to the one we were using. They would be able to ride obliquely across the open ground and catch us at the same time as the first group of horsemen. My wheellocks were all loaded but they would be of little use fired from the back of a galloping horse. I would have to use my sword. We were both lucky in that our horses were as powerful as the ones chasing us and as we did not wear plate they were not suffering as much as the ones who were pursuing us.

The latter group had closed the ground and when a pistol was fired I knew, without looking, that they were close enough to risk wasting a ball. The first one was a ranging shot. The ball whistled over my head. The ground was rising, and our horses were labouring. I saw the smoke from the chimneys of Podelwitz and knew that sanctuary was just ahead. When I looked behind, I saw that the cuirassiers were less than forty paces behind us. Had they risked their pistols and harquebuses they might have enjoyed some success, but I think that they were keen to capture us.

The ground levelled out and I saw the village ahead. Apart from the smoke from the chimneys it looked deserted.

"Head for the road through the village. We will have to rely on the Loberbach to stop them."

"Aye, Sir."

It was as we entered the village that I saw the Hunting Dogs. Corporal Simpson had hidden them and as we passed through, I heard the command, "Fire!"

More than fifty weapons belched balls at the cuirassiers. Some pinged from plate but one or two found flesh and I heard cries as men were dropped. A German voice shouted, "It is a trap! Back!"

I reined in and looked back. Four men had been hit and the others were all racing back to their camp. Tilly would now know that not only was the Swedish army coming, it was also close. I had to get to the king and tell him the size of the problem and the army that he faced.

"Sergeant Jennings, stay here and fortify the village. It will take the enemy a little time to realise what we intend. I will get to the king as soon as I can."

He nodded, "Don't worry, Colonel, Robbie has made a good start, but we can make it even better."

Captain of Horse

I galloped my weary horse north towards the army I knew was heading south. When I met Captain Friedrich, I was relieved beyond words, "Captain, hurry to Podelwitz. The enemy are alerted, and we need the village defending."

"Sir, Bretherton's Horse, at the gallop!"

I met the king and the advance guard led by Sir James. I pointed behind me, "We hold the village of Podelwitz, King Gustavus, but the enemy are moving towards it."

The king was decisive, and he said, "Sir James, take your musketeers and reinforce the village."

"Right, lads, at the double." I heard the collective groan as the men shouldered their muskets and muskettengabel and ran, like so many pack horses, towards the village.

The general pulled his horse to the side and his senior generals joined us. "Tell me all." I did so and he nodded, "We can keep our original formation, but I had planned on using the two villages to anchor my flanks."

I shook my head, "Göbschelwitz might be used for it is far enough from the boggy ground to allow you to manoeuvre, but Podelwitz lies almost on the boggy ground."

"Then, Elector, you place your Saxons with their flank against Göbschelwitz. General Horn, you will occupy the centre and I will take the right." He turned to me, "Thank you, Colonel, you may rejoin you regiment. They will be brigaded for the battle with the Finns." He saw my face and smiled, "The general who leads them is not a wild man. General Åke Henriksson Tott is steady. General Johan Banér will command."

I saluted, "Sir!"

Both men had a good reputation, but I would have preferred an independent command.

I whipped my horse's head around and galloped up the road. The musketeers had still to reach the village, but I saw the horse holders with mounts of the rest of the regiment, and that Sigismund had spread the men out in a long line on either side of the village. I saw that the two flanks were held by my lieutenants. They had the strongest companies and the most veterans.

As I reined in on a very weary animal, Sergeant Jennings shouted, "Sir!" He pointed and I saw some regiments of

Captain of Horse

Hungarian and Croat cavalry preparing to charge us. They knew the battlefield as well as we and they would try to dispute the crossing of the stream. We would be seen as a minor obstacle. They would come in a loose line and as I had witnessed with our Finns, such wild men were unpredictable. Until Sir James and his three regiments of musketeers arrived, we would have to hold them. The problem would be that they had weapons with the same range as us and they would be mounted. As there were four regiments we would be outnumbered by four to one! A fifth of our men were holding the reins of our horses. I knew that this might be bloody.

I threw off my helmet and red sash. Ashcroft handed me my hat and I walked to a place before the village where I could address the regiment. I had my back to the horsemen who were forming their lines just half a mile away.

"We have come a long way in a year. We are, in my view, the finest regiment in this army and I am eminently proud of each and every one of you. We are facing more than four times our number and these are wild men. Trust to your skill and the men alongside whom you stand. There may come a day when we will all fall in battle, and men will forget Bretherton's Horse, but it will not be today. Sir James Ramsay and his Scotsmen are coming to our aid. They are sent by King Charles, and they will not let us down. We fight this day for our cause which is just, but we also fight for our country. We were bred to be warriors. Let us show this Spanish king how we can fight."

Even as the men cheered Ashcroft shouted, "Watch out, Colonel!"

I turned and saw a Croat wielding a war hammer charge towards me; he had broken from the line of horsemen and was clearly intent on killing the foolish officer who turned his back on his enemies. I raised my pistol and aimed. I had one shot and if I failed then I would be dead. I took a deep breath and aimed just above his horse's head. Even in that moment I knew that if I hit his horse then the body of the animal would kill me. I fired and took a step to the right. The smoke filled the air before me, but I saw the Croat's head jerk back as my ball hit him. The cheer from behind confirmed that he was dead.

Lieutenant Stirling yelled, "Enough heroics, Sir!"

Captain of Horse

I ran and reached the green standard fluttering bravely above our heads and my core of men: Stephen, Ashcroft, Murphy and Gilmour. Stephen of Alnmouth said, quietly, "Nice speech, Colonel! We will all try not to die, eh?"

Captain Friedrich shouted, "Prepare weapons." I only had one loaded pistol left and I holstered the spent one and drew my second pistol and my sword. I rammed the sword's tip into the ground.

The Croats and Hungarians were screaming a war cry and saw their chance to destroy us while we were unsupported. Sigismund shouted, "Fire!"

Smoke billowed and I heard shouts and screams as the light horsemen were hit. Those of my men who had two pistols, and there were now many, fired a second volley. Others did as I had done and drew their swords. I holstered my pistol and drew my sword as the head of a small horse emerged through the smoke. I slashed at it with my blade and the animal was wise enough to jerk its head and body to the side. In doing so it exposed the Hungarian with the wicked looking sabre and I backhanded my blade into his leg. He had high boots and a leather jack but the cloth around his thighs did not halt my sharp sword. When the blood blossomed and bloomed, I knew he had a mortal wound. His horse's movement had also disordered the men behind. I knew that we were lucky for we had buildings behind us but the companies on the flanks had no such shelter.

There was such a cacophony of noise that it was hard to make sense of anything. I was just aware of the men and horses before me as I slashed and stabbed with my sword. In many ways I was lucky that this was a cuirassier's sword for it was longer than my own but I preferred the balance of mine. Gilmour had planted the standard. There would be no retreat and he was using a claymore two-handed. I saw it hack into the side of a horse's head and the animal fell in a heap. My standard bearer finished off the rider by hacking through his exposed neck.

Suddenly I heard a Scottish voice. It sounded far off as in a dream. It was Sir James, "Present! Fire!"

The noise of more than two hundred and fifty muskets was like the rippling crack of thunder that heralded a storm. Smoke billowed to our left and right. The horsemen before us paused and stared at this new threat.

Gilmour shouted, "At them boys!" He picked up the standard in his left hand and ran at the horsemen before us. Murphy blew the horn. I recognised no call. It was just a sound to encourage men. The effect was that the centre of our line lurched forward and, combined with the musketeers' attack on the flanks, made the Hungarians and Croats seek the shelter of their own lines. Sir James had arrived just in time.

My men stood cheering as the horsemen ran.

Captain Friedrich bellowed, "Now, before they return, take what you can. We eat horse this night!"

That brought a huge cheer. I looked around and saw nothing but smiling faces and, entering the village was King Gustavus and his generals. He raised his sword in salute, and I bowed. We had survived. My men had fought well but tomorrow or the day after would see our sternest test. We would fight in a major battle, and it would be another who commanded us and not Colonel James Bretherton.

Chapter 18

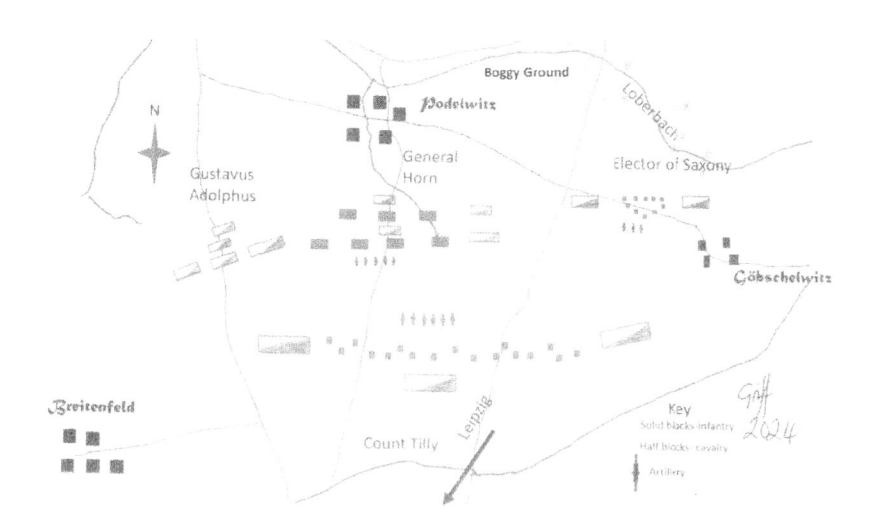

The opening positions 17th September 1631

Breitenfeld September 1631

We halted in our battle lines. We had no tents but we had fires close to the village. There the doctors set up the temporary hospital we knew would be needed. The baggage train, the tross, made an impromptu fort, and I knew that the women of the regiment would have food already cooking. Our six German drivers would know, better than anyone, the need to be vigilant. The Imperial Army was also arrayed in its battle lines. It took time for the artillery to be placed. General Torstensson was a master of his craft. Four 24-pounder guns, eight 18-pounder guns and 42 lighter regimental guns were spread out before our centre troops. The lighter regimental guns were distributed evenly before the infantry. I saw that while the enemy had fewer guns, many of them were far heavier than ours. However, they were also more spread out. We were on the right close to the king and I saw immediately the difference in the formations of the three armies. The Saxons emulated the Imperial Army with huge tercios. Some of the Catholic Alliance tercios had two thousand men in each one. Both our Saxon allies and the Imperialist Army also made huge blocks of horsemen. King Gustavus had our men in smaller more manoeuvrable blocks. We had two lines with supporting cavalry. Tilly had a long line with seventeen tercios, including some that held more than two thousand men in each block. The flanks were guarded by cavalry.

We were in the second rank. General Johan Banér commanded, and we had some musketeers. We were mainly the reserve cavalry but as the king was with us we knew that he would use us judiciously. We had thirty companies of cuirassiers and forty-eight companies who were a mixture of light horsemen and medium cavalry. The bulk of our heavy cavalry were on the left with General Horn.

The bombardment began at twelve. We were lucky for we were on the right flank and the enemy seemed intent upon destroying our centre and our Saxon allies. Tilly was attempting to destroy what he perceived as our weakness, the Saxons.

I soon noticed that our guns were firing at a rate of three to five volleys to one Imperial volley. The weight of shot proved decisive. It was hard to estimate numbers, but I thought that we killed twice the number of our enemy. It was a bizarre experience for we were almost bystanders. Whilst I was confident about the Swedish and Scottish regiments standing, the Saxons were already looking a little shaky. You can always tell when men are not happy on a battlefield and one or two were slipping silently away, even as we watched.

Stephen of Alnmouth shook his head and said, almost to himself, "Why do they just stand there? Why not move out of the way?"

We had just seen a twelve-pounder ball scythe through a file of musketeers. Eight of them were killed by the single ball which continued to bounce and roll along the ground.

"Discipline and they know that if they do move then they," I pointed at the waiting cuirassiers, "will be among them like wolves when the sheepdog has gone." Zu Pappenheim commanded seven regiments of elite cuirassiers. They were desperate to get to grips with the musketeers.

The artillery exchange lasted for two hours and it was clear that we were having the better of it. However, it was unpleasant to stand where we did as a south westerly breeze blew the smoke and dust into our faces. I know that in the grander scheme of things it was nowhere near as bad a fate as the centre and left endured, but the smoke made it hard for us to see.

Lieutenant Larsson was sent with orders, not just for us but the rest of the right wing.

"General Banér, the king asks that you echelon your men to the right so that the smoke is not in their faces."

"Very well, Lieutenant." He turned to an aide, "I hope that Count Tilly gives us time to accomplish this without interference."

While Tilly might have wished to consider his options, zu Pappenheim did not and we saw him forming up his cuirassiers with muskets and harquebusiers ready to support. He did not see a realignment but the preparations for a retreat. General Banér was no fool and seeing the cuirassiers form up, knew what was coming. He ordered the musketeers to place themselves up close to the cavalry and had our horsemen prepare their weapons. The king joined us. One thing I liked about the king was that he was brave, and he was not averse to putting himself in the front line.

He said to the general, "Unless I miss my guess, our opponent will perform a caracole."

"I agree, Your Majesty."

"Have the musketeers ready their weapons. I want a volley at point blank range. No one is to fire until they are within pistol range. Let them think they have caught us mid-manoeuvre."

The king was right. With the smoke on the battlefield and his experience of Imperial troops, General zu Pappenheim would expect us still to be turning but the discipline of the soldiers meant that we were ready. My horsemen had their pistols, muskets, calivers, and harquebuses prepared. If we fired at point blank range, then more than fifteen hundred weapons would all fire at once. We were still in the second rank despite the shift in our position. We watched as the glistening mailed warriors charged our musketeers and front-line cavalry. I could not help but wince when the first caracole emptied their pistols. However, the noise of the muskets and our own guns was even louder. We had regimental artillery with us and the little guns also did mighty damage. The cuirassiers and the accompanying musketeers made four more attacks before they regrouped. The wounded were taken away to the wagons and the doctors back at Podelwitz.

As the enemy regrouped Ashcroft asked, "Are we winning, Sir?"

I shook my head, "We are not losing, yet, and we do not know what is happening on the rest of the battlefield. Look to your front, Ashcroft, and fight what we see. It is many hours until sunset."

It was clear, when the next charge came, that zu Pappenheim had changed his plan. He extended his lines and sent men to charge around our right flank. The king commanded, "Reserve line take your places on the right."

The attack meant that we would be involved, and we moved along with the other brigades of cavalry and musketeers. The king's plan for strength in depth now paid off. However, without incredible discipline we could not have done this. General Åke Henriksson Tott was a disciplinarian and he was the one who tamed the wild Finns so that they followed his commands as meekly as lap dogs.

We had barely reached our allocated place in the line and, indeed, the regimental artillery was still unlimbering, when the cuirassiers pounced. General Tott roared, "We will fire when they have fired. We endure the pain. Present! Fire!" The first squadrons discharged their weapons, and we returned fire. We were enveloped in a wall of smoke. I knew why we had waited until they had fired. They were marginally closer to us and we emptied more saddles. I had six wheellocks with me and I had the luxury of being able to fire them as three pairs. I could not see the effect, but I did see the results of the Imperial attack. I saw men fall from their saddles or clutch wounds. There were not many but for a regiment that had lost few men hitherto they were damaging losses. We also lost generals in the fighting. I saw two cuirassier generals, Aderkas and Damitz, fall during these attacks.

King Gustavus and General Banér rode along our lines encouraging us. The enemy saw them and some drew their swords to end the battle with the death of the king. All of them were felled before they could harm our leaders. Lieutenant

Captain of Horse

Larsson was in the thick of it. He was learning, at last, what it was to be a soldier in a major battle.

By my reckoning it was about four o'clock in the afternoon when the rider came from General Horn. As luck would have it the king and General Banér were close enough for me to hear his words, "King Gustavus, the Yellow Regiment has attacked and there is a gap between Schleswig-Holstein-Gottorp's regiment and Piccolomini's harquebusiers and the main body of the enemy."

"Thank General Horn."

"He also said to tell you that the Saxons have fled, King Gustavus. We are now assaulted on two sides."

"Tell him to hold on." His voice sounded as though he had just been told what the weather would be like the next day. He was always calm and unflappable. The news was disastrous. We had lost one third of our army and we had yet to hurt the enemy. King Gustavus, however, saw the positive. "General Banér, rally the cavalry of Sperreuth, Stenbock, Soop, Tott, Stålhandske and Wunsch. I want you to lead them in a broad counter charge against both Pappenheim's cuirassiers and Piccolomini's and Merode's harquebusiers." He pointed to the enemy.

"Yes. King Gustavus. Cavalry commanders to me."

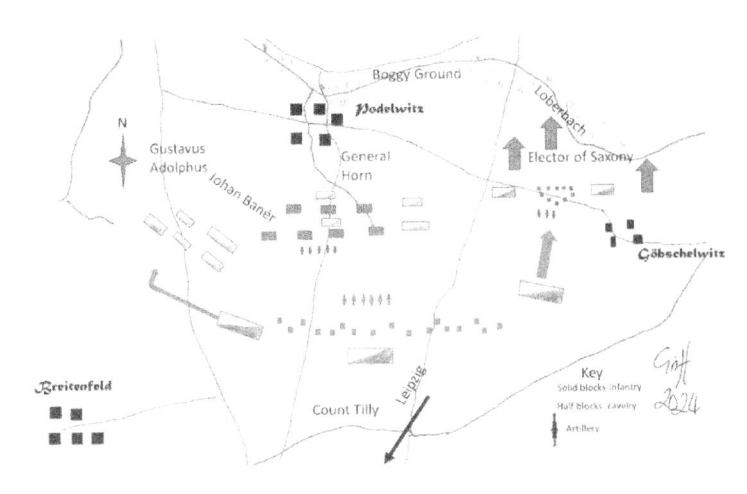

Pappenheim's attack and the flight of the Saxons

I turned to Sigismund, "You heard the order. We are to charge, prepare the men. Put the Wildcats in the front ranks and then the Wolves."

"Yes, Sir." He was grinning as he rode off.

"Gilmour, Murphy, stay close to me. Stephen, guard the colours and Ashcroft, guard Murphy." While we waited, I reloaded all my weapons.

All four of them shouted, "Yes, Colonel!" There was glee in their voices. It is hard to endure attack after attack and do nothing. Now we had the chance to do something. We could hit back. Now that Gilmour had his stirrup bucket fitted he had a free hand to wield a weapon. He could fight.

When General Tott came back we found that we were to be with the other light horsemen on the right. The Livonian and Curonian cuirassiers would be the point of our attack, and they would charge into zu Pappenheim's cuirassiers. The orders were for us to close to within pistol range, open fire and charge home with cold steel. I joined the Wildcat company. The enemy were regrouping after what must have been their ninth attack. I had lost count.

Dick Dickson was grinning. He looked more like a wild borderer than ever, "Now we shall show them what we can do. This would never have happened with Deschamps in charge, Colonel. Fancy us being in a cavalry charge." He tapped his sword, "These Germans will feel northern steel before the day is out."

I nodded, "Aye, Lieutenant, but listen for the horn. I want us to hold the line and to hit as one. When I sound recall, I want no one charging off into the wild blue yonder. We fight together. Understand?"

He looked offended and said, "Of course, Sir!"

General Banér's horn sounded, and we began to trot in a long line towards the cuirassiers, musketeers and harquebusiers who were still dressing their lines. I was riding Marcus, and he had endured the battle as we all had until now. He was eager to get to grips with the enemy and I had to rein him back in to obey my own orders and hold the line. We had Finns to the right of us and the Östergötland Horsemen to our left. The Swedes from Östergötland were a solid regiment of horsemen.

We had the advantage that we had all reloaded. The cuirassiers, as well as regrouping, were in the process of reloading and when we stopped just thirty paces from them and raised our weapons, I could see the men before us were slower to do so. It was a ragged volley from our line but the one in return was even more so. I fired two pistols and holstered them as General Banér sounded the charge.

"Murphy, the charge!" I knew that our own horn would inspire the regiment and drawing my own sword and not the cuirassier one I had used before, I spurred Marcus. Now I could let him have his head.

Our volley had emptied saddles and when we struck the enemy, we outnumbered the ones we faced. The Finns to our left had their wicked war hammers and axes. I heard the screams as the cuirassiers were butchered by wild men who were now well controlled by a stern leader. I pointed my sword at a German cuirassier who had drawn a second wheellock. Even as I closed with him, he fired. I should have been dead for he was so close to me, but he misfired. Perhaps he had loaded badly in the heat of battle, I know not, but the speed of my horse and my levelled sword ended his life, as the tip drove into his throat. I withdrew my weapon and looked for my next opponent.

We had passed through their front ranks and those behind had weapons ready, but our horses were now moving quickly. The cuirassier horses were skittish, alarmed by the smoke and noise. Even though pistols and wheellocks fired, the balls largely missed their targets and our swords reaped a fine harvest. The Finns to our right had not kept the same formation but that only helped us for their weapons had carved a hole deep into the enemy horsemen. Lieutenant Stirling had led his company to fill the gap they had created, and they had been followed by the Hawk Company. Badger Company had ridden to close with us and it meant we now had a two company front and, unlike the Finns, we still held our formation.

Fighting men with breastplates and backplates, not to mention helmets, meant my men and I had to think when we struck our blows. The border horse were all clever men, and they struck at any unprotected part of the enemy. It meant that we wounded more than we killed but that had an effect. A wounded man worries that he is going to die and looks for an excuse to run. Our charge caused a rout but the moment they ran was not a single one. It was as though the enemy line was punctured at different places and when they ran, the ones who had been holding firm found themselves surrounded and they ran. For us, we were slashing, stabbing and scything and suddenly, the men before us thinned and we saw, not the breast plates but the back plates. It is always easier to strike at the back of a fleeing man as he cannot fight back. I stood in my stirrups to bring the flat of my sword down hard onto the helmet of the cuirassier before me. He was wearing a head protector, but the woollen protector was there to absorb lighter blows rather than the mighty one I inflicted. He fell from his saddle. I do not think my blow killed him, but it rendered him unconscious. He died when he was trampled by the horses galloping behind me.

I suddenly recognised where we were. We were close to the place where Jennings and I had scouted. Breitenfeld lay just ahead.

"Murphy, sound reform!" Ours was the only horn that sounded. I knew that with the village just ahead it would become a choke point. I wanted my men to hit the men trapped there in a block. I felt, rather than saw, the loose lines of Finns and Swedes ride ahead of us. I was proud to see that we had solid lines.

"Murphy, the charge!"

The horses had enjoyed a few moments of rest, and we were now boot to boot as we charged. Behind us the Badger Company had still to discharge their weapons. That would prove vital. To my left I heard the volley as an Imperial tercio blasted at our horsemen. I ignored it for we had horsemen to fight before us. I was right, they were milling at the edge of the village as they sought a way through. Some turned to face us, and we charged into a mass of men and horses. This time it was breastplates and not the backs of men we faced. Standing in my stirrups would allow my opponent to have a free slash at me. I duelled with an officer wearing a red plume in his helmet. He had a longer sword, and he was skilled.

The voice from behind shouted, in English, "Lean to your left, Colonel."

Captain of Horse

I trusted all my men and I obeyed. I saw the frown on the officer's face as he raised his sword for the coup de grace. The frown became a look of horror as the trooper just behind me discharged his pistol into the officer's face. He fell from the saddle. The rest of the Badger Company did the same and the effect was astonishing. Saddles were emptied and the men before us began to surrender.

Our pursuit was halted by General Banér's horn. A messenger rode up to General Tott who shouted, "Light Horse, let the Livonian and Curonian cuirassiers continue the chase. Reload your weapons and turn to your left. We have a regiment of musketeers to destroy."

I shouted, "Bretherton's Horse reform. Stag, Fox, Otter and Hunting Dogs to the fore. Lieutenants Dickson and Stirling, secure the village."

"Sir!" I knew that my most senior officers would want to be in at the kill, but they saluted and obeyed orders.

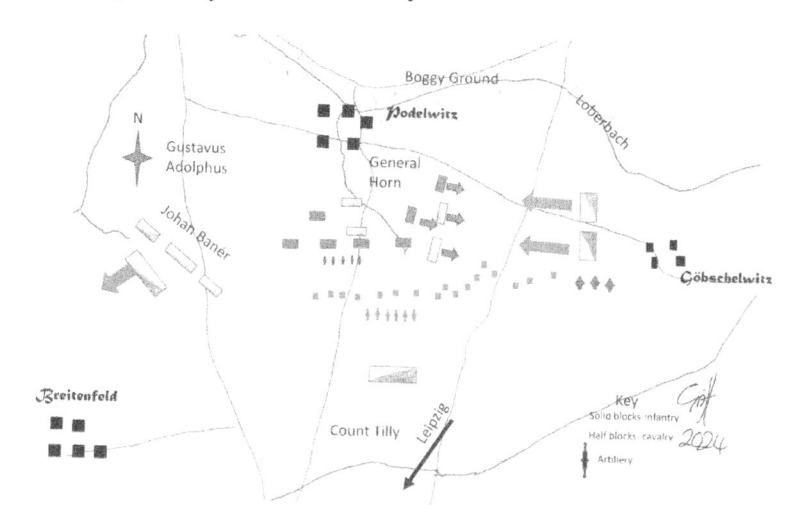

Pappenheim's flight and Count von Fürstenberg-Heiligenberg's attack

We formed lines and followed General Tott as we headed for the fifteen hundred musketeers of the Schleswig-Holstein-Gottorp regiment. General Horn had sent the Yellow Regiment to aid us and we all reined in to face the musketeers. The pikemen who had been protecting them had fallen and the harquebusiers

Captain of Horse

were all dead. The regiment was the last one holding the left flank of the Imperial line. They were obeying their orders.

"Fire!"

Almost two thousand weapons opened fire. We reloaded and fired again. I am not sure how many times we fired but eventually we heard General Banér shout, "Cease fire!"

When the smoke cleared, we saw the remnants of the musketeer regiment. There were just three hundred of them left alive. General zu Pappenheim and his cuirassiers were being chased all the way back to Leipzig. The Saxons had fled but we had turned the enemy left.

The battle had been going on for five hours. We had enjoyed a partial victory, but I could see, through the smoke of battle, twenty thousand Imperial troops preparing to attack General Horn. He had General Baudissin and the reserve cuirassier regiments for support but that was all. I saw Lieutenant Larsson and King Gustavus ride to the reserves, the Scottish regiments led by Colonel Hepburn. If the king was acting as a messenger, then things were in a parlous state.

"Murphy, sound the recall."

While most of my men had already reformed some, perhaps deafened by the cannon fire, were still chasing the odd Imperial soldier. I heard General Tott do the same.

The horns sounded and weary horsemen returned to their regiments. We had lost men. I saw gaps in some of the companies. The Wildcat and Wolf companies had suffered the greatest losses. That was to be expected but my two lieutenants along with their guidons still remained.

To my surprise the king and his aide rode directly to us. General Tott had moved his horse closer to mine so that we could talk but the arrival of the king pre-empted any conversation.

He had obviously been in action as his tunic was spattered with blood. His pistols had been discharged. This was a warrior king. He smiled, "Gentlemen you have done well but I need one last effort from you. I need your Hakkapeliitta, Bretherton's Horse, as well as the remnants of Stenbock's, Sperreuth's and Rheingrave's regiments." He drew his sword and pointed to the left of the Imperial line. "There is a gap there. I know that your horses are weary and we must charge uphill, but if we can take the artillery on the Galgenberg then we have a chance of defeating Tilly and winning this battle."

We all said, "Yes, Your Majesty."

Even before we had the chance to order our men to form lines he said, "Lieutenant Larsson, ask General Soop and his Västergötland cavalry to charge against Erwitte's open left flank."

"Sir."

"That should buy us time."

It was indeed a race against time. As Sigismund and I organised our depleted numbers I saw that General Horn was hard pressed. The Imperial cavalry that had chased the Saxons from the field now returned to attack his left flank. The enemy artillery was pounding his lines and while their rate of fire was not as high as ours, it was still causing too many fatalities. Would they break?

It took fifteen minutes for us to prepare. I had six loaded weapons and Marcus had recovered a little. My colour party was intact.

King Gustavus looked at the standard and said, "You shall soon have another battle honour, Colonel, Breitenfeld."

I hoped he was not jinxing us for the battle, despite our victory on the right, still hung in the balance.

Once we were ready, he led us, along with a returned Lieutenant Larsson and flanked by General Tott and General Banér, in a long line six regiments wide. We kept a steady pace for it was an energy sucking slope. I saw that Soop's regiment had driven back the enemy cavalry to disorder the massive tercios. The cuirassiers who faced us were driven off without us having to fire a single shot. They were demoralised and defeated. All those fruitless charges against our right flank had sucked the life from them. We did not even need to use our pistols. We slashed and hacked at the gunners who fell to a man. While we turned the guns to face the enemy, men who could fire the artillery were found. The king ordered our right flank to wheel. I saw, from the vantage point of the ridge called the Galgenberg, that the Scottish regiments led by colonels McKay and Munro had recaptured the Saxon guns and they were also being turned.

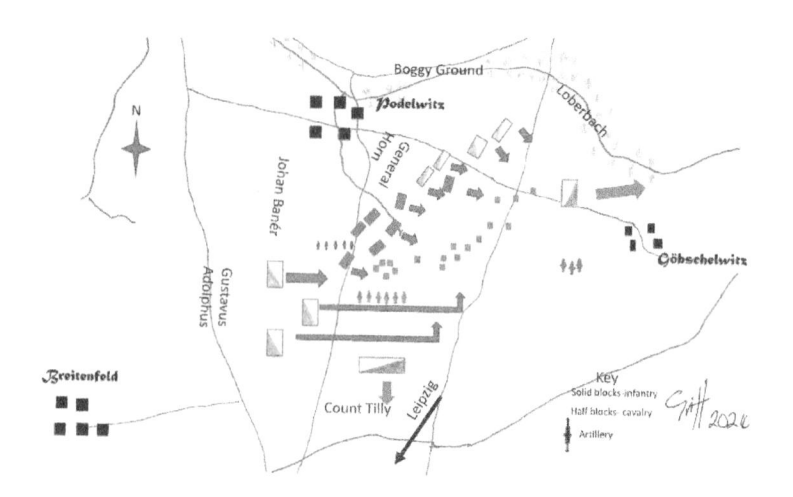

The end of the battle

I knew what was going to happen. Count Tilly's army was surrounded on three sides by artillery and men. Our numbers were almost equal, but the Catholic army had lost every battle except for the battle against the Saxons. When the cannons began to fire there was only one outcome, annihilation. The tercios broke and I knew that we had won. We had the field but the king wanted more.

"General Tott, the enemy are fleeing towards Leipzig. Let us see if we can capture more of them."

General Tott looked as weary as I felt. Like me he had few balls left and his sword was notched. I was lucky, I still had my cuirassier sword. "King Gustavus, it is almost six o'clock. It will be dark by nine."

"Then see how many men we can take before the sun does set." He gave a sad smile, "You have done your best and this last effort might win us the war. Think of that, we can all go home, and the Catholics will have been defeated."

As stirring speeches go it lacked something, but the king had led us from the front and General Tott nodded. He looked at me, "Your men and mine have still some spirit, Colonel, let us go amongst the Imperialists and see what we can take."

This time we rode in company order. There were two columns and even the Finns were no longer shouting and cheering. It cost too much energy. We took the Leipzig Road and took many hundreds of prisoners as we came upon dispirited men. The retreat stopped at the Linkelwald forest when General zu Pappenheim had organised many of the fleeing infantry into improvised tercios. We waited until the artillery summoned by General Tott arrived and when it did, we pounded the Imperial tercio. By the time darkness fell and the battle ended, over three and a half thousand men had been wounded, captured or killed. The six hundred survivors slipped away in the dark. We were too exhausted to follow, and we headed back to Podelwitz where there was hot food, ale and, most important for us, a bed. The battle was over.

Chapter 19

The Main River Autumn 1631
My men and my officers rose early. There was loot on the battlefield. On our way back to our camp some men had availed themselves of the chance to take from the bodies. The morning afforded more light. My men were excellent scavengers and knew the best places to search. After all, they had witnessed the slaughter of more horsemen than anyone else and it was the horsemen who had the fattest purses. We also buried the eighty men who had died. None had women and no one was married. Stephen of Alnmouth looked a relieved man to have survived.

At noon the king ordered the camp to be broken and we headed for Halle, luckily it was just sixteen miles away. The king and the generals held a council of war while we tended to our wounds and replenished our powder and ball. That we would be heading to war again was clear. The rumour was that we would head to Vienna. If we could take that Imperial city, then the war would be over. However, Count Tilly had headed south towards the Catholic state of Bavaria. I knew that King Gustavus would regard the task as half-finished if he did not defeat Count Tilly in a decisive battle. Darkness had robbed us of the chance of such a complete victory.

The next day Lieutenant Larsson, now sporting a scar on his cheek, came to give us the news that we were to head south towards Nördlingen where Count Tilly had set up his base. The king wanted to secure Saxony. The Elector of Saxony would head for Vienna. That made a sort of sense. There might be Saxon strongholds that were held by the Imperialists. It was better if they were taken by Swedes and Scots rather than Saxons. Our first target would be the city of Erfurt. Once more we were the scouts.

Before he left me Lieutenant Larsson gave me what many might consider gossip, but as he knew the feelings that Prince Francis Albert of Saxe-Lauenburg had for me he was just issuing a warning. "Prince Francis was unhappy that he did not lead German cavalry at the battle. He was angry that you, an Englishman, was given such a prominent position. He said so to the king." He shook his head, "It did not help that his cousin fought for the Imperialists. The prince wanted the chance to kill his cousin. He wishes for the Duchy to be his."

"But I had no say in the matter."

"The prince is not a reasonable man, Colonel. He is a spoiled noble." The lieutenant shrugged, "You are like me, Colonel, you have become a soldier as a profession. The prince sees it as a right. He does not understand war in the way that we do. The king recognises that, and it is why he keeps the prince close to him where he can do no harm."

"Yet the prince was not at his side when we charged the enemy."

"Exactly. He cannot trust him and he does not want the prince killed. He left him with his command. It did not please the prince. The man is petty and harbours grudges."

"Thank you for telling me but as I shall be scouting with my regiment, I do not think our paths will cross."

"Perhaps, but be careful, my friend."

That night, as we prepared to leave and while my men foraged all that they could from Halle, we said goodbye to Stephen of Alnmouth. He had his back pay, the money he had accrued as well as two horses and some plate armour. He did not go alone. Five others decided that they had done enough. In three of the cases, they had lost best friends, and I understood their reasons. The others were like Stephen and had made enough money. The six would be led by Stephen and they stood more chance of reaching England as they were travelling together. They were armed and it would be either a very brave or very foolish brigand who took them on. The journey would be a shorter one than we had taken the previous year as we were closer to Rotterdam. I rose early and saw them off.

"You have the letter for my wife, safe?"

"I do, Colonel, and trust me, I shall deliver it and tell her that when I left you, you were well." He hesitated, "Will you be home again?"

I shrugged, "If we had gone to Vienna then I would be more confident, but I shall endeavour to have a leave while we are in winter camp. It all depends upon the king."

He smiled, "I spoke with Lieutenant Larsson and told him I would be leaving, and he confided in me that the king holds you in the highest regard. I am confident he will allow you to visit with your family."

His words made my spirits rise. His leaving had made me sad but now I spied hope.

We had smaller companies now and were more akin to the other regiments. The Hunting Dogs had lost the fewest as they had not borne the brunt of the fighting. They ranged ahead. I had spoken to my two lieutenants and Sigismund. We all agreed that when we did enjoy winter quarters, Jennings would be promoted to lieutenant. He deserved it. In many ways he was the most reliable of all my officers, Sigismund included.

The king had set his plan in motion, and we rolled like a huge metal snake to Erfurt. We were now advancing upon Catholic strongholds or, at least, those cities which had been held by Count Tilly. Such was the scale of our victory that at the sight of our army the city threw open its gates and we took it without a fight. The ones who might have fought us were either dead or fled with Tilly. King Gustavus was not a vindictive leader, and his demands were not punitive. We did not pillage the city and the supplies we took were needed by the army.

At the start of October, we headed for the Main River. We took the town of Würzburg easily enough but the fortress of Marienberg held out. It had a garrison, and the castle had a prominent position. While the infantry and artillery besieged it the cavalry ranged ahead with King Gustavus leading it. While the guns and men were placed in position we scouted as far as we could towards Mainz. The next day the guns pounded at the walls. We had captured some large guns from the Imperialists, and they were used to break down the walls. On the eighth of October the assault began. Colonel Hepburn, now promoted to general had his Scottish soldiers lead the assault. They had lost fewer men in the battle than most and they had confidence for it was their resolute musketry that had held the vaunted Imperial tercios. The defenders stood no chance, and the fortress fell by the end of the day. The king made Würzburg his temporary base and the fortress his home.

Two days after the fortress had fallen, I was summoned to a meeting in the Great Hall of the fortress. His generals and General Baudissin were there, and they had a map before them.

"Colonel Bretherton, once more the Protestant cause needs your eyes and ears." All eyes were on me, but I was looking at the king's finger which was pointing at the map. "Here is the Main. It leads to the Rhine. I know that when you fought for the Dutch and the Danes this was the land that was lost. Mainz is vital to us, and I plan on taking it before Christmas. We will, God willing and our might of arms prevail, take it. I need your regiment to ride as far as you can along the river. Find the weaknesses and assess the opposition." He lifted his finger and sat back. "We have done well but the army needs time to recover. I intend to spend a month doing so. By that time, you will have a better picture of what lies between here and Mainz."

I leaned over the map and used the measuring device to estimate the distance. "It is sixty miles as the crow flies but the river twists and turns. It will be nearer a one-hundred-mile journey."

"It will and some places will oppose us while others may well do as Erfurt and Würzburg did and capitulate without a fight, but there may be another Marienberg Fortress. I am aware of the task I am setting for you."

We had done this before and even though we were fewer in number, I was confident that we could manage this. "How long do we have?"

"Could you do this in two weeks?"

"We could."

"General Baudissin, ensure that the colonel has all that he needs and make sure that his tross is protected while he is away."

The king's words were important. When the Saxons had fled the field some of their men had raided the baggage trains of some of the other regiments. Horses, food and treasure had been taken but worst of all some women had been raped. Thanks to our German drivers they had not attempted that at our tross. The Saxons' actions had angered my men, and it was good that the Saxon army was heading for Vienna.

As we walked to my camp the general said, "The king thinks highly of you. General Tott also spoke well of you. Next year may see you leading a brigade of cavalry. How do you feel about that, Colonel?"

I shook my head, "My men are not line cavalry, General, you know that. When we chased the cuirassiers we enjoyed some success, but we lost more men when we charged them at Breitenfeld. This task is better suited to them."

"You misunderstand me, Colonel. I am talking about you leading two or three regiments, not yours. Captain Friedrich is more than capable of leading the regiment is he not?"

His words took me aback and I stuttered out, "Well yes, of course, but which regiments? I would not like to usurp another."

He laughed, "There are many regiments with good colonels, but they do not have your skills of leadership. You saw how the king used our cavalry at Breitenfeld. Instead of using a mass of horsemen as zu Pappenheim did, he used smaller elements. You could lead one such brigade." He shook his head, "I am getting ahead of myself. The king has yet to plan the campaign for next year. I just wanted you to know the plans that are afoot. Do not become too attached to Bretherton's Horse. The king knows his good leaders and his weak ones. There are others who wish for such a command, but the king knows his own mind."

I suddenly realised that he was talking about Prince Francis Albert of Saxe-Lauenburg. Lieutenant Larsson must have known of this when he warned me. I would have to be careful.

I gathered my officers and told them of the plan. They were pleased that our wagons and women would be protected. I did not want them looking over their shoulders as we rode through the unknown lands of the Main Valley.

"Our aim is to find out where the king will have problems. To that end I want to use three columns. I will lead one with the Hunting Dogs and Wolves. Captain Friedrich will lead the Badgers, Foxes and the Otters. Lieutenant Dickson will lead the rest. My column will head down the river. Captain Friedrich will scout the north bank and Lieutenant Dickson the south. We identify and avoid any towns with garrisons. We camp and use smaller villages along the way." I pointed to the map on the table. "While we travel separately, we will camp together. Our first camp will be at Marktheidenfeld. General Baudissin told me that this was a Protestant town until Bishop von Mespelbrunn forced it to become Catholic."

Lieutenant Jennings nodded, "You are hoping that our presence will swing the town back to the Protestant cause, Colonel?"

"I am and that is why we use three columns to converge upon it. I want any Imperialist sympathisers to see us as a larger number than we actually are. We then move to Worth am Main and our last stop, before Frankfurt am Main, will be Hanau which is, I believe, Protestant. The king has given us two weeks. It will take three or four days to reach Hanau and that gives us enough time to be cautious."

The ride to Marktheidenfeld was relatively uneventful although we found evidence of the presence of Imperial deserters. Some farms and hamlets had been despoiled. The survivors cowered in their homes as we rode through. They were all Protestant and a Lutheran minister at Remlingen told us what had happened.

"It was in the last week of September. The men were in the fields harvesting their crops when Imperial soldiers appeared. They slaughtered the men and raped the women before taking all that there was to be had." He shook his head, "I was not here. I was visiting my family in Hanau. I came back to find this. The elector should have left men to protect his people. We are too close to Bavaria to be left so vulnerable."

I had no words of consolation. The village was too small to justify a garrison but perhaps a regular patrol of horsemen might have done some good. However, even as that thought came into my head the soldier in me dismissed it. Deserters would avoid regular troops. They would hide and choose their moment judiciously.

That night, as we enjoyed the hospitality of Marktheidenfeld who were grateful to have our regiment there, I spoke with my officers. "We need to find these deserters. They have not done as many of those captured after Breitenfeld and switch allegiances, they have chosen to become brigands. We hang them. When we scout, we look for men who hide."

The next day our vigilance was rewarded. My column saw no one but when Captain Friedrich and his men met us at Worth am

Main, he told us they had found a dozen deserters. The men had tried to fight back and flee. Ten died in the firefight and the other two were hanged. "I left the bodies swinging in the wind as a warning to the others, Colonel."

He was asking for my approval, and I nodded, "It is unpleasant but necessary."

So far, the scouting expedition was going better than we could have expected. So far as I could see the king would have no opposition on his ride to the Rhine.

The village of Sulzbach am Main changed that. It lay close to the Main and the Sulzbach rivers. We found a village not just raided but destroyed. The still smoking buildings spoke of a recent raid and the bodies were not yet decomposed. There were so many that we knew it was not the work of deserters. Even as we buried the bodies, Jennings and his scouts found the tracks of many horses. We knew how to determine a loose body of men and a more organised group and Jennings had identified the latter. "There had to be a hundred men or more, Colonel. They headed north and west."

"Do you know when this happened?"

I had my own ideas, but I valued my company commander's opinion, "Yesterday? The buildings are still smoking, and the foxes have not yet completely ravaged the bodies." He added, by way of explanation, "The burning buildings would have kept them away."

I nodded, "And we found no animals so whoever did this took them, eh?"

"That is how I read it, Colonel."

"Captain Friedrich is to the north of us. Send a man to find him and tell him we are hunting an organised body of cavalry. Have him join us."

"Sir."

When the bodies had been buried, I said some words over the graves. The words were inadequate but at least someone had said them. We followed the trail. More than a hundred men leave a clear trail. Horses leave dung, and branches are broken. Hooves trample vegetation and men drop things. They had raided and we found discarded bones from fowl, empty jugs of wine and ale and pieces of stale bread. They were still ahead of us but how far we did not know. We were just two miles from Hösbach when Captain Friedrich found us. His face was grim, and he told us that he had found the hamlet of Waldaschaff similarly devastated.

I looked at the sun. By my reckoning it was about three o'clock in the afternoon. My other column would be approaching the rendezvous and if we did not join them might worry. I turned to Ashcroft, "Roger, ride to the rendezvous and tell Lieutenant Dickson what we are doing. He is to remain at the rendezvous until we arrive."

"Sir."

Just then Lieutenant Jennings pointed, "Sir, smoke."

I looked and saw the spiral that bespoke not of a fire for cooking but one of destruction. "Hösbach?"

Jennings nodded, "That would be my reading of it, Colonel."

"Then let us catch these killers before they do more harm."

As we rode Lieutenant Friedrich said, "Colonel, this makes no sense to me. This is Bavarian as much as it is Saxon. Bavaria is a loyal part of the empire. Why would an Imperial regiment devastate its own allies?"

I shrugged, "I do not know but I know that as the rest of our army and the Saxon army is well to the east of us then it is not one of our regiments. We deal with whoever we find."

We heard the noise, not only of burning buildings but also the sound of combat and death. I drew my pistol as did the rest of our men. We were riding in a single column four men abreast. It was all that the narrow road would allow. We twisted and turned through trees and could see little, but we had the acrid smell of burning. I smelled burning bodies too.

When we burst into the open, we saw horsemen slashing and stabbing at men, women and children. Some men had their breeches around their ankles as they raped women. Hösbach was the largest settlement we had found since Marktheidenfeld and had side streets and some large buildings.

I shouted, "Murphy, sound the charge."

As the horn rang out the enemy, whoever they were, stopped and looked in our direction. Even before I thought to open fire, muskets were discharged in our direction. I levelled my pistol and aimed at the soldier who had just stood, his breeches still around his ankles, raising his harquebus. I fired before he did and he fell. I holstered my pistol and drew my sword. I did not wish to risk hitting the civilians who had endured enough. The enemy horn sounded and that told me that they were a regular regiment. It was then I saw their red sashes. They were Imperial troops.

I watched an officer mount his horse and speak to the trumpeter. I pointed my sword, "Take them!"

My men roared. I knew they would be angered by what they had seen and, like me, know that we had to use swords. The enemy could fire their weapons for they cared not who they hit. We did. I leaned from my saddle to hack into the side of the head of a man who was raising his own sword. He must have had too much to drink for his swing was wild and merely took the plume from my hat. My sword jarred against his skull as he slid to his death. The enemy were fleeing. The ones we killed, we took no prisoners, were the ones too far from their horses. Their dying helped more than half of the enemy to escape. We accounted for more than sixty men although we lost twelve good men in doing so. I sent Captain Friedrich to pursue them and I reined in. We had to find out who they were.

I dismounted and handed my reins to Murphy. My officers also dismounted and we wandered around the enemy seeking one who was alive. Most were dead or dying. We found one who cursed us in German before expiring. I had almost given up when I saw a man who had been slashed in the stomach. It was a mortal wound but one that might take more than an hour to kill him. His red sash blended into his bloody tunic.

Lieutenant Stirling and some of his men were with me and I said to the man, in German, "Who is your leader? Whom do you serve?"

He looked blankly at me and held the sash as though trying to stem the bleeding. A quiet voice next to me said, "Try English, Colonel."

The man heard the voice and looked up, recognition in his eyes.

I turned. The man who had spoken was Bill Burton. He said, "His name is Nathaniel Jackson, and he is a nasty man. He is a bastard! I served with him."

The man gave a wan smile and looked at Bill, "You were always a soft old bugger, Bill Burton. We were glad to be shot of you."

I said, "Who do you serve?"

The man coughed and blood came up. He grinned, "Wouldn't you like to know."

Bill said, "Heinrich Holk, Colonel. As evil a man as ever was. He was our leader."

"But didn't you fight for the Danes?" I asked the question of Burton.

"Aye, we did and after that battle, Holk joined the other side. He has no beliefs except one of self-preservation and lining his own purse."

Nathaniel Jackson winced, "The pain is too much. Kill me, eh? End my misery."

I might have done so for I am not a naturally cruel man, but Bill Burton said, "Let him die slowly, Colonel. One of the raped women we found had NJ carved into her forehead. That was the mark of Jackson."

I nodded, "Let us see to the townsfolk who are still alive. Kill any others like this." I gestured to the body of the man I had killed.

As we turned Jackson shouted, "Captain Holk will have you lot! He saw your standard and knows who you are. You are all dead men." It was ironic that in his curse the effort killed him, and he slumped to his death.

We headed back to Würzburg. We now had a picture of what the king faced. There were towns with garrisons, Haibach, Goldbach, Kleinwallstadt and Heimbuchental were the biggest, but none had a garrison large enough to slow down King Gustavus. His biggest problems would be deserters and rogue units like Holk's Horse.

Chapter 20

Frankfurt am Main December 1631
We found no more despoiled villages and reached Frankfurt am Main six days after leaving the fortress. The town offered little opposition. While most Imperial troops had fled further south with Tilly, there was still a garrison in the city and the Imperial standard still flew from the walls. Once we discovered the size of the garrison we headed back to the king. Twelve days after leaving for our scouting expedition we returned to Würzburg. I reported to the king and while he was pleased that he would be able to reach the Rhine with apparently little opposition he was concerned about what we had found: the deserters and Holk's Horse. We had learned the name of the unit when we reached Frankfurt. While they had not raided the town, they had passed through, and we learned that there were two hundred men in the regiment. We had accounted for sixty but as Burton told us, they would be able to recruit more men quickly. Heinrich Holk's cruelty attracted many men, and he was not choosy about who served under his standard.

It meant that when we left Würzburg on the nineteenth of November we had thirteen thousand men. The king left seven thousand in garrison at Würzburg. We had wagons and many foot soldiers and we travelled slowly. He wanted to ensure that there were no more deserters and that the likes of Holk's Horse were not in our line of march. He also had the garrisons of the towns we had identified to subdue.

Mindful of my words he offered each of the garrisons, there were seven of them, the opportunity to switch sides and join us. In that way our army was swollen as we headed for the Rhine. We ended up with more men when we reached Frankfurt am Main than we had when we had left Würzburg. In many ways the ravages of Heinrich Holk and his men had helped us. There was much anti-Imperial feeling in the Main Valley. The land was still largely Catholic, but being so close to Protestant lands meant that there were enough Protestants to make our passage easier. It helped that King Gustavus did not take everything from the people. We were fed and housed but that was all.

We set up siege lines around the city and prepared to use our artillery to batter the last major city on the Main into submission. It took some days to do this and during that time my men and I gathered supplies. We missed the preparations. When we watched the gunners as they aligned their weapons it proved to be a little anti-climactic. Before the guns could open fire, the city sued for peace, and we entered it without firing a shot or losing a man. They had hoped we would not actually attack. When we entered we found that they had few artillery pieces, and the garrison was very small.

Mainz would, the king thought, present a different problem. It was a huge fortress and one of the strongest in all Germany. With a fortified village, Kastel, on the right bank of the Rhine, it would be hard to take. While we enjoyed the hospitality of Frankfurt am Main the king held a council of war to decide how best to proceed. Thanks to my success I was included much to the obvious annoyance of Prince Francis Albert of Saxe-Lauenburg.

The king liked to hear ideas and suggestions from everyone, and he began by outlining the situation. "We have, for the first time, a major fortress before us. Frankfurt an der Oder was insignificant in comparison to the citadel of Mainz. General Torstenson, can we reduce its walls with artillery?"

The artilleryman nodded, "Of course." He paused and smiled, "It would take all of our powder and all of our ball. It would take many months in the depths of winter and, inevitably, many guns would be damaged, but it could be done."

King Gustavus gave a wry smile, "In other words, it is too difficult." The general nodded, "And by the same token a siege would cause many desertions, not to mention disease and starvation."

General Banér suggested, "Negotiation?"

The king nodded, "A good idea but if we began by negotiating then the enemy might realise that we were too weak to take the fortress. We do not need Count Tilly to be encouraged and bring his army from Nuremburg."

Samuel von Winterfield had rejoined us before Breitenfeld and he said, "There is another way." Every eye swivelled. "We send spies into the city to make contact with their leaders."

"A good idea but who? It is risky for any man and if the spies were caught…" The king was that rare creature, he cared for even the humblest of his men.

Samuel von Winterfeld smiled as his eyes swivelled to look at me, "Captain Friedrich has a sister who is married to one of the men on the council of the city. Walter von Schmidt is known as a moderate man. If Captain Friedrich and, say, Colonel Bretherton, were to seek an audience with him they could ascertain the mood and be assured of a welcome. With luck they could negotiate an arrangement and, at the very least would be able to tell us the size of the problem."

Silence filled the room as every eye looked at me. I could understand why Sigismund had been chosen but me. I was about to decline when I caught the look on the face of the prince. He was smiling for he thought I was going to refuse, and I was damned if I would give him the satisfaction. "Of course, King Gustavus, I am more than happy to serve but I cannot answer for Captain Friedrich."

The king nodded, "Time is of the essence. Lieutenant Larsson, bring the captain."

"Yes, Your Majesty."

"Now let us decide what to do when the city is ours; either through diplomacy or the unnecessary waste of a siege."

I listened but did not hear all that was discussed for my mind was already working out a plan to get into the city. The idea arrived before Sigismund did. We would play the parts of two mercenaries who had survived the Battle of Breitenfeld. We would live from our wits and let the attitude of the guards determine if we played Imperial soldiers or Swedes.

When Captain Friedrich arrived, he had the look on his face of a condemned man. I realised why. I was used to such councils, but Sigismund was not. Samuel von Winterfeld smiled, "No need to fear, Captain. You are here so that the king can ask you for a favour."

He looked relieved, "Whatever it is then I agree."

The king shook his head, "Listen before you agree. We wish you and Colonel Bretherton to enter Mainz as spies, speak to your brother-in-law and ascertain if we can negotiate a peaceful entry to the city."

Sigismund turned and looked at me. I nodded my agreement. He said, "Then I will happily do as you ask, King Gustavus, although I am doubtful as to the outcome. I have seen neither my sister nor her husband these many years. We are estranged."

The relief in the room was palpable. It was almost as though they had not heard his caveat. I had. "Good, then the First Minister of Brandenburg will brief you while we continue our discussion about the prosecution of this war."

As we followed the minister, Sigismund said quietly, "What have we got ourselves into, James?"

"I do not know. I did not realise you had a sister."

"I have three. I left our home long ago. Elizabeth was the youngest and she married well. I did not know that anyone knew of this."

Von Winterfeld said, over his shoulder, "When you were selected to bring the colonel from England, Captain, all things were considered. We know a great deal about you, and you will be serving not only Brandenburg but also Protestant Germany."

Sigismund's silence told me that he was not sure how to react to that information. It seemed that he had no secrets whether he wanted them known or not.

We entered a chamber and the Brandenburger sat and smiled. He said, "This is not as risky as it sounds. Your brother-in-law, Captain Friedrich, is a known moderate. He also has the backing of the Jews in Mainz. They represent a powerful body in the town for, while they are not Christian, they bring much prosperity into the city through trade. They do not want war, and I believe that von Schmidt can use them to influence the rest of the council."

"But how do we get into the city, my lord? You may be right but first we have to gain entry."

Samuel von Winterfeld smiled, "I believe I saw the colonel working that out while we waited for your arrival."

I now felt like Sigismund. Did I have no secrets? I addressed my friend, "We say we are from Breitenfeld battlefield. We do not profess which side."

He looked incredulous, "And that will work?"

I shrugged, "When Jennings and I scouted out Breitenfeld we found that confidence and bluff work well. The Imperial Army is made up of many disparate elements. We act as though we are Imperial soldiers and trust to God. If there is trouble then we whip our horses' heads around and flee. I will not attempt to gain entry if there is a chance we might be apprehended." I looked at the First Minister while I spoke.

He gave me an easy smile, "Of course, but for what it is worth, I think that your plan is a good one." He stood, "And now you had better prepare. I will have a letter written for you to deliver to your brother-in-law. It will obviate any suspicion of treachery." Such acts were not uncommon in a war about religion.

We both dressed in clothes that could have been worn by the officers of either side. Mine still had the blood and dirt upon it from the battle of Breitenfeld. Jane and the women had offered to wash them, but I had said I would wait until after Mainz. I was now glad I had done so. Half of my pistols had been taken from Imperial horsemen as had Sigismund's. I used the cuirassier horse and the captured sword. I wished to be anonymous once more.

My officers were less than happy about our orders. "Sir, let us take a company as an escort. I know the land to the south appears free from enemies but…"

I smiled, "Lieutenant Stirling, we need to be hidden from view. A company of horsemen will trumpet to the world that there are Imperialist enemies abroad." He nodded but I could see that he was unhappy as were my other officers.

We mounted our horses and left the safety of our camp to head down the road into potential death or capture. We slipped quietly away from the camp. I did not need to be flattered. I was a soldier of fortune who earned a living through his sword. That I believed in my cause was good, but I was not willing, as some were, to die for it. We rode down a well-used road and passed many travellers going in both directions. It was comforting. The journey was a relatively short one, just eighteen miles and the road had a good surface. We made good time. When we saw the fortified village and bridge ahead, we dismounted.

"Do you know where your brother-in-law and sister live, Sigismund?"

"I have never visited but I was told that they have a large house close to the Rathaus." He smiled, "My brother-in-law is a rich man. He is a banker and knows how to align himself with the powerful men in the city. He is on the city council not because of any altruistic reason or because he wishes to serve the community, but because he can make more money that way. I can see why von Winterfield sent us. He is right, being a banker, Walter is close to the Jews in Mainz."

"You do not like him."

He shook his head, "I am a loyal Brandenburger. I am willing to fight for my religion and my land. Walter looks out for himself."

"And your sister?"

"I have three sisters. The other two married hard-working men. Elizabeth was the youngest. She was spoiled by our parents and she is a magpie. She likes pretty, shiny things and fine clothes. Walter gives her those. I will do this because the king asked me, but I will not enjoy the visit. It is not that I am afraid of the danger but because I will have to speak to a man I do not respect and ask him for a favour."

I realised that neither of us had our hearts in this venture. I said, "We have tarried enough. Let us get this over with. I will let you speak, Sigismund. You accent is better than mine. They might be less suspicious of a German."

He nodded but added, "You are better at this sort of thing than I am. If I am making a mistake then jump in, eh?"

"I will."

We walked the horses to the gate at the fortified village. It was a stone wall with two wooden towers set upon it. I saw two small three pounder cannons poking from the top. The soldier who arrested our progress was a member of the town watch and he was an older man. His face and dress reminded me of Edgar. I could tell he was not a regular soldier from his clothes and weapons. There were three sentries and the one who spoke was clearly the leader. His beard was flecked with grey and the other two were striplings.

"Who are you and what do you want?"

Sigismund sighed and adopted a world-weary tone, "We are two soldiers who survived the bloodbath that was Breitenfeld, and we wish to go home. Mainz seems like a good place to rest for we have travelled far."

I saw the three men take in our clothes, horses and the blood on my uniform. The greybeard nodded, "You have travelled far. Tell me, was it as bad as people say?"

Sigismund asked, "Bad?"

"We were told of thousands falling to cannon, ball and sword."

Sigismund nodded, "It was bloody, and many men died."

The older man nodded and said to the two youths, "And that is what I keep telling you. War is not glorious. These fine horsemen have survived but that is all. Stay in Mainz and put from your heads any thoughts of glory. This madness will end and our land will become prosperous once more." They nodded and he turned back to us, "If you seek an inn that will not rook you and serves good ale and passable food then the *'Golden Ear'* in the main square will serve your needs. Look for the corn above the door and tell them that Heinrich sent you."

"We will and thank you."

We walked through the gate and the village. People gave us a cursory examination as we passed through. The wooden bridge that led across the river was just wide enough for a wagon. We were able to walk our horses side by side, our horses' hooves and our boots clattering on the planks as we walked. Even though we were alone we said nothing. We had learned nothing from the three men except that Heinrich had common sense. We had not been pushed about our allegiances. That might come at the main gate.

Surprisingly we were not stopped by the guards at the main gate. These were dressed in a uniform. They wore blue. I took comfort from the fact that none of the four wore red sashes which meant that while they were Imperial troops they were not suspicious of us. They studied us but said nothing. I assumed that they thought we had endured a more rigorous interrogation at Kastel. We kept walking our horses. The town was crowded. There must have been a market and Christmas would soon be upon us. People were stocking up. The crowds helped us to blend in and when I saw some Imperial soldiers, horsemen, wearing red sashes then I was glad that we had walked our horses and not ridden them. We were hidden from them as they caroused and smoked pipes outside the tavern we passed. It was a warning that there was a strong Imperial presence. As we entered the main square we looked around for the Rathaus. It was a fine building. I looked around the square for the house that might belong to Sigismund's brother-in-law. As I did so my heart almost stopped for I saw a face I recognised. It was Don Alessandro, and he was coming out of the Rathaus. With him were three men. None looked Spanish.

Sigismund had not seen him, and he turned to speak to a stall holder, "Which is the house of Walter von Schmidt?"

The middle-aged woman selling pots and earthenware pointed to a building three doors from the Rathaus, "You see that building with the fancy filigree, the one that looks like a gingerbread house?" Sigismund nodded, "That is the home of the spider and his greedy wife."

Sigismund said, "Spider?"

She cackled, "Aye, he is like a spider. He makes webs and sooner or later everyone has to come to him for money. He bleeds us dry, and his wife gains more pretty things."

We nodded and pushed our way through the crowds. Don Alessandro and the three men had disappeared down a side street. I was not sure that the king's plan would succeed. He might have power but if people did not like him then how could he persuade them to support him?

There were two men at the door. These were not like the ancient gatekeeper and the youths. These were professionals. I saw the cudgels they held as well as the swords. They were there to protect the banker. They were not intimidated by our array of weapons, "Can we help you," the man who spoke, a huge ox of a man, paused to give us a contemptuous look, "gentlemen?"

"I am here to visit with my sister, Elizabeth von Schmidt."

Neither was expecting that answer and confusion replaced the contempt, "Does the mistress know that you are coming?"

Sigismund shook his head and said, simply, "No."

The one who had done all the talking frowned and said, "How do we know you are who you say you are?"

Sigismund smiled, "That is simple, my friend, fetch my sister and if she does not know me then you can bar our entry."

He looked at his companion who shrugged and said, "I could take them to the stable and then ask the mistress what we should do. Karl and Viktor can watch them."

Relieved that he had been given an answer the ox nodded, "Good idea."

The man said, "Follow me," and we were led through the gateway into the courtyard. The yard was cobbled, and we clattered our horses across it. Two men came out of the stables at the noise of our approach and the man who had led us said, "Keep an eye on these two, eh?"

They nodded.

As we waited, I decided that Sigismund's brother-in-law might not be a warrior, but he had surrounded himself with men who could fight. Karl and Viktor looked like two ex-soldiers. I saw them scrutinising our horses just as much as us two.

It took some time but eventually the man returned. He said to Karl and Viktor, "You can stable their horses. The mistress seems to think, from my description, that you are her brother. Come with me."

We handed our reins to the two men and followed the man, not to the front entrance, but the servants' entrance at the rear. We were led through the kitchen and a warren of corridors. When we emerged into the hall it was as though we had entered a different world. The unpainted plaster of the dimly lit kitchen and corridors was now replaced by a beautifully furnished and painted, well-lit residence. It was palatial.

A liveried butler waited for us. He nodded to the guard who left us. "Your names?"

"Captain Sigismund von Friedrich." I realised it was the first time that Sigismund had used his full title. He was clearly intimidated.

"Colonel James Bretherton." Even as I used my title, I realised that I, too, was intimidated.

"Follow me." It sounded like a command rather than a request. The butler looked like he could handle himself too. He led us to a large pair of doors. He opened them and I saw that we were in a fine drawing room. A roaring fire burned, and the couches were well padded and covered in fine cloth. Tapestries and paintings adorned the walls. I saw a portrait of a young woman in a woodland glade.

"Sigismund von Friedrich and Colonel James Bretherton."

The two occupants made no attempt to rise although I did see a smile on the face of his sister. She was pretty, or, rather, she had been pretty when she had been young. I glanced up at the portrait. I saw what she had looked like once but time, rich living and age had caught up with her. She was not fat but her puffed cheeks showed that she was heading in that direction. Her husband, in contrast, had hawklike features and a lean and hungry look.

Sigismund's sister said, "Sigismund, I have not seen you for years! This is most unexpected."

It was hardly a warm welcome for she made no attempt to rise. He looked at me and I nodded, "We are here, Elizabeth, at the request of the Swedish King. King Gustavus Adolphus has sent the colonel and I with a message."

If we had thrown cold water on the two of them, we could not have had a greater effect. Walter von Schmidt raced across the room, threw open the doors and peered outside. He commanded, "Adolf, see that we are not disturbed."

A disembodied voice, I guessed it was the butler, said, "Yes, my lord."

He strode back into the room and said to Sigismund, "The king sent a message to me?"

Sigismund turned to me, and I spoke, "To the council really. The king has an army ready to take Mainz, but he does not wish the slaughter and bloodshed that would inevitably follow." I waved a hand, "I have not seen evidence of large numbers of Imperial troops. He could take it easily but there would be much damage and death." I was exaggerating a little for our army was not particularly big.

The banker nodded, "There is a squadron of Spanish cuirassiers in the city but you are right, there are not enough men to defend the walls." I could see his mind working. He said, "How do we know you are from the Swedish king? My wife has not heard from her brother since we married. This might all be a ruse from my enemies. There are many on the council who wish to dispossess me of my position."

I reached into my tunic and like a conjuror performing a slight of hand I proffered the letter.

While he read it, I wondered if brother and sister might speak to each other but there was mutual silence. Samuel von Winterfield must have known that the siblings did not get on and yet he had still risked our lives.

The letter read, the banker said, "A large army?"

I continued with the illusion, "Less than a day from the river."

Ignoring us two he said to his wife, "The council is split and wavering. The Spaniard who addressed us yesterday spoke of an Imperial Army coming here in the spring." He held up the letter, "This and the presence of a large army on our doorstep might well swing the mood. It would bring great benefit to us, my love. We would have saved the city from destruction and we could profit from this." She rose and kissed his hand.

I felt nauseated. No wonder Sigismund had been reluctant to come.

"So, my lord, you will agree to the king's request?"

"This is not yet done. I will have to arrange an extraordinary meeting of the council. It cannot be before tomorrow. I will go now and set the wheels in motion." Still clutching the letter, he headed for the door. A thought struck him, "I suppose you two will have to stay the night. See to it, Elizabeth."

"Of course, my husband."

When he had gone she stood and gestured with her hand, "Come with me."

A servant was helping her husband to don his cloak and Sigismund's sister said to the butler, "Adolf, have my brother and the colonel housed in the guest room. You know the one." He nodded, "Tell the cook that we will have two extra guests for dinner."

"Yes, my lady."

She smiled as false a smile as I have ever seen and said, "It is good to see you, Sigismund. I am sure you will wish to freshen up before we dine and I have much to do." She rushed off and we followed the butler.

When we reached the room, I saw that there were two beds but as it was in the part of the house far from the main stairway, I guessed it was not the best guest room. I knew that when we passed from well-lit and decorated corridors to one with plain plaster. Here there were no paintings hung on the wall and just one lamp burned in a sconce. Inside the room there was a jug of water and a bowl as well as a large pot for us to make water.

The butler pointed to a rope hanging down, "If you need anything then pull that rope, gentlemen and a servant will come." He gave a thin smile, "Better you do not wander as you might get lost. I will fetch you when it is time to dine."

We each sat on a bed when he had gone and Sigismund said, "Hardly the warmest of welcomes, eh, James?"

I smiled, "We did not come for that, we came to save the lives of our men and, it seems to me, we now have a good chance of that. Your brother-in-law seemed optimistic."

He almost spat his reply out, "He saw a way to become richer. Now do you see why we are estranged? Had this been one of my other two sisters we would have enjoyed a warm welcome and genuine smiles. The room we would be given would be a better one."

"Never mind. If all goes well then on the morrow, after the council meeting, we can leave and rejoin our men. If we have good news for the king, then…"

He smiled, "You are right, and I should not let the harpy that is my sister get under my skin."

When we were summoned to dinner Elizabeth was alone. "My husband has still to return. He would not want the food to be wasted, sit and enjoy."

I had no sisters but if this was in England and Roger and Peter, the nearest thing I had to a past family, were dining with me then the conversation would flow. We three enjoyed each other's company and were comfortable with one another. Here there was silence punctuated by the chink of knives and spoons on fine china and the clink of glasses. The food was well cooked and delicious, but I did not enjoy it for the room felt awkward. It was almost a relief when Walter von Schmidt returned, an exultant look upon his face.

He did not look at us when he spoke but his wife whose face lit up when he entered the room, "I think I have done it. I managed to arrange a council meeting for the morrow, and I have spoken with enough people privately to be confident in a successful outcome."

I knew that the successful outcome would be more money and power for the banker.

I said, "And the Imperialist supporters?"

He looked at me as though I was an imbecile, "They are irrelevant. The Spaniard was less than happy but what can he do?" He rubbed his hands, "It has given me an appetite." I was not so sure. Don Alessandro did not seem to me the sort of man who would accept such a decision. I had witnessed, in Bärwalde, how ruthless he could be.

Sigismund and I were ignored for the rest of the meal. We retired as soon as we had finished and neither of our hosts seemed concerned. Once in the room he said, "We have achieved what we needed to then."

I shook my head, "When your brother-in-law has the agreement of the council and we are back in Frankfurt am Main reporting to the king, then we will have success. Until then it is like the Battle of Breitenfeld, all hangs in the balance."

The banker did not want us with him at the meeting. I suspected he wanted the glory to himself. Our presence would tell the others that he was a broker. He wanted to be the mastermind behind the political stroke that would ensure the prosperity of Mainz and the survival of the rich. We ate breakfast and waited.

He returned at noon and was elated. "It was harder than I thought. The Imperialists brought their horsemen with the breastplates and helmets outside the Rathaus. I think they thought to intimidate the council." He laughed, "If so, it did not work. The motion was passed, and Mainz will not oppose King Gustavus." He handed me a parchment. I saw the signatures of the council and, at the top was the name of Walter von Schmidt. We had, by our actions, made him the most powerful man in Mainz.

I said, "Thank you, we should leave now."

"Of course." He added, "I have ensured that the gates are double manned, and the sentries warned that you should be allowed to pass without hindrance."

Neither of them came to see us off. They were both too concerned with planning how they would benefit from the arrival of the king. The bodyguards and grooms were a little less distant as we mounted our horses. I saw that the animals had been well looked after and fed well. Their coats gleamed. I put the letter from the council in the saddlebags and fastened it tightly. As we passed through the gates the ox, whose name we had learned was Friedrich, said to me, "There are men watching the house, Colonel." He shrugged, "I thought you should know."

"Thank you."

I had expected nothing less. While we had been waiting Sigismund and I had made sure that our weapons were cleaned and loaded, and our swords sharpened. Knowing that we were watched helped me to identify the watchers. I recognised, as we passed them, that one was Don Alessandro. That was no surprise. With him were two cuirassier officers. I took comfort that none of them were mounted. I was also happy the regiment was not there to bar our egress. Once we had passed through Kastel we would ride as though the devil was behind us. That we were expected was clear and we were waved to the bridge. As we rode across the bridge to Kastel I looked behind. No horsemen followed us. They were different men at the gates of Kastel, but they had been forewarned and they waved us to pass.

As soon as we were through the gates, I slapped my horse's rump, "Let us ride!"

We galloped. Our horses had been rested and well fed. Used to the carrying of men with breast and backplates, we were lighter burdens. They ate up the ground. We had passed through the hamlet of Hochheim am Main and were about to pass through a forested section when my horse neighed and raised his head. He was not my horse, but I respected his instincts. Something ahead had alerted him and I reined in. Sigismund rode another five paces before he stopped.

"Colonel, what is amiss? I thought you wanted to make the best time we could."

"I do but my horse tells me there is something wrong." At that moment Sigismund's horse also neighed and raised his head. I could see nothing ahead. Suddenly, there was a ripple of smoke followed by the pop of weapons from the trees. I saw Sigismund clutch his left arm as he was struck by a ball. Even as I drew a brace of wheellocks I saw the dozen cuirassiers break from cover. They each fired a second pistol as they raced at us.

As I fired, I shouted, "Sigismund, get behind me." With one arm he would be impaired when it came to fighting. I had six pistols, and the enemy had discharged their weapons. I aimed at the leading riders and fired. I holstered them and drew two more. My vision was slightly obscured by the smoke. I heard Sigismund fire one of his pistols as I drew two more and fired my next two. The ping of ball on plate told me that men had been hit but I could not see the effect. When I had fired my last two pistols and Sigismund had fired a second, I drew my sword, and it was not a moment too soon. A cuirassier corporal had emerged from the smoke and was pointing his long sword at me. I had a weapon that was as long, and I parried his blow. Even as I deflected it a second rider came at me. This one had been hit by a ball, but he held a sword. Sigismund bravely pushed his horse forward as, one armed, he tried to defend me.

The cuirassier whose sword I had deflected wheeled his horse and as I did the same, I saw that just one man was on the ground. That we had hit others was clear but the two of us were outnumbered. Once the rest closed with us and surrounded us then we were dead men. I would not go down without a fight and knowing that Sigismund was wounded made me fight all the harder. As my opponent wheeled, I riposted his strike and used my quick hands to flick my sword at his neck. His helmet was a burgonet type with a moveable nasal guard. He too had quick hands, and he deflected the sword up. For him it was a mistake. The tip slid past the nasal guard and into his eye. He screamed and reeled.

I heard the cry, "James!"

As I wheeled, I saw that while Sigismund had killed his first opponent he was being attacked by two men and one, even as I watched, slid his sword into Sigismund's side. The remaining cuirassiers were loading their weapons. Once they did so we would be dead. I spurred my horse at the two men fighting Sigismund. I slashed at the arm of one. I heard wheellocks being primed and as I lunged across Sigismund to his second enemy, I heard an English voice shout, "Fire!"

Captain of Horse

The smoke and flame that erupted before me did not come from Imperial weapons but the wheellocks and harquebuses of the Hunting Dogs. The voice I had heard was Jennings. Four saddles were emptied and the survivors, realising that they were well outnumbered, fled past us.

I shouted, "The captain is hurt, see to him!"

Jennings shouted, "McHale, see to the captain. Peterson, get some men to take the horses and strip the dead." He grinned at me, "Lieutenant Dickson thought it might be a good idea to do a little hunting close to Mainz, fortunate, eh Colonel?"

"Fortunate indeed. Now let us get back to Frankfurt am Main before the rest of the Spanish squadron get here."

Epilogue

Mainz December 11th, 1631

Sigismund was lucky. The ball that struck him did not break a bone and the doctors were able to clean it well. We knew that such a wound, even when healed would still ache in cold and damp weather. He would remember the encounter on the road for the rest of his life. It was a small price to pay. The sword strike had also avoided anything major, but it needed to be stitched. The captain refused to be left in Frankfurt am Main and he came with us as we entered Mainz. The king allowed us to be with him and his generals at the fore.

Walter von Schmidt was dressed in his best when he greeted us on the steps of the Rathaus. He had a fur about his shoulders and looked almost regal. The king accepted the surrender of the town and the army cheered. The banker did not even glance at his brother-in-law. My friend would still be estranged from his sister and her husband.

I was happy. I liked neither of them and the most important thing was that we had taken another city without loss. We had ended the year with a bloodless victory and with the whole of the Main Valley in Swedish hands.

The day after our arrival Sigismund and I were summoned to the king. "Captain Sigismund, we owe much to you and your family." Sigismund said nothing. I knew why. His brother-in-law had done what he had done for personal gain. "You have shown yourself to be a fine officer. I would like you to raise a regiment of Brandenburger horsemen, Colonel Friedrich."

My friend was almost stumped for words; he eventually muttered, "I am honoured, King Gustavus. Thank you."

"Your First Minister will provide the funds. I believe he is anxious for new blood to enjoy success. Yours will be the premier Brandenburg regiment and I hope that it will be the nucleus of an army that I can rely upon. We need strong allies, and you seem, to me, the perfect man to lead them."

I watched Sigismund grow a handspan.

He turned to me, "Colonel, you have done all that I have asked of you. There is a chest of reichsthalers waiting for you, but I believe that a greater reward will be the two months leave I am authorising. I need you back here on the last day of February."

"Thank you, King Gustavus, for both offers. I will return."

"And when you do, we shall end this war and take back Germany from the papists."

My men were delighted that I had been rewarded. I promoted Stirling to captain and Jennings to lieutenant. We also promoted more men to be sergeants. Another six men had decided that they wished to return to England, including Sergeant White and his wife and child. They would not hinder us as they would ride. The women of the regiment were hardy souls. I would not be travelling alone, and we left Mainz for the two hundred and fifty miles journey to Rotterdam. With luck I would make it home for Christmas as I had the previous year. I had then been a Captain of Horse and now I was a Colonel of Horse. I knew that there were plans for me to lead brigades in the future. Who knew what might be possible?

The End

Glossary

Bidet - another name for a nag or poor-quality horse
Gott mit uns - God with us
Haliwerfolc - the men of the saint (Cuthbert)
Knacker's yard - horse abattoir
Landsberg - Gorzow (Poland)
Muskettengabel - a rest for a musket
Reichsthalers - the coins of the Empire: 25–26 grams of fine silver
Secrete - a small helmet hidden beneath a cap or hat
Serpentine - the match holder for the lighted fuse on a matchlock
Stirrup bucket - a way to attach a standard to a saddle
Swetebags - bags containing herbs and concealed beneath clothes to take away the stink of sweat
Tross - the German and Swedish term for the baggage train and camp followers
Quillon - the crosspiece of a sword of the period
Quilitz - Neuhardenberg
Walthame Cross - Waltham Cross

Canonical Hours

Matins (nighttime)
Lauds (early morning)
Prime (first hour of daylight)
Terce (third hour)
Sext (noon)
Nones (ninth hour)
Vespers (sunset evening)
Compline (end of the day)

Captain of Horse

Historical Background

This series will be about the war between the Catholics and the Protestants in the early seventeenth century. It was a bloody war that devastated huge tracts of Europe. Between 5 and 9 million soldiers and civilians died in the 20-year conflict. The Spanish and Imperial troops were first faced by mercenaries, the Dutch and the Bohemians. Once the Danes and Swedes became involved then the conflict spread. James Bretherton is an amalgam of the mercenary leaders who fought in Europe. Despite being mercenaries, they all believed in their cause. These were not the condottiere who just fought for pay. I have used real battles and events as my structure. I have not glossed over the battles nor made them unduly heroic. They were not. I write about war from the perspective of the soldiers and not the generals.

Southwark Cathedral only became The Cathedral and Collegiate Church of St Saviour and St Mary Overie in 1905. Before that, it was a parish church serving those who lived close to London Bridge.

When Gustavus finished dealing with the Poles then he entered the war and that saw a huge increase in the use of mercenaries from Germany, Scotland and England.

Frankfurt an der Oder, Landsberg, Tangermünde, Burgstall and all the other skirmishes and battles did take place with the results I describe. The fiction is the involvement of my hero and his eponymous regiment. Werben happened the way I wrote it. Count Tilly waited for a day as he realised the Swedish defences were too good and when fog masked the field the next day he made his move. The fog evaporated exposing his men and as a result he lost 6,000 men compared with 200 on the Swedish side.

Arminianism: Arminian theology emphasised clerical authority and the individual's ability to reject or accept salvation, which opponents viewed as heretical and a potential vehicle for the reintroduction of Catholicism.

Cavalry at this time fought in a predictable way. They either used the caracole, lines of horsemen riding, firing their weapons and circling while they reloaded, or they halted, fired their weapons and then charged home. There were lancer regiments that did not use gunpowder weapons but there were few of them. The irregulars, the Croats, Hungarians and Finns fought much in the way their ancestors had done. They used weapons at close hand.

Count Tilly was ill served by Graf zu Pappenheim. The massacre at Magdeburg was not Tilly's doing but zu Pappenheim. When he took his two thousand horsemen to attack the king he lied to Count Tilly about the size of the opposition. He ordered the charge on King Gustavus without asking the count's permission. Like Ney at Waterloo, he cost his leader many horsemen and that would prove fatal. He was a brave and reckless horseman. He is in the mould of Murat, Jeb Stuart, Prince Rupert and George Armstrong Custer. Cavalry leaders like John Gaspard Le Marchant and Lord Uxbridge are rarer.

Heinrich Holk was a real leader. He did switch sides when captured, many men did so on both sides, but he was renowned for his cruelty and the rape and pillaging by his men. He will return in the next book.

Books used in the research:

- The English Civil War - Peter Gaunt
- The Thirty Years' War 1618-1648 - Richard Bonney
- Imperial Armies of the Thirty Years War Infantry and Artillery - Brnardic and Pavlovic
- Imperial Armies of the Thirty Years War Cavalry - Brnardic and Pavlovic
- The Army of Gustavus Adolphus 1 Infantry - Brzezinski and Hook
- The Army of Gustavus Adolphus 2 Cavalry - Brzezinski and Hook
- The English Civil War Armies - Young and Roffe
- Lutzen 1632 - Brzezinski and Turner
- The English Civil Wars - Blair Worden
- The Tower of London - Lapper and Parnell
- Dutch armies of the 80 Years War 1568-1648 Cavalry and Artillery - Groot and Embleton
- Dutch armies of the 80 Years War 1568-1648 Infantry - Groot and Embleton

Captain of Horse

Other books by Griff Hosker

If you enjoyed reading this book, then why not read another one by the author?

Ancient History

The Sword of Cartimandua Series
(Germania and Britannia 50 A.D. – 128 A.D.)
Ulpius Felix- Roman Warrior (prequel)
The Sword of Cartimandua
The Horse Warriors
Invasion Caledonia
Roman Retreat
Revolt of the Red Witch
Druid's Gold
Trajan's Hunters
The Last Frontier
Hero of Rome
Roman Hawk
Roman Treachery
Roman Wall
Roman Courage

The Wolf Warrior series
(Britain in the late 6th Century)
Saxon Dawn
Saxon Revenge
Saxon England
Saxon Blood
Saxon Slayer
Saxon Slaughter
Saxon Bane
Saxon Fall: Rise of the Warlord
Saxon Throne
Saxon Sword

Captain of Horse

Medieval History

The Dragon Heart Series
Viking Slave *
Viking Warrior *
Viking Jarl *
Viking Kingdom *
Viking Wolf *
Viking War*
Viking Sword
Viking Wrath
Viking Raid
Viking Legend
Viking Vengeance
Viking Dragon
Viking Treasure
Viking Enemy
Viking Witch
Viking Blood
Viking Weregeld
Viking Storm
Viking Warband
Viking Shadow
Viking Legacy
Viking Clan
Viking Bravery

Norseman
Norse Warrior

The Norman Genesis Series
Hrolf the Viking *
Horseman *
The Battle for a Home *
Revenge of the Franks *
The Land of the Northmen
Ragnvald Hrolfsson
Brothers in Blood
Lord of Rouen

244

Captain of Horse

Drekar in the Seine
Duke of Normandy
The Duke and the King

Danelaw
(England and Denmark in the 11th Century)
Dragon Sword *
Oathsword *
Bloodsword *
Danish Sword*
The Sword of Cnut

New World Series
Blood on the Blade *
Across the Seas *
The Savage Wilderness *
The Bear and the Wolf *
Erik The Navigator *
Erik's Clan *
The Last Viking*

The Vengeance Trail *

The Conquest Series
(Normandy and England 1050-1100)
Hastings*
Conquest

The Aelfraed Series
(Britain and Byzantium 1050 A.D. - 1085 A.D.)
Housecarl *
Outlaw *
Varangian *

The Reconquista Chronicles
Castilian Knight *
El Campeador *
The Lord of Valencia *

Captain of Horse

The Anarchy Series England
(1120-1180)
English Knight *
Knight of the Empress *
Northern Knight *
Baron of the North *
Earl *
King Henry's Champion *
The King is Dead *
Warlord of the North*
Enemy at the Gate*
The Fallen Crown*
Warlord's War
Kingmaker
Henry II
Crusader
The Welsh Marches
Irish War
Poisonous Plots
The Princes' Revolt
Earl Marshal
The Perfect Knight

Border Knight
(1182-1300)
Sword for Hire *
Return of the Knight *
Baron's War *
Magna Carta *
Welsh Wars *
Henry III *
The Bloody Border *
Baron's Crusade*
Sentinel of the North*
War in the West*
Debt of Honour
The Blood of the Warlord
The Fettered King
de Montfort's Crown

Captain of Horse

The Ripples of Rebellion

Sir John Hawkwood Series
(France and Italy 1339- 1387)
Crécy: The Age of the Archer *
Man At Arms *
The White Company *
Leader of Men *
Tuscan Warlord *
Condottiere*
Legacy

Lord Edward's Archer
Lord Edward's Archer *
King in Waiting *
An Archer's Crusade *
Targets of Treachery *
The Great Cause *
Wallace's War *
The Hunt*
The Prince and the Archer

Struggle for a Crown
(1360- 1485)
Blood on the Crown *
To Murder a King *
The Throne *
King Henry IV *
The Road to Agincourt *
St Crispin's Day *
The Battle for France *
The Last Knight *
Queen's Knight *
The Knight's Tale

Tales from the Sword I
(Short stories from the Medieval period)

Tudor Warrior series

Captain of Horse

(England and Scotland in the late 15th and early 16th century)
Tudor Warrior *
Tudor Spy *
Flodden*

Conquistador
(England and America in the 16th Century)
Conquistador *
The English Adventurer *

English Mercenary
(The 30 Years War and the English Civil War)
Horse and Pistol
Captain of Horse

Modern History

East India Saga
East Indiaman

The Napoleonic Horseman Series
Chasseur à Cheval
Napoleon's Guard
British Light Dragoon
Soldier Spy
1808: The Road to Coruña
Talavera
The Lines of Torres Vedras
Bloody Badajoz
The Road to France
Waterloo

The Lucky Jack American Civil War series
Rebel Raiders
Confederate Rangers
The Road to Gettysburg

Captain of Horse

Soldier of the Queen series
Soldier of the Queen*
Redcoat's Rifle*
Omdurman*
Desert War

The British Ace Series
1914
1915 Fokker Scourge
1916 Angels over the Somme
1917 Eagles Fall
1918 We will remember them
From Arctic Snow to Desert Sand
Wings over Persia

Combined Operations series
(1940-1945)
Commando *
Raider *
Behind Enemy Lines
Dieppe
Toehold in Europe
Sword Beach
Breakout
The Battle for Antwerp
King Tiger
Beyond the Rhine
Korea
Korean Winter

Tales from the Sword II
(Short stories from the Modern period)

Books marked thus *, are also available in the audio format. For more information on all of the books then please visit the author's website at www.griffhosker.com where there is a link to contact him or visit his Facebook page: Griff Hosker at Sword Books or follow him on Twitter: @HoskerGriff or Sword (@swordbooksltd)

Captain of Horse

If you wish to be on the mailing list then contact the author through his website.: Griff Hosker at Sword Books

Printed in Great Britain
by Amazon